Cecily wasn't beautiful, but she had a way about her.

She was intelligent, lively, outrageous and she made him feel good inside. She could have become his world, if he'd allowed her to.

Unexpectedly, Tate reached out and touched her soft cheek with just his fingertips. "I'm Native American," he said quietly. "You're not."

"There is," she said unsteadily, "such a thing as birth control."

His face was very solemn and his eyes were narrow and intent on hers. "And sex is all you want from me, Cecily?" he asked mockingly. "No kids, ever?"

It was the most serious conversation they'd ever had. She couldn't look away from his dark eyes. She wanted him. But she wanted children, too, eventually. Her expression told him so.

"No, Cecily," he continued gently. "Sex isn't what you want at all. And what you really want, I can't give you. We have no future together. If I marry one day, it's important to me that I marry a woman with the same background as my own. And I don't want to live with a young, and all too innocent, white woman."

"I wouldn't be innocent if you'd cooperate for an hour," she muttered outrageously.

"You'll tempt me once too often," he bit off. "This teasing is more dangerous than you realize."

"Nobody tops Diana Palmer...I love her stories."
—Jayne Ann Krentz

DIANA PALMER

Paper Rose

MIRA

ISBN 1-55166-539-5

PAPER ROSE

Copyright © 1999 by Diana Palmer.

Visit us at www.mirabooks.com

Printed in U.S.A.

For Glenda and Doris, with love.

Prologue

Cecily Peterson twirled a beautiful red paper rose between her fingers, staring at its perfection with eyes full of shattered dreams. She was in love with a man who was never going to be able to return that love. Her life was a paper rose, an imitation of beauty forever captured in a medium that would not age, or decay, or die. But it was cold. It was dead and yet it had never lived. Tate Winthrop had brought her the delicate crimson rose from Japan. At the time, it had given her hope that he might one day learn to care for her. But as the years passed, and hope dwindled, she finally realized that the paper rose was making a statement for him. He was telling her in the nicest possible way that his feelings for her were only an imitation of passion and love. He was saying, without speaking one word, that fondness would never be a substitute for love. She remembered so vividly how their turbulent relationship began so many years ago...

Eight years earlier...

There was dust coming up the long winding road from Corryville, South Dakota. Tate Winthrop's black eyes narrowed as he turned on the top rung of the makeshift corral fence to watch the progress of a beat-up gray pickup truck. That would be carrying the order he'd placed with the Blake Feed Company in town.

No sense in starting his young mare on the leading rein right now, he thought, climbing back down. The old jeans he wore clung close to his tall, powerful body. He was lean and fit, with elegant hands and big feet. His straight black hair, which fell to his waist when it was loosened, was braided and held by a black band at his nape. His mother's grandfather had been at the Little Bighorn and later went with a delegation to Washington, D.C., for Teddy Roosevelt's inauguration. One of the elders said that Tate resembled the old warrior in some ways.

He pulled out the barely touched Cuban cigar he'd placed in its carrier in the pocket of his chambray shirt and struck a match to light it between his cupped hands. The boys at the agency always wanted to know how he managed to get contraband cigars. He never told them anything. Keeping secrets was a way of life with him. They went with his job.

The truck pulled up onto the rise and came in sight of the small house and big barn, and the makeshift corral where a snow-white filly was prancing impatiently, tossing her mane.

A young, slender girl got out of the old truck's cab. She had blond hair cut short and green eyes. He was too far away to see those eyes, but he knew them better than he wanted to. Her name was Cecily Peterson. She was the stepdaughter of Arnold Blake, the man who'd just inherited full ownership of the Blake Feed Company; and the only employee who wasn't afraid to come up here with Tate Winthrop's order. Not too many miles from the Pine Ridge Sioux Reservation, Tate's ranch sat just outside the southern boundary of the Wapiti Ridge Sioux Reservation. Corryville itself sat on the Big Wapiti River, juxtapositioned between the Badlands and the reservation. Tate's mother, Leta, lived on the Wapiti Reservation, which was just a stone's throw from Corryville. Tate had grown up with discrimination. Perhaps that was why, when he could afford it, he'd bought a ranch outside the tribe's boundaries.

Tate Winthrop didn't like most people, and he steered clear of white women. But Cecily had become his soft spot. She was a gentle, kind girl of seventeen, and she'd had a hard life. Her invalid mother had died a short while ago and she was now living with her stepfather and one of his brothers. The brother was a decent sort, old enough to be Cecily's grandfather, but the stepfather was a layabout and a drunkard.

Everyone knew that Cecily did most of the work at the feed store that had been her late father's. Her stepfather had inherited it when Cecily's mother died recently, and he was apparently doing everything in his power to bankrupt it.

Cecily was just a little over medium height and slender as a reed. She would never be beautiful, but she had an inner light that changed her green eyes and made them like peridots in the sunlight.

He scoffed at his own fancies. She was just a child and his only contact with her was through the orders he placed at the feed store. It pleased him that she was interested in his ancestry, and not in any faddish way like some aficionados of Native Americans who dressed in buckskins and bought trinkets and tapes and tried to act as if they belonged there. He had no time for Sunday Indians from the city. But Cecily was another matter entirely. She knew something of the culture of the Oglala Lakota and she had a feel for its history. He'd found himself instructing her in little-known customs and mores before he realized it.

But her bond with him didn't become really apparent until her mother's death. It wasn't to her stepfather or her stepuncle or any of the townspeople that she went the day her mother died. It was to Tate, her eyes red-rimmed, her face tear-streaked. And he, who never let anyone get close to him except his own mother, had held her and comforted her while she cried. It had been the most natural thing in the world to dry her tears. But later, he was worried by her growing attachment to him. The last thing in the world he could allow was for her to fall in love with him. It wasn't only the life he led, dangerous and nomadic and solitary. It was the scarcity of pure Lakota blood left in the world. In order to preserve it, he must marry within the Sioux tribe somewhere. Not among his relatives, but among the other Sioux. *If* he married…

His mind came back to the present, to Cecily stopping the truck nearby and getting out. He deliberately didn't go to meet her.

She noticed that with a wry smile and went to him. She brought an invoice for him to sign. Her hands were shaking a little with the usual effect he had on her, but she tightened them on the pen and paper as she approached him. Even in her thick-heeled working boots, he was far taller than she was. She had on a checked man's shirt and jeans. He'd never seen her wear anything revealing or feminine.

She handed him the invoice without meeting his eyes. "My stepdad said this was what you ordered, but to check with you before I unloaded it," she said.

"Why does he always send you?" Tate asked the girl deliberately as he scanned the list.

"Because he knows I'm not afraid of you," she said.

His black eyes lifted from the paper and met hers. They were scary sometimes; like a cobra's, steady and intent and unblinking. They'd made her want to back away when she first met him. They didn't frighten her anymore, though. He'd been tender with her, more than anyone in her life had ever been. She knew, as most other people locally didn't, that there was more on the inside of Tate Winthrop than he ever allowed to show.

"Are you sure that you aren't afraid of me?" he asked in a soft drawl.

She only smiled. "You wouldn't slug me over a messed-up order," she said dryly, because she'd heard that he did exactly that once, when her stepfather had neglected to bring the feed he'd ordered in a blizzard and he'd lost some calves because of it.

She was right. He would never hit Cecily for any reason. He took the pen from her and signed the invoice before he handed it back. "That's everything I ordered, all right."

"Okay," she said brightly. "I'll unload it."

He didn't say a word. He put out the cigar, stuck it back into his pocket and followed her to the truck.

She gave him a hard look. "I'm no cream puff," she scoffed. "I can unload a few little bags of feed."

"Sure you can." He glanced at her and a smile lit his black eyes for a few seconds. "But you're not going to. Not here."

"Tate," she groaned. "You shouldn't be doing this! My stepfather ought to be here. If he's going to run the place, why won't he run it?"

"Because he's got you to do it for him." He stopped suddenly in the act of reaching for a heavy bag of fertilizer and stared at her intently. "What happened to your throat, Cecily?" he asked abruptly.

She put a hand to it, feeling the bruise there. She'd had her collar buttoned, but it had been too hot to keep it that way. She didn't realize that it would show.

He took off his work gloves, tossed them into the bed of the pickup with the feed and began to unbutton her blouse.

"Stop that!" she exclaimed. "Tate, you can't...!"

But he already had. His eyes blazed like black diamonds in fire. His hands gripped hard on the fabric as he saw the other bruises just at her collarbone, above the tattered little bra she wore—bruises like the imprint of a man's fingers. His jaw clenched hard. It infuriated him to see bruises on that pale skin. It was almost as bad to see the state of her clothes—he knew that she hadn't had anything new for a very long time. Presumably her stepfather kept her destitute, and probably on purpose so he wouldn't lose his mainstay. His eyes shot back up to catch hers and held them relentlessly. She was flushed and biting her lip. "I won't embarrass you any more than this, but you're going to tell me if those same kind of bruises are on your breasts."

Her eyes closed and tears slid past the closed eyelids. "Yes," she bit off.

"Was it your stepfather?" he asked shortly.

She swallowed. Since she couldn't meet his eyes, she merely nodded.

"Talk to me."

"He was trying to feel me...there. He was always trying, even when he first married Mama. I tried to tell her, but she didn't want to hear. He flattered her and they both liked to drink." She folded her arms over her breasts. "Last night he got stinking drunk and came into my room." She felt nauseated from the memory. "I was asleep." She looked up at him with the repulsion she felt showing in her eyes. "Why are men such animals?" she asked with a cynical maturity far beyond her years.

"Not all of us are," he replied, and his voice was like ice. He buttoned her blouse with a deftness that hinted of experience. "You don't even have a proper bra."

She flushed. "You weren't supposed to see it," she said mutinously.

He buttoned her up to her chin and then rested his hands lightly on her shoulders. They were good hands, lean and dark and warm and strong. She loved the feel of them.

"You aren't being subjected to that sort of lechery again."

Her eyes widened. "What?"

"You heard me. Come on. Let's get this unloaded. Then we'll talk and make decisions."

A short time later, he had her by the hand and all but dragged her into the house. He pulled out a chair for her, poured coffee from a coffeemaker into a cup and put it in front of her.

Stunned by his actions, she sat and stared around her. She'd never been in his house, and it was surprising to find that it wasn't at all what it appeared to be on the outside. It was full of electronic equipment, computers and laptops and printers, a funny-looking telephone setup and several short-wave radios. There was even a ham radio set. On the wall were collections of pistols and rifles, none of which looked like anything she'd ever seen.

The furnishings were impressive, too. She remembered then the whispers she'd heard about this reclusive man who was Lakota but didn't live on a reservation, who had a mysterious background and an even more mysterious profession. Unlike many Lakota who were victims of prejudice, nobody pushed Tate Winthrop. In fact, most people around Corryville were a little afraid of him.

She glanced at his taciturn face, wondering why she'd been hijacked into his house. He usually signed the invoice, unloaded the supplies, and when they talked, it was always outside. Not that he didn't watch her like a hawk when he was in town and she was anywhere around. Over the past year, he'd always seemed to be watching her. And today he'd seen the truth of her miserable home life all too starkly.

He sat down and leaned back in his chair. He dropped his hat on the floor and stared at her intently.

He made an angry sound and took another draw from the cigar. "Did he have you last night?" he asked bluntly.

She blushed violently and closed her eyes. It was useless not to tell him the truth. "He tried to," she choked. "I hit him and he...grabbed me. He was pretty drunk, or I'd never have got away, even if I got pretty bruised doing it. He'd always bothered me, but it wasn't until last night..." She lifted an anguished face to his. "I hid in the woods until he passed out, but I didn't dare go back to sleep." Her face tautened. "I'd rather starve to death than let him do it," she bit off. "I mean it!"

He watched her quietly while the smoke from his cigar went sailing up into the fan. He'd seen enough of her to know that she never shirked her duties, never complained, never asked for anything. He admired her. That was rare, because he had a fine contempt for most women. Especially white ones. The thought of her stepfather assaulting her made him livid. He'd never wanted so badly to hurt a man.

He flicked ashes into a big glass ashtray and didn't say anything for a minute or two.

She sipped coffee, feeling uncomfortable. He was still almost a stranger to her and he'd seen her in her underwear. It was a new, odd uneasiness she couldn't remember feeling with anyone else, especially with another man.

"What do you want to do with your life, Cecily?" he asked unexpectedly.

"Be an archaeologist," she blurted out.

His eyebrows arched. "Why?"

"We had a science teacher just before I graduated. He was an archaeologist. He'd actually help excavate

Mayan ruins down in the Yucatan." Her green eyes almost glowed with excitement and enthusiasm. "I thought how wonderful it would be, to bring an ancient civilization out into the light and show it to the world like that..." Her voice trailed off as she realized how impossible that dream was. She shrugged. "There's no money for that, though. Mama had a little savings, but he spent it all. She said he had no business sense, and I guess it's true, because he's all but ruined daddy's business."

"How long has your father been dead?"

"Six years," she said. "Then Mama married *him* last year." She closed her eyes and shivered. "She said she was lonely, and he paid her a lot of attention. I saw right through him. Why couldn't she?"

"Because some people lack perception." His black eyes narrowed as they measured her. "What sort of grades did you make in school?"

"A's and B's," she replied. "I was good in science." She had a sudden unpleasant thought. "Are you going to try to have my stepfather locked up?" she asked worriedly. "Everybody would know," she added, feeling ashamed.

He searched her eyes, feeling the fear she had of public recrimination, the trial, the eyes staring at her. "You don't think rape warrants it?"

"He didn't," she said. "But you're right. He's probably been sitting at home thinking about it all day. By tonight, I won't stand a chance. Not even if I hide in the woods."

He leaned forward, one elbow on the beautiful

cherry wood of the table, and stared right into her eyes.

She felt nauseous. She folded her arms over her breasts and stared into space, shivering. It was the worst nightmare she'd faced in her young life.

"All right, don't go into mental convulsions over it," he said quietly. He looked as if nothing ever ruffled him. In fact, very little did. "He won't touch you, I guarantee it. I have a solution."

"A solution?" Her green eyes were wide and wet, and full of hope.

"I know of a scholarship you can get at George Washington University, outside Washington, D.C.," he said, thinking how good it was that he'd learned to lie with such a straight face, and never thinking this lie might come back to haunt him. "Books and board included. It's for needy cases. You'd certainly qualify. Interested?"

She was hesitant. "Yes. But...well, how would I get there, and apply?"

"Forget the logistics for now. They aren't important. They have a good archaeology program and you'd be well out of reach of your stepfather. If you want it, say the word."

"Yes, I want it!" she said. "But I'll have to go back home..."

"No, you won't," he said shortly. "Not ever again." He threw his legs off the chair and got up, reaching for the telephone. He punched in a number, waited, and then began to speak in a language that was positively not English.

She'd lived around Lakota people most of her young life, but she'd never heard the language spoken like this. It was full of rising and falling tones, and sang of ancient places and the sound of the wind. She loved the sound of it in his deep voice.

All too soon he ended the conversation. "Let's go."

"The truck, the other orders," she protested weakly.

"I'll have the truck taken back to your stepfather, along with a message." He didn't mention that he planned to deliver both.

"But where am I going?"

"To my mother on the reservation," he said. "My father died earlier this year, so she's alone. She'll enjoy your company."

"I don't have clothes," she protested.

"I'll get yours from your stepfather."

"You make this sound so easy," she said, amazed.

"Most things are easy if you can get past the red tape. I learned long ago to cut it close to the bone." He opened the door. "Coming?"

She got up, feeling suddenly free and full of hope. It was like one of those everyday miracles people talked about. "Yes…"

Chapter One

Present day
Washington, D.C.

Cameras were flashing all around Cecily Peterson. Microphones wielded by acrobatic television journalists were being thrust in her face as she walked quite calmly out of the fund-raising dinner that Senator Matt Holden was hosting.

Behind her, a furious tall man with a long braid of black hair was waiting for a tureen of expensive crab bisque to complete its trip down the once-spotless dress slacks of his tuxedo before he tried to move. The diamond-festooned blond socialite with him was glaring daggers at Cecily's back.

Cecily kept walking. "Film at eleven," she murmured to no one in particular, and with a bright little smile.

She didn't really look like a woman whose entire life had crashed and burned in the space of a few minutes. Her life was like Tate Winthrop's tuxedo—in ruins. Everything was going to change now.

She went to the big black utility vehicle that her date had driven her here in, to wait for him to join her. Her high heels were damp from the grass. She could feel her medium blond hair coming down from its high, complicated coiffure. The street and traffic lights were blurs of color to her pale green eyes because she wasn't wearing her glasses and she couldn't use contacts. She had on a black dress with tiny little straps, and the black shawl she was wearing with it didn't provide much warmth. She couldn't get into the vehicle without the key, but that didn't matter. She was too numb to feel the chill of the night air anyway, or care about the busy Washington, D.C. street traffic behind her. She was furious that she'd had to learn the truth about her financial status and her supposed educational grant from that dyed blonde who Tate Winthrop was escorting around town these days. Her mind wandered back to a day two years ago, when everything had seemed so perfect, and her dreams had hovered on the cusp of fulfillment....

The airport in Tulsa was crowded. Cecily juggled her carry-on bag with a duffel bag full of equipment, scanning the milling rush around her for Tate Winthrop. She was wearing her usual field gear: boots, a khaki suit with a safari jacket and a bush hat hanging

behind her head by a rawhide string. Her natural
blond hair was in a neat braided bun atop her head,
and through her big-lensed glasses, her green eyes
twinkled with anticipation. It wasn't often that Tate
Winthrop asked her to help him on a case. It was an
occasion.

Suddenly there he was, towering over the people
around him. He was Lakota Sioux, and looked it. He
had high cheekbones and big black, deep-set eyes under a jutting brow. His mouth was wide and sexy,
with a thin upper lip and a chiseled lower one and he
had perfect teeth. His hair was straight and jet-black;
it fell to his waist when he wasn't wearing it in a
braid, as he was now. He was lean and striking, muscular without being obvious. And he'd once worked
for a secret government agency. Of course, Cecily
wasn't supposed to know that; or that he was con-
sulting with them on the sly right now in a hush-hush
murder case in Oklahoma.

"Where's your luggage?" Tate asked in his deep,
crisp voice.

She gave him a pert look, taking in the elegance
of his vested suit. "Where's your field gear?" she
countered with the ease of long acquaintance.

Tate had saved her from the unsavory advances of
a drunken stepfather when she was just seventeen.
He'd taken her to his mother on the Wapiti Ridge
Sioux Reservation near the Black Hills, and there
she'd stayed until he got her a scholarship and a grant
and enrolled her in George Washington University,

down the street from his apartment in Washington, D.C. He'd been her guardian angel through four years of college and the master's program she was beginning now—doing forensic archaeology. She was already earning respect for her work. She was an honors student all the way, not surprising since she had no social life and could devote all her time to her studies. She didn't need to date; she had eyes for no man in the world except Tate.

"I'm security chief of the Hutton corporation," he reminded her. "This is a freelance favor I'm doing for a couple of old friends. So this *is* my working gear."

She made a face. "You'll get all dusty."

He made a sound deep in his throat. "You can brush me off."

She grinned wickedly. "Now that's what I call incentive!"

He chuckled. "Cut it out. We've got a serious and sensitive situation here."

"So you intimated on the phone." She glanced around the airport. "Where's baggage claim? I brought some tools and electronic equipment, too."

"How about clothes?"

She stared at him blankly. "What do I need with a lot of clothes cluttering up my equipment case? These are wash-and-wear."

He made another sound. "You can't expect to go to a restaurant in that!"

"Why not? And who's taking me to any restaurant?" she demanded. "*You* never do."

He shrugged. "I'm going to do penance while we're out here."

Her eyes sparkled. "Great! Your bed or mine?"

He laughed in spite of himself. She was the only person in his life who'd ever been able to make him feel carefree, even briefly. She lit fires inside him, although he was careful not to let them show too much. "You never give up, do you?"

"Someday you'll weaken," she assured him. "And I'm prepared. I have a week's supply of Trojans in my fanny pack...."

He managed to look shocked. "Cecily!"

She shrugged. "Women have to think about these things. I'm twenty-three, you know." She added, "You came into my life at a formative time and rescued me from something terrible. Can I help it if you make other potential lovers look like fried sea bass by comparison?"

"I didn't bring you out here to discuss your lack of lovers," he pointed out.

"And here I hoped you were offering yourself up as an educational experience," she sighed.

He glared down at her as they walked toward baggage claim.

"Okay," she said glumly. "I'll give up, for now. What do you want me to do out here?" she added, and sounded like the professional she really was. "You mentioned something about skeletal remains."

He looked around them before he spoke. "We had a tip," he told her, "that a murder could be solved if we looked in a certain place. About twenty years ago, a foreign double agent went missing near Tulsa. He was carrying a piece of microfilm that identified a mole in the CIA. It would be embarrassing for everybody if this is him and the microfilm surfaced now."

"I gather that your mole has moved up in the world?"

"Don't even ask," he told her, then, with a smile he added, "I don't want to have to put you in the witness protection program. All you have to do is tell me if this DB is the one we're looking for."

"Dead body," she translated. Then she frowned. "I thought you had an expert out here."

"You can't imagine what sort of damned expert these guys brought with them."

Yes, she could, but she didn't say anything.

"Besides," he added with a quick glance, "you're discreet. I know from experience that you don't tell everything you know."

"What did your expert tell you about the body?"

"That it's very old," he said with exaggerated awe. "Probably thousands of years old!"

"Why do you think it isn't?"

"For one thing, there's a .32 caliber bullet in the skull."

"Well, that rather lets out a Paleo-Indian hunter," she agreed.

"Sure it does. But I need an expert to say so, or

the case will be summarily dropped. I don't know about you, but I don't want a former KGB mole making policy for me.''

''Me, neither,'' she said inelegantly. ''You do realize that somebody could have been out to the site and used the skull for target practice?''

He nodded. ''Can you date the remains?''

''I don't know. Carbon dating is best, but it takes time. I'll do the best I can.''

''That's good enough for me. Experts in Paleo-Indian archaeology aren't thick on the ground in the 'company' these days. You were the only person I could think of to call.''

''I'm flattered.''

''You're good,'' he said. ''That's not flattery.'' Changing the subject, he asked, ''What have you got in those cases if you didn't bring clothes?''

''A laptop computer with a modem and fax, a cellular phone, assorted digging tools, including a collapsible shovel, two reference works on human skeletal remains.''

She was struggling with the case. He reached out and took it from her, testing the weight. ''Good God, you'll get a hernia dragging this thing around. Haven't you ever heard of luggage carriers?''

''Sure. I have three. They're all back in D.C. in my closet.''

He led the way to a sport utility vehicle. He put her bags in the back and opened the door for her.

Cecily wasn't beautiful, but she had a way about

her. She was intelligent, lively, outrageous and she made him feel good inside. She could have become his world, if he'd allowed her to. But he was full-blooded Lakota, and she was not. If he ever married, something his profession made unlikely, he didn't like the idea of mixed blood.

He got in beside her and impatiently reached for her seat belt, snapping it in place. "You always forget," he murmured, meeting her eyes.

Her breath came uneasily through her lips as she met that level stare and responded helplessly to it. He was handsome and sexy and she loved him more than her own life. She had for years. But it was a hopeless, unreturned adoration that left her unfulfilled. He'd never touched her, not even in the most innocent way. He only looked.

"I should close my door to you," she said huskily. "Refuse to speak to you, refuse to see you, and get on with my life. You're a constant torment."

Unexpectedly he reached out and touched her soft cheek with just his fingertips. They smoothed down to her full, soft mouth and teased the lower lip away from the upper one. "I'm Lakota," he said quietly. "You're white."

"There is," she said unsteadily, "such a thing as birth control."

His face was very solemn and his eyes were narrow and intent on hers. "And sex is all you want from me, Cecily?" he asked mockingly. "No kids, ever?"

It was the most serious conversation they'd ever

had. She couldn't look away from his dark eyes. She wanted him. But she wanted children, too, eventually. Her expression told him so.

"No, Cecily," he continued gently. "Sex isn't what you want at all. And what you really want, I can't give you. We have no future together. If I marry one day, it's important to me that I marry a woman with the same background as my own. And I don't want to live with a young, and all too innocent, white woman."

"I wouldn't be innocent if you'd cooperate for an hour," she muttered outrageously.

His dark eyes twinkled. "Under different circumstances, I would," he said, and there was suddenly something hot and dangerous in the way he looked at her as the smile faded from his chiseled lips, something that made her heart race even faster. "I'd love to strip you and throw you onto a bed and bend you like a willow twig under my body."

"Stop!" she whispered theatrically. "I'll swoon!" And it wasn't all acting.

His hand slid behind her nape and contracted, dragging her rapt face just under his, so close that she could smell the coffee that clung to his clean breath, so close that her breasts almost touched his jacket.

"You'll tempt me once too often," he bit off. "This teasing is more dangerous than you realize."

She didn't reply. She couldn't. She was throbbing, aroused, sick with desire. In all her life, there had been only this man who made her feel alive, who made her feel passion. Despite the traumatic experience of her teens, she had a fierce physical attraction to Tate that she was incapable of feeling with any other man.

She touched his lean cheek with cold fingertips, slid them back, around his neck into the thick mane of long hair that he kept tightly bound—like his own passions.

"You could kiss me," she whispered unsteadily, "just to see how it feels."

He tensed. His mouth poised just above her parted lips. The silence in the car was pregnant, tense, alive with possibilities and anticipation. He looked into her wide, pale, eager green eyes and saw the heat she couldn't disguise. His own body felt the pressure and warmth of hers and began to swell, against his will.

"Tate," she breathed, pushing upward, toward his mouth, his chiseled, beautiful mouth that promised heaven, promised satisfaction, promised paradise.

His dark fingers corded in her hair. They hurt, and she didn't care. Her whole body ached.

"Cecily, you little fool," he ground out.

Her lips parted even more. He was weak. This once, he was weak. She could tempt him. It could happen. She could feel his mouth, taste it, breathe it. She felt him waver. She felt the sharp explosion of his breath against her lips as he let his control slip. His mouth parted and his head bent. She wanted it. Oh, God, she wanted it, wanted it, wanted it....

* * *

The sudden blare of a horn made her jump, brought her back to the painful present in the chill of the nation's capitol, outside the exclusive restaurant where she'd just made the evening news by attacking Tate Winthrop with a tureen of crab bisque.

She stretched, hurting as she let the memory of the past reluctantly slip away. A car horn had separated her from Tate two years ago, too. He'd withdrawn from her at once, and that had been the end of her dreams. She'd helped solve his murder mystery, which was no more than a Paleo-Indian skull with a bullet in it, used in an attempt to frame an unpopular member of congress. Any anthropologist worth her salt would have known the race from the dentition and the approximate age from the patination and the projectile points and pottery that the would-be framer hadn't realized would help date the remains.

Tate had involved Cecily, a student, and that had given her hope. But fate had quickly taken hope away with a blare from an impatient driver's horn. From that moment on, Tate had put her at a distance and kept her there, for the two years of her master's studies in forensic archaeology. Their close friendship had all but vanished. And tonight had shattered her world.

Her doctorate was a fading dream already. Since Tate had rescued her from her abusive stepfather at the age of seventeen and taken her to live with his mother on the Wapiti Ridge Sioux reservation, which was near the Pine Ridge Sioux Reservation, he'd acted in stead of a guardian. But he'd told her that she had a grant to pay for her education, her apartment, her clothing and food and other necessities. She had a bank account that it paid into. All her expenses had been covered for the past six years by that anonymous foundation that helped penniless young women get an education. At least that's what Tate had told her. And tonight she'd discovered that it had all been a lie. Tate had been paying for it, all of it, out of his own pocket.

She pulled the shawl closer as a tall, lithe figure cut across the parking lot and joined her at the passenger door.

"You're already famous," Colby Lane told her, his dark eyes twinkling in his lean, scarred face. "You'll see yourself on the evening news, if you live long enough to watch it." He jerked a thumb over his shoulder. "Tate's on his way right now."

"Unlock this thing and get me out of here!" she squeaked.

He chuckled. "Coward."

He unlocked the door and let her climb in. By the time he got behind the wheel and took off, Tate was striding across the parking lot with blood in his eye.

Cecily blew him a kiss as Colby gunned the engine down the busy street.

"You're living dangerously tonight," Colby told her. "He knows where you live," he added.

"He should. He paid for the apartment," she added in a sharp, hurt tone. She wrapped her arms closer around her. "I don't want to go home, Colby. Can I stay with you tonight?"

She knew, as few other people did, that Colby Lane was still passionately in love with his ex-wife, Maureen. He had nothing to do with other women even two years after his divorce was final. He drank to excess from time to time, but he wasn't dangerous. Cecily trusted no one more. He'd been a good friend to her, as well as to Tate, over the years.

"He won't like it," he said.

She let out a long breath. "What does it matter now?" she asked wearily. "I've burned my bridges."

"I don't know why that socialite Audrey had to tell you," he muttered irritably. "It was none of her business."

"Maybe she wants a big diamond engagement ring, and Tate can't afford it because he's keeping me," she said bitterly.

He glanced at her rigid profile. "He won't marry her."

She made a sound deep in her throat. "Why not? She's got everything...money, power, position and beauty—and a degree from Vassar."

"In psychology," Colby mused.

"She's been going around with Tate for several months."

"He goes around with a lot of women. He won't marry any of them."

"Well, he certainly won't marry me," she assured him. "I'm white."

"More a nice, soft tan," he told her. "You can marry me. I'll take care of you."

She made a face at him. "You'd call me Maureen in your sleep and I'd lay your head open with the lamp. It would never work."

He drew in a long breath. His lean hands tightened on the wheel. One of them was artificial. Colby had lost an arm in Africa. He was a mercenary, a professional soldier. Sometimes he worked for various covert government agencies, sometimes he freelanced. She never asked about his frequent travels. They were companions who went out together occasionally, fellow sufferers of unrequited passions for other people. It made for a close friendship.

"Tate's a damned fool," he said flatly.

"I don't appeal to him," she corrected. "It's a shame I'm not Lakota."

"Leta Winthrop would argue that point," he murmured with an amused glance. "Didn't you lobby for sovereignty at that Senate hearing last month?"

"Me and several other activists. Some of the Lakota resent having a white woman plead their case, but I've been trying my best."

"I know."

"Thanks for your support." She leaned back against the car seat. "It's been a horrible night. I guess Senator Holden will never speak to me again, much less invite me to another political banquet."

"He'll love the publicity he gets from your exit," he corrected with a chuckle. "And I believe he's been trying to persuade you to assume the position of assistant curator in charge of acquisitions with his new Native American Museum project in D.C."

"So he is. I may have to take it now. I can't see going on with my studies under the circumstances."

"I've got some cash in Swiss banks. I'll help you."

"Thanks, but no, thanks. I'm going to be totally independent."

"Suit yourself." He glanced at her. "If you take that job, it won't get you any points with Tate. He and Matt Holden are bitter enemies."

"Senator Holden doesn't favor allowing a casino on the Wapiti reservation. Tate does. They've almost come to blows on the issue twice."

"So I heard. And that's not all I've heard. Holden is sticking his nose into a hornet's nest in the Indian Affairs committee, and he's had some public and all but slanderous things to say about the push for a casino at Wapiti."

"There are other Sioux casinos in South Dakota," she replied. "But Senator Holden is fighting this one all the way. Nobody knows why. He and Tate have had some real battles over this."

"That's just an excuse and you know it. Tate hates the man." Colby pushed back a strand of straight black hair that fell into his eyes. Unlike Tate, his hair was short. "I know I said this before, but it bears repeating. You know Tate won't like you staying with me."

"I don't care," she said bitterly. "I don't tell him where to sleep. It's none of his business what I do anymore."

He made a rough sound. "Would you like to guess what he's going to assume if you stay the night in my apartment?"

She drew in a long breath. "Okay. I don't want to cause problems between you, not after all the years you've been friends. Take me to a hotel instead."

He hesitated uncharacteristically. "I can take the heat, if you can."

"I don't know that I can. I've got enough turmoil in my life right now. Besides, he'll look for me at your place. I don't want to be found for a couple of days, until I can get used to my new situation and make some decisions about my future. I want to see Senator Holden and find another apartment. I can do all that from a hotel."

"Suit yourself."

"Make it a moderately priced one," she added with graveyard humor. "I'm no longer a woman of means. From now on, I'm going to have to be responsible for my own bills."

"You should have poured the soup in the right lap," he murmured.

"Which was?"

"Audrey Gannon's," he said curtly. "She had no right to tell you that Tate was your benefactor. She did it for pure spite, to drive a wedge between you and Tate. She's nothing but trouble. One day Tate is going to be sorry that he ever met her."

"She's lasted longer than the others."

"You haven't spent enough time talking to her to know what she's like. I have," he added darkly. "She has enemies, among them an ex-husband who's living in a duplex because she got his house, his Mercedes, and his Swiss bank account in the divorce settlement."

"So that's where all those pretty diamonds came from," she said wickedly.

"Her parents had money, too, but they spent most of it before they died in a plane crash. She likes unusual men, they say, and Tate's unusual."

"She won't go to the reservation to see Leta," she commented.

"Of course not." He leaned toward her as he stopped at a traffic light. "It's a *Native American* reservation!"

She stuck her tongue out at him. "Leta's worth two of Audrey."

"Three," he returned. "Okay. I'll find you a hotel. Then I'm leaving town before Tate comes looking for me!"

"You might hang a crab on your front door," she said, tongue-in-cheek. "It just might ward him off."

"Ha!"

She turned her eyes toward the bright lights of the city. She felt cold and alone and a little frightened. But everything would work out. She knew it would. She was a grown woman and she could take care of herself. This was her chance to prove it.

Chapter Two

There was film at eleven. Senator Holden found it hilarious, and when Cecily phoned to ask him about the job at the new museum that he'd offered her, he told her so. He didn't ask any questions. He accepted her application over the phone and gave her the job on the spot.

Early Monday morning, Cecily found a small apartment that she could manage on the salary she'd be making and she moved out of the apartment Tate had been paying for. She pulled out of her master's classes and withdrew from college. From now on, she was paying her own way. And one day, she'd pay Tate back, every penny. For the time being, shell-shocked and sick at heart that she was nothing more than a charity case to him, she wanted no more to do with the man she'd loved for so long. No wonder he'd thought of her as his ward. She was obligated to him for every crumb she put in her mouth. But no more. She was her own woman now. She'd support herself. Maybe later she could finish her master's degree. She had plenty of time for that. At least she had a job to see her through this difficult transition.

She was forced to use her small bank account to pay the deposit on the new apartment, to pay for movers to transport her few possessions and for enough food to keep her going until she drew her first paycheck. She was so sick at heart that she hated the whole world. She couldn't even talk to Tate's mother, Leta.

The new apartment was small, and not much to look at, but at least she'd be responsible for herself. Unlike the old one, it was unfurnished, so she started out with very little. She didn't even have a television set. At least the new place was closer to the museum. She could ride the bus to work every day, or even take the metro if she liked.

Colby came by to help her unpack, bringing a pizza with him and a small boom box with some cassettes as a house-warming present. They munched while they unwrapped lamps and dishes, sipping beer because it was all he brought for them to drink.

"I hate beer," she moaned.

"If you drink enough of it, you won't care about the taste," he assured her.

She gave the can a dubious stare, shrugged, closed her eyes, held her breath and drank heavily. "Yuck!" she said.

"Keep going."

She finished half of the can and ate some more pizza. After a few minutes, sure enough, it didn't taste half-bad.

He watched her grin and nodded. "That's the first smile I've seen in days."

"I'm getting through it," she assured him. "I start work next Monday. I can't wait."

"I wish I could be around to hear about your first day, but I've got another overseas assignment."

She suspended the pizza at her mouth. Putting it down, she said worriedly, "Colby, you've already lost an arm..."

"And it will make me more careful," he told her. "I lost it because I got drunk. I won't let that happen again." He glanced at the can. "Beer doesn't affect me these days. It's just a pleasant diversion." He looked at her. "I'm through my worst time. Now I'm going to help you through yours. When I get back."

She grimaced. "Well, don't get killed, okay?"

He chuckled. "Okay."

During Colby's absence, she celebrated her twenty-fifth birthday with a cupcake, a candle and a card from Leta, who never forgot. Tate apparently had, or he was holding a grudge. For the first time in eight years, her birthday passed unnoticed by him.

She was now firmly entrenched at the museum and having the time of her life. She missed college and her classmates, but she loved the work she was doing.

Acquisitions would be part of her duties as assistant curator, and she got to work in her own forensic archaeology field, Paleo-Indian archaeology. She didn't really miss forensics as much as she'd expected to. It was almost as exciting to have access to rare collections of Folsom Clovis, and other projectile points, which were thousands of years old, along with bola stones, chippers and other stone tools and pottery fashioned by long-dead hands.

Her new phone number was unlisted, but Tate called her once at the museum. She put the phone down, gently but firmly. He didn't call again.

Senator Holden did. "It's my birthday Saturday night," he said. "I want you and Colby to come."

"He's out of town. But I'd love to."

"Great! We can talk about some new projects I've got in mind."

"We can?" she asked, grinning because she knew how much he loved the museum; it had been his idea to open it. He was a fanatic in the field of Native American culture. He wasn't Sioux, but his mother had taught on the Wapiti Sioux reservation. Like Cecily, he had an affinity for the Lakota nation.

He chuckled. "I'll tell you all about it on Saturday. Six sharp at my house. Don't be late. It's a buffet."

"I won't eat for days," she promised.

When she hung up she realized what she'd said. She did eat more frugally than before. She spent more frugally than before. Her surroundings weren't lavish.

But she wasn't having to depend on anyone's charity. She was twenty-five and self-supporting. It felt good.

Cecily phoned Leta to let her know that she planned to fly out to Rapid City and drive over to the Wapiti Ridge Sioux Reservation near Custer State Park in South Dakota for the tribe's annual celebrations. There would be a large contingent of Lakota at the three-day September event, and native dancing and singing as well. She'd already bought her plane ticket and reserved a rental car. She wasn't going to back out of the event just because she and Tate weren't speaking. Anyway, there wasn't a chance that Tate would go now.

"Tate hasn't called recently," Leta mentioned when they'd discussed the event. "I phoned to see if he was at his apartment, and that Audrey Gannon answered. She told me he was out of the country on some job for his boss, Pierce Hutton."

Cecily felt a lump in her throat. She swallowed before she replied. "I didn't know she was living with him," she said, trying to sound nonchalant.

"He's secretive, isn't he, baby? I guess he must feel something for her," Leta replied irritably. "She hates what he is, she hates the reservation and she was barely civil to me when I told her who I was. If he's as crazy about her as she says he is, she could turn him against his own people, even against me."

"Surely she wouldn't," Cecily tried to reassure her.

"Surely she would. She's against native sovereignty." There was a hesitation. "I'm glad you're coming out here. I miss seeing you. Since you went to live in Washington, I hardly get to have you out here at all."

"I miss you, too," Cecily said warmly.

"I need something to lift my spirits," Leta continued. "We've just lost the hope of getting an ambulance and a new community clinic, because the funds that were budgeted have disappeared."

"Disappeared? Where to?" Cecily said.

"Nobody knows," Leta said. "Tom Black Knife, you remember our tribal chief, says it's probably a math error. I'm not so sure. There are some real suspicious comings and goings around here lately. Especially since the paperwork for the proposed casino was sent off. I guess you haven't been able to get Senator Holden to listen to you about our side of the story?" she added, a curious inflection in her voice.

"Matt Holden is one hundred percent against the casino, despite all my pleading," Cecily said sadly. "Not that I haven't bombarded him with information. I'm going to his birthday party. Maybe I can waylay him there and do us some good."

"Yes. His birthday. He's inflexible when anything goes against his principles," Leta murmured.

"You sound as if you know him!" Cecily teased.

There was a long pause and when Leta spoke, her voice was strained. "I know of him. Everybody here does."

"Why don't you come to Washington later in the year and talk to him personally?" Cecily asked. "You can stay with me."

"What, in that fancy apartment?" she said, distracted.

Cecily winced. "I've…moved. I have a new place. It's smaller, and a little shabby, but it's homey. You'll like it. I have a sofa that folds out into a bed. I can sleep there and you can have the bedroom."

Leta paused. "I'd love to see you. But I don't know about getting on an airplane. I'll have to think about that. You and Tate and I could go on the town, if I did. It might be fun, at that!"

Cecily hesitated. "Tate and I aren't speaking, Leta," she said tautly.

"Why not?"

"I found out who's been paying all my expenses."

"It's some foundation, isn't it?" Leta asked in all innocence. "What would that have to do with you and Tate not speaking? So, who's really behind it?" she added in a teasing tone. "Is it some gun runner or maybe one of those international terrorists we read about?"

Leta didn't know that Tate had been supporting her! Well she couldn't discuss it on the phone. Time for that when she flew out to South Dakota.

"I'll tell you all about it when I get there," Cecily promised. "See you soon."

"Okay. Take care, baby."

"You take care, too." She put down the receiver.

Leta was going to be hurt that her "children" were at war. She frowned, remembering what Leta had said about losing some tribal funds. She wondered what was going on at Wapiti.

Saturday came and Colby was unexpectedly back in the country, so she asked him to go with her to Senator Holden's birthday party. He agreed, but he sounded solemn. When he came to pick her up, she could see how tired he was.

"I shouldn't have asked you," she said gently, knowing better than to ask him what was wrong.

He shrugged. "It beats sitting at home, thinking." He smiled wanly. "I'm bad company. But I'll give it a shot."

They left Cecily's apartment and drove to the Senator's residence.

Cecily stared around her at the elegant company of politicians, millionaires and other guests assembled in the huge ballroom of Senator Matt Holden's Maryland home. Her upswept medium blond hair was neatly done and her knee-length black cocktail dress, while off the rack, was tasteful. But her pale green eyes were restless. She felt vulnerable without her glasses. She hadn't wanted to bother with them, since Colby was driving. And she hated the worry of trying to wear contact lenses. Besides, who did she need to see, anyway? She and Colby had arrived just in time to wander through the buffet and nibble at the delicious spread. There was everything from caviar to champagne.

Now that they'd finished eating, she wished he would hurry back with the coffee. She was uncomfortable among people whose casual conversation centered around investments, foreign travel and upcoming appropriation bills. She didn't travel in monied circles. As she studied the people around her being offered drinks by a white-coated, white-gloved waiter, she grinned to herself thinking that her usual companions these days were skeletons. She glanced at the tureen in the waiter's hands and had an attack of conscience.

She draped her small evening bag over one shoulder and wandered quietly through the room of guests, nodding and smiling politely at people she knew mainly from the nightly news. She was in glittering company, but she was a stranger, alone in this packed gathering. She'd have been more at home in her office at the museum. Or on the reservation with Leta.

It was an unusually quiet cocktail party, she thought, and conversation was muted and somber around her. Recent turmoil in Washington, D.C., had thrown a shroud over the celebration of Senator Holden's birthday. Holden was the senior Republican senator from South Dakota, a fiery, difficult man who made enemies as easily as he ran the Senate Committee on Indian Affairs, of which he was chairman. He had his finger in plenty of political pies and some private ones. His most recent private one was private sector funding for his pet project, the newly created Anthropological and Archaeological Museum of the Native American where Cecily now worked.

She spotted Matt Holden and her eyes began to twinkle. He was a handsome devil, even at his age. His wife had died the year before, and the husky black-eyed politician with his glimmering silver hair and elegant broad-shouldered physique was now on every widow's list of eligibles. Even now, two lovely elderly society dames were attacking from both sides with expensive perfume and daring cleavage. At least one of them should have worn something high-necked, she mused, with her collarbone and skinny neck so prominent.

Another pair of eyes followed her amused gaze. "Doesn't it remind you of shark attacks?" a pleasant voice murmured in her ear.

She jumped, and looked up at her companion for the evening. "Good grief, Colby, you scared me out of a year's growth!" she burst out with a helpless laugh.

Colby only smiled. "Here's your coffee. It's not bad, either."

He handed her the cup and sipped from his own. She wondered why he'd been out of the country at the same time as Tate, and why. Then she shut Tate out of her mind. She wasn't going to think about him tonight.

"You never did say where you went," she told the lithe congenial man at her side.

He mentioned a war-torn country in Africa, then murmured, "And you didn't hear that from me."

She sobered quickly. Everyone knew about the strife and the terrible aftermath of surreptitious bombings. It was all that people talked about. "Those poor people."

"Amen."

She glanced up at him. "I suppose you were involved somehow in the capture of the suspects?"

He only smiled. He would never talk about assignments. Colby wasn't a handsome man, especially with all the scars on his lean face. His thick, faintly wavy short black hair was his best asset. Still he did have a dangerous magnetism that Cecily knew didn't go unnoticed by the ladies. Unfortunately he was too stuck in the past to even look at another woman twice. His wife of five years had left him two years back and found someone else; someone who was at home more, already had two children of his own and didn't risk his life for his job. His benders since her departure were legendary. Cecily's intervention with the Maryland psychologist had saved him from certain alcoholism, but he still teetered dangerously on the edge of ruin. A pity, she thought, to love someone so much and lose them and be unable to let go. Just like herself mooning over Tate, she thought with bitterness.

"Seen Tate lately?" Colby asked carelessly.

She stiffened. "No."

He looked down at her with a wry grin. "It was a

boring banquet, anyway. You made all the news shows that night, and I hear one of the bigger late-night television hosts did a monologue about it!''

"Go ahead," she invited with a gesture. "Rub it in.''

"I can't help myself," he said with an involuntary chuckle. "I believe it's the first time in American political history that an ex-CIA agent was baptized with a tureen of crab bisque right in the middle of a televised political affair.'' Colby had to work hard not to crack a smile. He sipped his coffee instead. Before he met Cecily, he couldn't have imagined any woman doing that to tall, handsome, elegant Tate Winthrop. "Matt Holden seems to have forgiven you," he added.

She smiled wickedly. "He loved it," she said. "Just between you and me, he thrives on publicity.''

Colby's dark eyes went to Holden. "You might also have been invited because he likes embarrassing Tate,'' he mused. "Talk about natural enemies!''

Cecily shifted from one leg to the other. Her high heeled shoes were getting uncomfortable. She didn't go out much formally. "I know. Tate's gung ho for that proposed casino on the Wapiti Ridge Sioux Reservation in South Dakota to help raise tribal funds and support more programs for teens, to help cut down on alcoholism and violence. The senator, on the other hand, is violently opposed to the casino project on Wapiti. They've locked horns over that issue and several others involving Lakota sovereignty.''

Colby's brows drew together. "Isn't the senator Lakota?"

Cecily grinned. "His father was from Morocco," she said. "He hasn't got a drop of Lakota blood. But he looks it, doesn't he? Maybe that's why he gets the Lakota vote every election. That, and the fact that his mother used to teach at the Lakota school on Wapiti Ridge, or so I've heard." Thinking about that, she wondered if Leta had ever met Matt in her youth. They were about the same age.

"Did he know Tate's family then?"

"He may have known of them, but he ran for congress before Tate was even born, and he came to D.C. as a freshman senator the same year in a landslide victory."

"You didn't know him until this museum thing came up."

"That's true." She smoothed down the narrow skirt of her dress and glanced with irritation at a mud spot on her black suede sling-backs. "Darn," she said. "It was raining and I had to walk on the grass. I've got mud all over my shoes. They're brand-new, too."

"I'll carry you across the grass on the return trip, if you like," Colby offered with twinkling eyes. "It would have to be over one shoulder, of course," he added with a wry glance at his artificial arm.

She frowned at the bitterness in his tone. He was a little fuzzy because she needed glasses to see at distances.

"Listen, nobody in her right mind would ever take you for a cripple," she said gently and with a warm smile. She laid a hand on his sleeve. "Anyway," she added with a wicked grin, "I've already given the news media enough to gossip about just recently. I don't need any more complications in my life. I've only just gotten rid of one big one."

Colby studied her with an amused smile. She was the only woman he'd ever known that he genuinely liked. He was about to speak when he happened to glance over her shoulder at a man approaching them. "About that big complication, Cecily."

"What about it?" she asked.

"I'd say it's just reappeared with a vengeance. No, don't turn around," he said, suddenly jerking her close to him with the artificial arm that looked so real, a souvenir of one of his foreign assignments. "Just keep looking at me and pretend to be fascinated with my nose, and we'll give him something to think about."

She laughed in spite of the racing pulse that always accompanied Tate's appearances in her life. She studied Colby's lean, scarred face. He wasn't anybody's idea of a pinup, but he had style and guts and if it hadn't been for Tate, she would have found him very attractive. "Your nose has been broken twice, I see," she told Colby.

"Three times, but who's counting?" He lifted his eyes and his eyebrows at someone behind her. "Well, hi, Tate! I didn't expect to see you here tonight."

"Obviously," came a deep, gruff voice that cut like a knife.

Colby loosened his grip on Cecily and moved back a little. "I thought you weren't coming," he said.

Tate moved into Cecily's line of view, half a head taller than Colby Lane. He was wearing evening clothes, like the other men present, but he had an elegance that made him stand apart. She never tired of gazing into his large black eyes which were deep-set in a dark, handsome face with a straight nose, and a wide, narrow, sexy mouth and faintly cleft chin. He was the most beautiful man. He looked as if all he needed was a breastplate and feathers in his hair to bring back the heyday of the Lakota warrior in the nineteenth century. Cecily remembered him that way from the ceremonial gatherings at Wapiti Ridge, and the image stuck stubbornly in her mind.

"Audrey likes to rub elbows with the rich and fa-mous," Tate returned. His dark eyes met Cecily's fierce green ones. "I see you're still in Holden's good graces. Has he bought you a ring yet?"

"What's the matter with you, Tate?" Cecily asked with a cold smile. "Feeling…crabby?"

His eyes smoldered as he glared at her. "What did you give Holden to get that job at the museum?" he asked with pure malice.

Anger at the vicious insinuation caused her to draw back her hand holding the half-full coffee cup, and Colby caught her wrist smoothly before she could sling the contents at the man towering over her.

Tate ignored Colby. His eyes began to glitter as he looked at Cecily. "Don't make that mistake again," he said in a voice so quiet it was barely audible. He looked as if all his latent hostilities were waiting for an excuse to turn on her. "If you throw that cup at me, so help me, I'll carry you over and put you down in the punch bowl!"

"You and the CIA, maybe!" Cecily hissed. "Go ahead and try...!"

Tate actually took a step toward her just as Colby managed to get between them. "Now, now," he cautioned.

Cecily wasn't backing down an inch. Neither was Tate. He'd gone from lazy affection and indulgent amusement to bristling antagonism in the space of weeks. Lately he flew into a rage if Cecily's name was mentioned, but Colby hadn't told her that.

"You have no right to make that kind of insinuation about me," she said through her teeth. "I don't get jobs lying on my back, and you know it!"

Tate's black eyes narrowed. He looked formidable, but Cecily wasn't intimidated by him. She never had been. He glanced at her hands, which were clenched on her cup, and then back to her rigid features. It had infuriated him to be the object of televised ridicule at the political dinner, and Audrey's comments had only made things worse. He was carrying a grudge. But as he looked at Cecily, he felt an emptiness in his very soul. This woman had been a thorn in his side for years, ever since an impulsive act of compassion had made her his responsibility. In those days, she'd been demure and sweet and dependent on him, and her shy hero worship had been vaguely flattering. Now, she was a fiery, independent woman who didn't give a damn about his disapproval or, apparently, his company, and she had done everything except leave town to keep out of his way.

She was still like an adopted daughter to his mother, but Tate couldn't get near her now. He didn't like admitting how much it hurt to have Cecily turn her back on him. All Audrey's charms hadn't been able to erase the memory of Cecily's wounded, accusing eyes when Audrey had told her the truth about her so-called grant. He wished he'd never confided in the socialite. In the early days of their relationship, he'd been more forthcoming about the past than he should have been. It never occurred to him that Audrey would tell everything she knew to everyone who came within speaking distance. Amazing that he could be so easily taken in by a pretty face. Not that he hadn't learned his lesson. Audrey heard nothing from him now that he wouldn't mind having the media overhear. But the damage was done. It was standing in front of him with blazing green eyes and clenched hands. And to have Colby Lane, his friend, on the verge of an affair with Cecily...

"Why are you in town?" he asked Colby abruptly.

"I wasn't needed any longer," the other man replied with a grin. "Apparently my methods of interrogation were a little too...intense for some of our politically correct colleagues. They sent me home."

"Marshmallows," Tate muttered. "And did you see who was handling the investigation?"

"I did." Colby finished his coffee. "Whatever happened to the good old days when the "company" handled overseas intelligence?" he wondered.

"Oh, no," Audrey said in her husky voice as she joined them, ravishing in a red satin dress with a matching chiffon overlay. It looked like couture, and frightfully expensive. It probably was. She was dripping diamonds. "No shop talk," she continued, pressing Tate's arm to her breasts. She gave Cecily a cursory, contemptuous glance and transferred her blue eyes to Colby with a flirtatious smile. "Hi, Colby. Long time, no see."

He smiled back, but his eyes didn't. "I've been busy."

"Too busy to come and see your best friend?" she chided. "We've invited you for dinner twice and you always have an excuse."

Insinuating, of course, that she and Tate were living together, which Cecily already knew because of what Leta had told her. Cecily didn't react visibly. Inside, she was slowly dying at the images of Tate and Audrey together.

"I've been out of the country for a week, myself, upgrading the security on one of our new oil rig pro-

jects in the Caspian Sea," Tate replied. "We've had
a few problems."

"So I heard," Colby said. "Brauer had friends,
didn't he?" he added, mentioning the German national who'd involved Tate's employer in a kidnap-
ping scheme. "I guess even from prison he can hire
cleaners."

Tate shrugged. "Pierce and I can handle it." He
smiled down at Audrey. "I'm not ready to cash in
my chips yet."

Cecily unobtrusively slid her free hand into
Colby's real one for comfort. Surprised, his fingers
tightened around it.

"Well, it was nice to see you," Colby said, reading
the tiny signal, "but we need to leave pretty soon."

At the coupling of their names, Tate glanced spec-
ulatively from one of them to the other. Everyone
knew that Colby was still in love with his ex-wife,
but he was holding Cecily's hand and acting protective of her. He didn't like that. Colby was teetering
on alcoholism, and Tate didn't want Cecily's life ruined by him. He'd have to think of some way to handle this; for her own good, of course, he decided
firmly.

"So you did show up, after all," Matt Holden said
shortly, joining the small group. He glared at Tate.
"I'm not giving one inch on the casino issue, just in
case you wondered," he said without preamble.

Tate glared back at him. "You're one man. You
won't stop progress."

"Yes, I will," Holden said in a clipped, hostile tone. "I'm not having organized crime at Wapiti Ridge, and if you don't like it, you know what you can do."

"Bull! There's no connection to organized crime at Wapiti. That's just an excuse. But you don't own the governor or the state attorney general," Tate told him. "And you have no influence whatsoever on the res."

"Do you really want to be partners with men who'll take eighty percent of the profit and shoot anybody who tries to stop them?" Holden asked. "I won't have organized crime making a living at the expense of children's food and clothing and housing!"

Tate took a step toward the man, who was a head shorter than he was, and his black eyes were every bit as intimidating as Holden's. "That's strong talk from a big shot Washington bureaucrat who rides around in chauffeured limousines and has his meals on china plates! What the hell do you know about children whose parents can't even afford heat in the winter, who live on a reservation that hasn't even got a damned ambulance to take injured people to the clinic?"

"I know more about it than you think you do," Holden shot back. "Listen here…"

Cecily walked between them, just as Colby had gotten between her and Tate minutes earlier. She smiled at Holden. "My boss at the museum told me that you had a collection of projectile points dating back to the Folsom point," she said. "I don't suppose there's any chance of your showing them to me?"

Holden stood for a moment vibrating with unexpressed anger, but as he looked at Cecily, his rigid features relaxed and he smiled self-consciously. "Yes, I do have such a collection. You really want to see it?"

"Paleo-Indian archaeology is still my first love," she replied. "Yes, I'd very much enjoy that."

He took her arm. "If you'll excuse us?"

Cecily didn't look back. She went right along with the senator, apparently hanging on every word.

"Why do you do things like that?" Audrey asked snappily, glancing around to find some people still watching them in the wake of the very audible disagreement. "He's a very powerful man, you know. And I think he's right about casinos." She tossed back her shoulder-length blond hair. "There shouldn't even be any reservations in the first place," she muttered, missing Tate's angry stare. "We're all Americans. It's stupid to support a bunch of people who'd rather live with bears than in cities. They should just phase out the reservations and let everybody live together."

Colby pursed his lips and glanced at Tate. He spoke a few words, softly, in a gutteral language that the other man understood very well.

"Why are you dating Cecily?" Tate asked instead of answering the question he'd been asked in Lakota.

Colby looked nonchalant. "She's single. I'm single. I like her."

"I can't imagine why you'd agree to be seen with her in public," Audrey sniffed. "She has no breeding and she's a social disaster."

"Listen, she didn't pour crab bisque all over me," Colby said with a deliberately provoking glance at Tate. "She wouldn't have poured it on you if you'd told her the truth from the beginning. Cecily hates lies. I can't imagine that you've known her for eight years without realizing that."

"She has the pride of Lucifer," he returned. "She'd never have gone to college in the first place if I hadn't paid for it. She's self-supporting and able to take care of herself. It was worth every penny."

"She is going to pay you back, now that she knows, isn't she?" Audrey asked. "You don't owe her anything, Tate. You were stuck with her, and you're certainly not a relative or anything."

"There are things about my obligation to Cecily that you don't understand," Tate told the woman. He drew in a short breath as he watched Cecily cling to Holden's arm on the way out of the room.

"Like what?" Audrey persisted. "Don't tell me you were lovers!"

"Of course not," Tate said irritably. "And that's all I'm going to say on the subject."

"She's not much to look at even now." Audrey was also staring after Cecily and Holden. "He does like her, doesn't he?" she drawled. "He could afford to keep her. They must spend a lot of time together now that he's involved in that museum.''

That had just occurred to Tate, too, and he didn't like it. Holden was years too old for Cecily.

Colby caught that disapproval in his face, but he didn't remark on it. He held up his empty cup. ''I need a refill. Excuse me.''

He left them together. Audrey leaned against Tate's muscular arm with a soft sigh. ''Why did you want to come to this boring party?'' she asked. ''We could have gone to the ballet with the Carsons instead.''

''I hate ballet.''

''You like opera.''

''There's a difference.'' He was still glaring at the doorway through which Holden and Cecily had vanished. ''What does she see in him?'' he wondered.

''Maybe he likes to dig up dead people, too,'' she said with a contemptuous laugh.

Tate could feel the heat rising over his cheekbones. ''I'm still trying to understand why you told Cecily that I paid for her education.''

She looked up at him innocently. ''You never said I couldn't. She's too old to need a guardian, you know. It was only ever just an excuse to hang around you, getting in my...in *our* way. She'll get over it.''

''Get over what?'' he asked with a scowl.

''Her infatuation.'' She patted his arm, oblivious to the shock on his face. ''All young girls go through it. Someone had to show her that she has no place in your life now.'' She looked up at him adoringly. ''You have me, now.''

He went with her to the punch bowl, still frowning and feeling vague disquiet. Audrey was constantly in his face, getting the manager to let her into his apartment at all hours, even phoning him at work. She was possessive to a frightening degree. He didn't understand why. She was someone to take around, but he wasn't intimately involved with her. She was acting as if they were attached at the hip, and he didn't like it. Her attitude toward Cecily chafed. ''What makes you think she's infatuated with me?'' he asked conversationally.

''Oh, Colby told me once, when he was a little tipsy. It was before they started going around together,'' she said airily. ''He felt sorry for her, but I don't. There are plenty of eligible men in the world. She isn't very attractive, but she'll find someone of her own one day. Maybe even Colby,'' she added thoughtfully. ''They seem very close, don't they— even closer than she and Matt Holden. She might be just the woman to help him get over his ex-wife!''

Chapter Three

The annual Pow Wow on the Wapiti Ridge Sioux reservation in southwestern South Dakota was Cecily's favorite event. She'd promised Leta that she'd show up for it, and she had, begging an extra day off past the weekend on the excuse that she was going to look into buying some handicrafts from the reservation for the museum. Tate wasn't likely to be here. Colby had mentioned that he was abroad again, so Cecily felt safe, for the moment. It would have hurt Leta's feelings if she hadn't come, since Leta didn't know why there was a rift between her son and Cecily.

She looked around at the beautiful costumes, many made of fringed buckskin and very old, some of more recent vintage. Most Pow Wows were held in the summer months. Then she reminded herself that mid-

September was still summer, even if there was a nip in the air here.

She didn't have a drop of Lakota blood, but she had closer connections to this branch of the Oglala tribe than most whites. Tate Winthrop and his mother Leta had given Cecily refuge when she was still in her teens. She and Tate still weren't speaking after the crab bisque attack, but Leta was like the mother she'd lost.

"I see a lot more people here this year," Cecily told Leta, scanning the colorful crowd while sitting on hay bales around a circle where a dance competition was being held to the throbbing beat and chant of the drummers.

"They advertised it more this year," Leta replied with a grin. She was young-looking for fifty-four, a little plump but with a pretty face, dark brown eyes and braided silver-flecked dark hair. She was dressed in fawn buckskins and boots with beaded, feathered ornaments in her hair. One of the ornaments was a circle with a cross inside, denoting the circle of life.

"You look lovely," Cecily said with genuine affection.

Leta made a face. "I'm fat. You've lost weight," she added. Her eyes narrowed.

Cecily stretched lazily. She was wearing a simple blue checked shirt with a denim skirt and boots. Her long blond hair was braided and circled around the crown of her head. Pale green eyes behind large framed glasses stared into nothing.

"Remember what I told you on the phone, that I found out the truth about the grant that was paying all my expenses?" she asked.

Leta nodded.

"Well, it wasn't a grant that was paying for my education and living expenses." She took a harsh breath. "It was Tate."

Leta scowled. "Are you sure?"

"I'm very sure." She glanced at the older woman. "I found out in the middle of Senator Matt Holden's political fund-raiser, and I lost my temper. I poured crab bisque all over your son and there were television cameras covering the event." She turned her wounded eyes toward the dancers. "I was devastated when I found out I'm nothing more than a charity case to him."

"That isn't true," Leta said gently, but a little remotely. "You know Tate's very fond of you."

"Yes. Very fond, the way a guardian is fond of a ward. He owned me." She stared at the brown grass under her feet, grimacing at the memory. "I couldn't bear the humiliation of knowing that. I guess he thought I wouldn't be able to make it on my own. I wasn't really very mature at seventeen. But he could have told me the truth. It was horrible to find it out that way, especially at my age." She took a deep breath. "I quit school, moved out of the apartment and took the job Senator Holden was asking me to take at the new museum he helped open. He's a nice man."

Leta looked away nervously. "Is he?" she asked in a curiously strained tone.

"You'd like him," she said with a smile, "even though Tate doesn't."

Leta's shoulders moved as if she were suddenly uncomfortable. "Yes, I know there's friction between them. They don't agree on any Native American issues, most especially on the fight to open a casino on Wapiti Ridge."

"The senator seems to think that organized crime would love to move in, but I don't think there's much danger of that. Other Sioux reservations in the state have perfectly good casinos. Anyway, it's the tribes in other states trying to open casinos that are drawing all the heat from gambling syndicates."

Leta hesitated. "Yes, but just lately…" She caught herself and smiled. "Well, there's no use talking about that right now. But, Cecily, what about your education?"

Of course, Leta knew that Tate had enrolled her in George Washington University near his Washington, D.C., apartment, so that he could keep an eye on her. He worked as security chief for Pierce Hutton's building conglomerate now, a highly paid, hectic and sometimes dangerous job. But it was less wearing on Leta's nerves than when he worked for the government.

"I can go back when I can afford to pay for it myself," Cecily returned.

"There's something more, isn't there?" Leta asked in her soft voice. "Come on, baby. Tell Mama."

Cecily grimaced. She smiled warmly at the older woman. She'd just turned twenty-five, but Leta had been "Mama" since hers had died and left her penniless, at the mercy of a drunken, lusting stepfather.

"Tate's new girl," she said after a minute. "She's really beautiful. She's thirty, divorced and she looks like a model. Blond, blue-eyed, perfect figure, social graces and she's rich."

"Bummer," Leta said drolly.

Cecily burst out laughing at the drawled slang. Leta was one of the most educated women she knew, politically active on sovereignty issues for her tribe and an advocate of literacy programs for young Lakota people. Her husband had died years before, and she'd changed. Jack Yellowbird Winthrop had been a brutal man, very much like Cecily's stepfather. During the time she spent with Leta, he was away on a construction job in Chicago or she'd never have been able to stay in the house with them.

"Tate's a man," Leta continued. "You can't expect him to live like a recluse. His job involves a lot of social events. Where Hutton goes, he goes."

"Yes, but this is...different," Cecily continued. She shrugged. "I saw him with her last week, at a coffeehouse near my apartment. They were holding hands. She's captivated him."

"The Lakota Captive." Leta made a line in the air with her hand. "I can see it now, the wily, brave

Lakota warrior with the brazen white woman pioneer. She carries him off into the sunset over her shoulder…''

Cecily whacked her with a strand of grass she'd pulled.

"You write history your way, I'll write it my way," Leta said wickedly.

"Native Americans are stoic and unemotional," Cecily reminded her. "All the books say so."

"We never read many books in the old days, so we didn't know that," came the dry explanation. She shook her head. "What a sad stereotype so many make of us—a bloodthirsty ignorant people who never smile because they're too busy torturing people over hot fires."

"Wrong tribe," Cecily corrected. She frowned thoughtfully. "That was the northeastern native people."

"Who's the Native American here, you or me?"

Cecily shrugged. "I'm German-American." She brightened. "But I had a grandmother who dated a Cherokee man once. Does that count?"

Leta hugged her warmly. "You're my adopted daughter. You're Lakota, even if you haven't got my blood."

Cecily let her cheek fall to Leta's shoulder and hugged her back. It felt so nice to be loved by someone in the world. Since her mother's death, she'd had no one of her own. It was a lonely life, despite the excitement and adventure her work held for her. She wasn't openly affectionate at all, except with Leta.

"For God's sake, next you'll be rocking her to sleep at night!" came a deep, disgusted voice at Cecily's back, and Cecily stiffened because she recognized it immediately.

"She's my baby girl," Leta told her tall, handsome son with a grin. "Shut up."

Cecily turned a little awkwardly. She hadn't expected this. Tate Winthrop towered over both of them. His jet-black hair was loose as he never wore it in the city, falling thick and straight almost to his waist. He was wearing a breastplate with buckskin leggings and high-topped moccasins. There were two feathers straight up in his hair with notches that had meaning among his people, marks of bravery.

Cecily tried not to stare at him. He was the most beautiful man she'd ever known. Since her seventeenth birthday, Tate had been her world. Fortunately he didn't realize that her mad flirting hid a true emotion. In fact, he treated her exactly as he had when she came to him for comfort after her mother had died suddenly; as he had when she came to him again with bruises all over her thin, young body from her drunken stepfather's violent attack. Although she dated, she'd never had a serious boyfriend. She had secret terrors of intimacy that had never really gone away, except when she thought of Tate that way. She loved him....

"Why aren't you dressed properly?" Tate asked,

scowling at her skirt and blouse. "I bought you buck-skins for your birthday, didn't I?"

"Three years ago," she said without meeting his probing eyes. She didn't like remembering that he'd forgotten her birthday this year. "I gained weight since then."

"Oh. Well, find something you like here..."

She held up a hand. "I don't want you to buy me anything else," she said flatly, and didn't back down from the sudden menace in his dark eyes. "I'm not dressing up like a Lakota woman. In case you haven't noticed, I'm blond. I don't want to be mistaken for some sort of overstimulated Native American groupie buying up artificial artifacts and enthusing over citi-fied Native American flute music, trying to act like a member of the tribe."

"You belong to it," he returned. "We adopted you years ago."

"So you did," she said. That was how he thought of her—a sister. That wasn't the way she wanted him to think of her. She smiled faintly. "But I won't pass for a Lakota, whatever I wear."

"You could take your hair down," he continued thoughtfully.

She shook her head. She only let her hair loose at night, when she went to bed. Perhaps she kept it tightly coiled for pure spite, because he loved long hair and she knew it.

"How old are you?" he asked, trying to remember. "Twenty, isn't it?"

"I was, five years ago," she said, exasperated. "You used to work for the CIA. I seem to remember that you went to college, too, and got a law degree. Didn't they teach you how to count?"

He looked surprised. Where had the years gone? She hadn't aged, not visibly.

"Where's Audrey?" she asked brightly, trying to sound nonchalant about it when her heart was breaking.

Something changed in his face. He looked briefly disturbed. "She couldn't get away," he said in a tone that didn't invite questions. "One of her friends was having a tea, and she promised to help. I flew out alone."

Cecily wondered if it was really because of a party that Audrey had stayed behind, or if his society girl-friend didn't want to be seen on an Native American reservation. Tate had mentioned once or twice that Audrey had asked him repeatedly to get a conservative haircut. As if he'd ever cut his hair willingly. It was a part of his heritage, of which he was fiercely proud. At least she didn't have to worry about him marrying Audrey. He might be smitten, but he'd said for years that he wasn't going to dilute his Lakota blood by mingling it with a white woman. He wanted a child who was purely Lakota, like himself. If he ever married, it would be to a Lakota woman. The first time he'd said that, it had broken Cecily's heart. But she'd come to accept it. When she realized that she was never going to be able to have Tate, she gave up and devoted herself to her studies. At least she was good at archaeology, she mused, even if she was a dismal failure as a woman in Tate's eyes.

"She's been broody ever since we got here," Leta said with pursed lips as she glanced from Tate to Cecily. "You two had a blowup, huh?" she asked, pretending innocence.

Tate drew in a short breath. "She poured crab bisque on me in front of television cameras."

Cecily drew herself up to her full height. "Pity it wasn't flaming shish kebab!" she returned fiercely.

Leta moved between them. "The Sioux wars are over," she announced.

"That's what you think," Cecily muttered, glaring around her at the tall man.

Tate's dark eyes began to twinkle. He'd missed her in his life. Even in a temper, she was refreshing, invigorating.

She averted her eyes to the large grass circle outlined by thick corded string. All around it were makeshift shelters on poles, some with canvas tops, with bales of hay to make seats for spectators. The first competition of the day was over and the winners were being announced. A women-only dance came next, and Leta grimaced as she glanced from one warring face to the other. If she left, there was no telling what might happen.

"That's me," she said reluctantly, adjusting the number on her back. "Got to run. Wish me luck."

"You know I do," Cecily said, smiling at her.

"Don't disgrace us," Tate added with laughter in his eyes.

Leta made a face at him, but smiled. "No fighting," she said, shaking a finger at them as she went to join the other competitors.

Tate's granitelike face had softened as he watched his mother. Whatever his faults, he was a good son.

"She's different since your father died," Cecily commented, sitting down on one of the bales of hay, grateful for the diversion. "I've never seen her so animated."

"My father was a hard man to live with," he replied quietly. "If he hadn't spent most of his life away on construction jobs, I'd probably have killed him."

She knew he wasn't kidding. Jack Winthrop had beaten Leta once, and Tate had wiped the floor with him after coming home unexpectedly and finding his mother cut and bruised. By then, he'd been in espionage work for some time. Jack Winthrop, big and tough as he was, was no match for the experienced younger man. It was the last time Leta ever suffered a beating, too. Jack became afraid of his son. Cecily remembered that Jack had never spoken one kind word about his only child. Oddly he seemed to hate Tate.

"You didn't like your father much, did you?" Cecily remembered.

"He wasn't a likable man." He sat down beside her.

She felt the warm strength of him and closed her eyes briefly to savor it. He hardly ever touched people, not even his mother. In all the long years she'd been part of his life, he'd never touched her with intent. Not to hold her hand, kiss her even on the cheek, brush back her hair. That one time, when she'd flown to Oklahoma to help him with his case was the closest they'd come to intimacy, and that was anticlimactic, even if she had lived on it for weeks afterward. She'd ached for any contact at all, but that wasn't Tate's way. Yet she'd seen him holding hands with Audrey that day in the coffee shop. Nothing had ever hurt so much. It was an indication of the attraction he felt for the gorgeous socialite.

She smiled as she watched Leta doing the intricate steps of the dance inside the circle. All the women were wearing buckskins, a feat of endurance because it was almost ninety degrees in the South Dakota September sun.

"That was a nasty crack I made about you and Senator Holden at his birthday party," he said after a minute. "I didn't mean it."

It was the closest he came to an apology. She was tired of arguing, so she took the olive branch for what it was. "I know."

The mention of birthdays reminded him that he'd deliberately ignored Cecily's this year. It wasn't a pleasant memory. He shifted on the hay, staring at his mother in the circle. "Do you like the job at the museum?"

"Very much. I'll be in charge of acquisitions, which is one reason I came out here. I want to exhibit some Oglala pottery and beadwork."

He didn't look at her. "How did you get to know Holden?"

"He's good friends with a member of the faculty at George Washington University," she said. "I ran into him in the hall one day. He knew me from one of the hearings..." She stopped, because this was part of her life she hadn't shared with Tate.

"Hearings?" he prompted.

She folded her hands on the warm fabric of her skirt. The sun was beating down on her uncovered head. "It was a public hearing on Native American sovereignty. I went to speak in favor of it before the Senate Committee on Indian Affairs, speaking for a committee from the Wapiti reservation. Holden is the chairman of the Senate committee." She kept her eyes on the circle of dancers. "It was Leta's idea," she added quickly. "She said Senator Holden was impressed by anthropology graduates, and I was the only one they could dig up at such short notice."

"I didn't know you involved yourself in political issues."

She glanced at him wryly. "Of course you didn't. You don't know a lot about me."

He scowled as he turned his attention to the circle and watched his mother dance, resplendent in her beautiful buckskins. No, he didn't know a lot about Cecily, but he did know how devastated she'd been to discover he'd paid her way through college, absorbed all her expenses out of pity for her situation. He was sorry for how much that had hurt her. But over the past two years, he'd deliberately distanced himself from her. He wondered why...

"I had dinner with Senator Holden last week," she said conversationally, deliberately trying to irritate him. "He wanted to point me toward some special collections for the museum."

He stared at his mother in the circle, but he was frowning, deep in thought. "I don't like Holden," he said curtly.

"Yes, I know. You'll be delighted to hear that he returned your sentiment," she said with a chuckle at his scowl. "He's really stubborn on the issue of a casino on the Wapiti reservation. We've pointed out the benefits to the tribe time and time again, but he won't give an inch," she recalled. "We could build a bigger clinic, buy an ambulance and train and hire an EMT to drive it. We could fund recreational programs for teens to keep them from drinking and getting into trouble. We could have prenatal programs..."

He was staring at her openly. "When did you talk to him about that?" he asked.

"I've been a thorn in his side for months," she said easily. "I've left him e-mail messages, put notes under his door, left voice mail, sent tapes of the poverty on the reservation through the mail. He knows me very well indeed. But most recently I got him to listen to me over a nice dinner at the local cafeteria between Senate sessions,'' she recalled. "He's afraid of organized crime. He seems to have some suspicions about the motives of the tribal chief who's so determined to get the casino approved by the state government for Class III gambling.''

"Tom Black Knife," he said, nodding, because he knew the tribal chief, and there had been some gossip about the way he earmarked tribal funds. Not a lot of money was going into the reservation's projects right now, and nobody seemed to know exactly where the money was going. Some was even missing, if Tate had understood a random comment one of his cousins had made earlier today. Tom was a good man with a kind heart, the softest touch on the reservation. Odd that his name would be connected with anything as unsavory as embezzlement. "But Holden is overlooking the benefits of the money the casino would bring in. Several Native American tribes have instituted casinos and had to fight state government all the way to get them. There are other casinos on Sioux land right here in our own state, but Holden is fighting our proposed compact with everything he's got. Holden's opposition hurts us in South Dakota, because he has powerful political allies in Pierre and no scruples about using them against us. One of them," he added darkly, "is the state attorney general herself!''

"I know," she said. Her pale eyes gazed into his dark ones. "But I'm working on the senator.''

He didn't even blink. "Working on him, how?''

Here we go again, she thought with resignation. Her eyebrows lifted. He was acting as if she'd already seduced the man! On second thought, why not live down to that image? She leaned forward avidly. "Well, first I smeared him with honey and licked my way down to his throat..." she began earnestly.

He cursed sharply.

She laughed helplessly. "All right, it was just dinner. But he really is a very nice man, Tate," she said.

He gave her a hard glare. "Listen, Cecily, going around with a man old enough to be your father isn't the way to fight your hang-ups."

"My hang-ups?" She glared at him. "Do feel free to elaborate."

"You have friends instead of lovers," he said curtly.

"I'm a modern woman," she said coolly. "That means I have the right to decide what I do with my body. Some women, I might add, advocate using men only for breeding purposes. I myself think they'd be more useful as house pets."

His black eyes twinkled. He waved to his mother who was just dancing past them with an ear to ear smile. "All the same, I don't like seeing you with Holden."

"I don't particularly care what you like," she said and smiled sweetly at him.

He hated that damned smile. It was like a red flag. "Listen, kid, you don't know beans about some of the political superstars in Congress, and Holden is an unknown commodity. He guards his privacy like a mercenary. I don't like him and I don't trust him. He's too secretive.''

"Look who's talking!" she exclaimed. "You could probably topple governments with things you know and don't tell!''

"Sure I could," he agreed. "But I'm not shady.''

She just looked at him. It was a speaking look.

"Maybe a little shady," he conceded finally. "A man has to have a few secrets.''

"So does a woman.''

He smoothed a hand down the buckskin leggings on one of his powerful thighs. "I hope you aren't going to let what happened to you in Corryville ruin the rest of your life," he said without looking at her. "You should go around with men your own age.''

She met his narrowed eyes. "I had my share of dates when I started college. It's amazing that every single one of them thought he was entitled to my bed in return for a nice dinner and some dancing. And you know what I got when I said no? They told me I wasn't liberated.'' She threw up her hands. "What does liberation have to do with rejecting a man with bad breath who looks like a lab rat?''

"You won't get around me by changing the subject," he continued doggedly. "Holden isn't the sort of man you need in your life and neither is Colby Lane.''

The silence beside her was thick with suppressed anger. Colby was ex-CIA, too, now a mercenary who did freelance work for various organizations, including, so rumor had it, the government. He was almost as tough as Tate. But he had a few more visible flaws. Tate was his friend and he couldn't miss the fact that Cecily and Colby were close—even Audrey had pointed it out to him. But he didn't like having Cecily dating the man, and Cecily knew it by his very silence.

She held up a hand before he could continue. "I know he's had his problems in the past…"

"He can't keep his hands off a liquor bottle at the best of times, and he still hasn't accepted the loss of his wife!"

"I sent him to a therapist over in Baltimore," she continued. "He's narrowed his habit down to a six-pack of beer on Saturdays."

"What does he get for a reward?" he asked insolently.

She sighed irritably. "Nobody suits you! You don't even like poor old lonely Senator Holden."

"Like him? Holden?" he asked, aghast. "Good God, he's the one man in Congress I'd like to burn at the stake! I'd furnish the wood and the matches!"

"You and Leta," she said, shaking her head. "Now, listen carefully. The Lakota didn't burn people at the stake," she said firmly. She went on to explain who did, and how, and why.

He searched her enthusiastic eyes. "You really do love Native American history, don't you?"

She nodded. "The way your ancestors lived for

thousands of years was so logical. They honored the man in the tribe who was the poorest, because he gave away more than the others did. They shared everything. They gave gifts, even to the point of bankrupting themselves. They never hit a little child to discipline it. They accepted even the most blatant differences in people without condemning them.'' She glanced at Tate and found him watching her. She smiled self-consciously. ''I like your way better.''

''Most whites never come close to understanding us, no matter how hard they try.''

''I had you and Leta to teach me,'' she said simply. ''They were wonderful lessons that I learned, here on the reservation. I feel…at peace here. At home. I belong, even though I shouldn't.''

He nodded. ''You belong,'' he said, and there was a note in his deep voice that she hadn't heard before.

Unexpectedly he caught her small chin and turned her face up to his. He searched her eyes until she felt as if her heart might explode from the excitement of the way he was looking at her. His thumb whispered up to the soft bow of her mouth with its light covering of pale pink lipstick. He caressed the lower lip away from her teeth and scowled as if the feel of it made some sort of confusion in him.

He looked straight into her eyes. The moment was almost intimate, and she couldn't break it. Her lips parted and his thumb pressed against them, hard.

''Now, isn't that interesting?'' he said to himself in a low, deep whisper.

"Wh...what?" she stammered.

His eyes were on her bare throat, where her pulse was hammering wildly. His hand moved down, and he pressed his thumb to the visible throb of the artery there. He could feel himself going taut at the unexpected reaction. It was Oklahoma all over again, when he'd promised himself he wouldn't ever touch her again. Impulses, he told himself firmly, were stupid and sometimes dangerous. And Cecily was off limits. Period.

He pulled his hand back and stood up, grateful that the loose fit of his buckskins hid his physical reaction to her.

"Mother's won a prize," he said. His voice sounded oddly strained. He forced a nonchalant smile and turned to Cecily. She was visibly shaken. He shouldn't have looked at her. Her reactions kindled new fires in him.

He reached down suddenly and caught her arms, pulling her up with him, deliberately closer than he needed to. He drew her a step closer, so that he could feel the whip of her excited breath against his throat. His fingers tightened on her arms, almost bruising them. Time seemed to stop for a space of seconds. He didn't even hear the drums or the chants or the murmur of conversation around them. For the first time in memory, he wanted to crush Cecily down the length of his body and grind his mouth into hers. The thought shocked him so badly that he let her go all at once, turned and walked toward the circle without even looking back.

Cecily stared after him and her legs shook. She must have dreamed what just happened, she told herself. It was years of hunger for Tate that had made her mind snap. Besides, he wasn't even attracted to her. Yes, she thought, moving toward Leta like a sleepwalker, it had only been a dream. Only another hopeless waking dream.

Cecily had planned to stay overnight and fly out the next morning, but when she and Leta went back to the small frame house in the headquarters village where Leta lived, Tate was sprawled in the easy chair watching the color television he'd given Leta last Christmas. She had good furniture and propane gas heat, one of the few houses to boast such luxuries. Tate made sure Leta lacked for nothing. It was a different story elsewhere, with elderly people trying to keep warm in fifty-below-zero temperatures with woodstoves in houses that were never tight enough to keep in the heat. The reservation was small and poor, despite the efforts of various missionary groups and some government assistance. Education, Cecily thought, was certainly the key to prosperity, but that was another difficulty that needed to be overcome. Native American colleges were springing up these days when funding could be had, places where the people could keep their traditions and their culture alive while learning the skills that would give them good jobs. It was one of Leta's dreams to have such a place on the Wapiti Ridge.

"You still here?" Leta asked her son with a broad grin.

"I thought I'd stay until tomorrow," he replied without looking at Cecily.

"I have to get to the airport," Cecily remarked cheerfully, her eyes cautioning Leta not to contradict her. "I'm due back at work Monday morning."

She and Leta knew that wasn't true, but Cecily couldn't imagine staying under the same roof with Tate. Not now.

"How about some coffee?" Tate asked his mother as he rose from the chair and turned off the television.

"I'll make it," Leta volunteered and hurried to the small kitchen to hide her glee.

Tate moved close to Cecily, an unusual thing for him to do. He never liked her closer than arm's length. Having him so close now made her nervous.

"There's a dance tonight," he told her. "We're going."

"I think Leta's had enough dancing," she began.

He shook his head. "You and I are going."

Her eyebrows lifted. "I wasn't asked."

Without counting the cost, he framed her face in his lean, warm hands and brought his mouth down gently on her shocked lips.

She made a sound that aroused and delighted him. He gathered her in, riveting her to the length of him while the kiss suddenly became hungry, demanding, intimate.

It was like falling. It was like having every single dream of her adult life come true. His mouth was hard and slow and exquisitely sensuous. She didn't like knowing how he'd gotten the experience that made him such a tender lover, but the wonder of it erased the jealousy. She held to his hard arms to keep from falling down and tried to respond enthusiastically, if a little inexperienced. He tasted of heaven. She opened her lips a little more to tempt him, and her hands tightened on the hard muscles of his arms, trying to hold him where he was. Years of dreaming of this, waiting, hoping, and it was actually happening! He was kissing her as if he loved her mouth...

His head lifted. His black eyes told her nothing as they searched her face intently. His hands on her arms were bruising. "We'll have supper before we go to the dance," he said, his voice a little strained.

"What do you want to eat?" Leta called suddenly from the kitchen.

"Sandwiches," he called back. "Okay?"

"Okay! I'll make some."

Tate's eyes went back to Cecily. She was looking at him as if he were the very secret of life. He was in over his head already, he reasoned. He might as well go the rest of the way. His body throbbed all over with just that one small taste of her. He had to have more. He had to, and damn the consequences!

He bent, lifting her in his arms like precious treasure, and carried her back to the armchair with his heart threatening to push through his chest. He settled down in it, his hand pressing her cheek to his buck-skin-clad shoulder as he bent again to her mouth before she could speak.

The seconds lengthened, sweetened. Cecily's hands explored his long hair, his cheeks, his eyebrows, his nose as if she'd never touched a man in her life. It was delicious, taboo, forbidden. It was exquisite. She moaned softly, unable to contain the sheer joy of being in Tate's arms at last. He heard the tiny sound and his mouth suddenly became demanding, insistent.

Kissing was suddenly no longer enough. His lean hand went to her rib cage and slowly worked its way up over one of her small, firm breasts. He lifted his head to search her eyes as he touched the hardness there, because this was difficult territory for her, with her memories of her stepfather. The man had all but raped her. Even therapy hadn't completely healed her fears of intimacy after eight years.

She read that thought in his eyes. "It's all right," she whispered, worried that he was going to stop.

In fact, he was. He searched her bright eyes and smoothed his hand deliberately over her small, hard-tipped breast, but guilt consumed him. She'd never even had a lover. It wasn't fair to treat her like this, not when he had no future to offer her. "You shouldn't have let me do that, Cecily," he said quietly.

He propelled her out of the chair and onto her feet,

holding her firmly by the shoulders for a few seconds until he could breathe normally. "Go help Leta in the kitchen."

"Bossy," she accused breathlessly. The kisses had her reeling visibly.

"Thousands of years of conditioning don't vanish overnight," he mused. He searched her face with traces of hunger still in his eyes. "Do you still carry that week's supply of prophylactics around with you?" he added wickedly.

She actually blushed. "I gave up on you and threw them out years ago."

His eyes went up and down her soft body like hands. "Pity."

"You said you wouldn't, ever!" she protested.

One eyebrow arched and his lips pursed. He was trying to lighten the tension, but just looking at her now aroused him. "So I did. Eloquently, too."

She was trembling. She wrapped both arms around herself to fight the emotion that was consuming her. She looked up at him accusingly. "You enjoy tormenting me, don't you?"

He scowled. "Maybe I do."

She turned away. "I'm flying out tonight."

"No need. I'm not staying." He went around her to the kitchen and kissed Leta goodbye where she stood at the counter making sandwiches.

"Make up before you go," she pleaded with her son.

"I did," he lied.

She touched his cheek sadly. "Stubborn," she murmured, then she smiled. "Like your father."

The mention of Jack Winthrop closed his face. "I've never hit you."

She caught her breath and her hand came down. She gnawed her lower lip. "Someday," she said hesitantly, "we must have a talk."

"Not today," he countered, oblivious to the guilt in her face. "I've got to get back to work."

"You don't like Senator Holden." She said it abruptly and without thinking, just as she'd said he was like his father. He didn't know who his father was. She still couldn't bring herself to tell him.

He turned. "There's no one I like less," he agreed. "He's wrong down the line about Wapiti Ridge and what's good for us, but he won't see reason. He doesn't know a thing about the Lakota, and he couldn't care less!"

"He grew up here," she said slowly.

"What?"

"He grew up here," she continued. "Before his mother was a widow, she came here to teach at the school. He had friends on the reservation, including Black Knife."

"You never told me that you knew him," he accused.

"You never asked me. I've known him for a long time."

He stared at her curiously. "If he knows the situation here, why is he fighting us on the idea of the casino?''

"He hates gambling," she said. "I haven't seen him in many years," she added, "not since he married that pretty white woman and ran for the senate the first time."

"His wife is dead."

She nodded. "I read it in the papers." Her eyes searched his. "Cecily says you have a pretty white woman of your own."

"Damn Cecily!" he said through his teeth, hating his own stupidity for touching Cecily in the first place and frustrated by the painful attraction he couldn't satisfy. "What I do is no business of hers! It never was, and it never will be!"

"Amen to that," Cecily said from the doorway, a little less confident because of his biting remarks, but calm just the same. "Why don't you go home to Audrey?"

"I don't understand this," Leta said worriedly as she studied her son. "You keep saying you don't want to be involved with a white woman…"

"Only with a plain white woman," Cecily corrected. "Isn't that right, Tate? But Audrey is beautiful."

It was only then that he realized how Cecily must feel about his relationship with the other woman, as if he'd bypassed her because she was no beauty. It wasn't true. He'd been responsible for her for years, even if she hadn't known it until recently. He'd fought his attraction to her because it was like exploiting her, taking advantage of her gratitude for what he'd done for her. How did he explain that without making matters worse than they already were?

Leta could have wept for Cecily, standing there with such dignity and poise, even in the face of Tate's hostility.

"It has nothing to do with beauty," Tate said finally.

Cecily only smiled. "I'll finish the sandwiches while you see Tate off," she told Leta.

"Cecily..." Tate began hesitantly.

"We all act on impulse occasionally," she said, meeting his eyes bravely. "It's no big thing. Really." She smiled, avoiding Leta's probing gaze, and turned to the refrigerator. "Are you eating before you go?"

He scowled fiercely. She thought he regretted touching her. Perhaps he did. He couldn't remember being so confused.

"No," he said after a minute. "I'll get something at the airport."

Leta went with him and waited while he got his suitcase and carried it out to his rental car, which was parked beside the one Cecily had rented. The reservation was a long drive from the airport, so a car was a necessity.

"You two used to get along so well," Leta murmured.

"I've been blind," he said through his teeth. "Stark staring blind."

"What do you mean?"

He stared out across the rolling hills that were turning golden as autumn approached. "She's in love with me."

It was a shock to hear himself say it. Until then, he hadn't really considered it. But Cecily had lain in his arms as trusting as a child, clinging to him. Her eyes had been rapt with pleasure, joy glistening in them. Why hadn't he known? Or was it that he hadn't wanted to know?

"You mustn't let her see that you know," Leta instructed grimly. "She is proud."

"Yes." He touched his mother's shoulder. "There are so few of us left who are full-bloods," he said, wondering why Leta grimaced. Perhaps she'd hoped that he might marry Cecily one day, despite her pride in their heritage.

"And you won't marry a white girl," she said.

He nodded solemnly. "Audrey is costume jewelry. I wear her on my arm. She's sophisticated and savvy and shallow. It means nothing. Just as the other handful meant nothing."

Leta's eyes fell to his chest. "That isn't all."

He sighed. "I've taken care of Cecily for eight years," he reminded her. "Even without the cultural differences, I'm in the position of a guardian to her, whether she likes it or not. I can't take advantage of what she feels for me."

"Of course you can't." Leta linked her fingers together. "Drive safely."

He pulled a small package from his jacket pocket. "Give this to her after I'm gone. It's her birthday present." He smiled ruefully. "We weren't speaking, so she didn't get it on her birthday."

"She may not want it."

He knew that. It hurt. "Try."

She watched him drive away down the winding dirt road that cut through to the main highway. She knew that one day soon she was going to have to share a painful truth with him. Things were happening that he didn't know about. Things that involved herself and Matt Holden and some vicious men in chauffeured limousines and the tribal chief. It was not a prospect she relished.

Chapter Four

Cecily lived on dreams for a week while she tried to come to grips with the monumental change in her relationship with Tate. Even if he'd resorted to bad temper to get out of a potentially embarrassing situation, he'd felt something. Lying in his arms, feeling his hungry kisses on her mouth, the touch of his hands on her face and her throat, she could sense his hunger for her. The wonderful thing was that she hadn't been afraid. It occurred to her that the revulsion she felt with other men wasn't completely because of her traumatic flight from home. Part of it was because her heart was set on Tate. He was the only man for her. She'd always known that he was fond of her. Until he kissed her, though, she hadn't known that he wanted her, too.

But it was obvious that Tate wasn't going to give in to his feelings, regardless of how strong they were.

In a way she couldn't blame him. They'd had this discussion before, almost two years ago, when she'd teased him about the mythical prophylactics she carried around with her. By exaggerating her feelings for him, she'd hidden them. But now, after her headlong response, he probably knew the truth. It had been, she recalled, much too obvious that she loved his kisses.

She wasn't sure that she could handle seeing him again so soon. She stayed away from the coffee shop she'd seen him frequent. There was a nice little seafood restaurant near her new office at the museum, and she started having lunch there, since she knew Tate didn't care for fish.

But one day at lunch she did spot a familiar face. Senator Matt Holden was standing just inside the doorway, with his hands jammed deep in his pockets and a ferocious scowl on his face. He was looking around as if searching for someone when he spotted her and made a beeline for her table.

She paused with her fork in midair. "Why, Senator…" she began.

He held up a hand, pulled a chair up close to her and leaned forward with his forearms on the table. "Cecily, I'm up to my neck in trouble. I need to speak with you privately, as soon as possible."

This was unprecedented, and a little flattering. If he had a problem she could help him with, certainly she would, although she couldn't think how someone like herself could help a powerful senior United States senator. Still she owed him her new job. So, having already paid for her lunch, she put down her fork, and followed him out to his waiting limousine.

He closed the curtain between them and the driver and leaned back.

"What is it?" Cecily asked.

He held up a hand and shook his head. "I thought you might appreciate a ride back to your office," he said lazily, as if he didn't have a problem in the world. "And I need to speak with your boss about that new exhibit in the Sioux section."

Cecily caught on at once. "I'm grateful for the lift. In fact, I wanted to ask what you thought of the beaded moccasins and the textile samples I brought back from my trip to the Wapiti Ridge reservation."

"I'd love to see them!" he said with a grin.

They rode in silence the few blocks to the new museum, where the driver let them out. Senator Holden sent him off with instructions to return in an hour. He took Cecily's arm and led her up the steps to the shining new building, where workmen were still scattered around adding glass panels and wallpaper and paint to the few areas that hadn't been completed on schedule. The interior decorator was there, too, pointing out flaws in workmanship while a morose man in white painter's clothing sighed helplessly.

Cecily opened the door to her office, noting that her secretary, Beatrice, had left a note on the computer keyboard reading, Gone To Lunch.

Senator Holden glanced at it before he followed Cecily inside and closed the door. He leaned back against it, staring at Cecily as she dropped into her swivel chair and waited.

"You're quick," he said with admiration. "I didn't want to talk in front of the chauffeur. He's a replacement for my regular one and I don't trust him. Hell, I don't trust anyone right now except you."

"I'm flattered. What's wrong?"

"Has Leta mentioned anything about a gambling syndicate sniffing around the reservation?" he asked bluntly.

She frowned. "Gambling syndicate?"

He sighed angrily. "She hasn't. Maybe she doesn't even know what's going on." He ran a hand through his thick silver hair and began to pace. "I'll be damned if I know what to do! I can't back down now. These people are dangerous. If they aren't stopped, they'll get a stranglehold on the reservation that nothing can ever break. Besides that," he continued, oblivious to Cecily's puzzled stare, "I've just given a freelance job to Tate Winthrop, upgrading the security in my office after the attempted shooting a few months ago in the capitol building. If that gets out, I could find myself in front of an investigating committee. I have to pull him off the job, and he isn't going to understand why. And I can't tell him!" He glanced at her and saw her confused expression. He smiled wanly. "You haven't got a clue what I'm talking about."

"Fair assessment," she agreed. "Why don't you sit down and stop pacing?"

"I'll go mad."

"Please?"

He hesitated for a few seconds before he resigned himself to sitting in the chair beside her desk. He leaned forward, deeply troubled. "What do you know about Tate Winthrop's...father?"

The pause between those words was curious, but she answered him without pondering them. "Not a lot. He was mostly away on construction jobs while I stayed with Leta, and I only know about him from her. He was a brutal man who drank to excess when he was at home and beat Leta and hated his only child," she said simply. "Leta said that Jack Winthrop tormented Tate every chance he got, and if she interfered, he knocked her around. At least, he did until one day Tate came home unexpectedly and found her after Jack had finished with her. They still talk about Jack Winthrop running like a madman from his son afterward, barely able to get out of the way in the condition he was in." She wondered about the look on Holden's face. He was furious. "Tate said once that if Jack Winthrop hadn't died of natural causes, he'd probably have killed him one day. I don't think he was kidding."

Holden stared at his big hands. "Leta's such a tiny little thing," he said quietly, almost to himself. "I can't imagine anyone brutal enough, cruel enough, to hurt her deliberately."

"You know Leta?" she asked abruptly.

"Most of my life," he replied gruffly. "My mother

taught at the school on the reservation after my father died. I grew up around the Lakota. In fact, Tom Black Knife and I served together." He glanced at her. "I've heard rumors that he's on the take. I'll never believe it. He's one of the most honest men I've ever known. He wants the casino, but he wouldn't resort to underhanded means to get it, and he's the last man who'd embezzle tribal funds."

"What does any of this have to do with Leta and Tate?" she asked, genuinely puzzled.

He leaned forward. "Can you keep a secret? A big secret?"

"If keeping it won't hurt anyone," she said finally.

"Telling it will hurt people more," he assured her. "Cecily, thirty-six years ago, about the time I won my first senate race, I had an affair with a lovely Lakota girl I'd known since childhood. But I had just married and my wife was my chief backer in the campaign. I couldn't have won without her support." He picked at a fingernail. "I chose position above passion, and there hasn't been a day in my life that I haven't regretted it." He looked up. "But there was a complication that she never told me about. There was a child. And now there's a renegade gambling syndicate on the outs with the Vegas group that's trying to leech its way onto Wapiti Ridge, where it can have total control over the casino it wants there. Since Wapiti is small, and near a major tourist attraction, it has the potential to draw a lot of customers. There's big money involved and this syndicate has ties to some rather nasty people up north.''

"Good Lord,'' she exclaimed. "I had no idea.''

"Neither did I until about a month ago when I started hearing rumors about it. I did some investigating and dug out enough to warrant an investigation. But the syndicate got wind of it, and now it's threatening to go public with the whole sordid mess unless I stop looking for missing tribal funds and support the casino. And the tricky part is that my son doesn't even know about me. He thinks another man was his father.''

Cecily's face paled. She stared at Holden, and it suddenly occurred to her that he was talking about Leta, and that he had more than a surface resemblance to Tate Winthrop. In fact, when he scowled, he looked just like Tate.

"Tate...'' she whispered.

"Is my son,'' he said, almost strangling on the word. "My son! And I didn't know until today, until this morning, when I had a visit from a man who works for the gambling syndicate. If I don't back down, he's going to the media with it.''

Cecily sat back in her chair with a rough sigh. "Tate thinks he's full-blooded Lakota. He's fanatical about it, obsessed with preserving the bloodlines of his culture. He'll go mad if he knows the truth!''

"He can't know,'' Holden said shortly. "Not yet.'' He looked every year of his age. "Maybe not ever, if I can find a way out of this mess I'm in.'' He ran his hands restlessly through his hair again. "I thought I'd die childless, Cecily. My wife never wanted children." His eyes closed. "Leta didn't tell me. She was probably afraid to tell me, because she knew my political career meant everything to me." He looked up. "And you know what? Money and power are hollow, empty things when you can't share them. I have a son, and I can't tell him." He laughed mirthlessly. "Ironic, isn't it?"

She winced. "It isn't fair to let him go through life thinking Jack Winthrop was his father."

"It isn't fair to destroy his illusions of who he is, either. That's why I've got to stop these people, while there's still time. I need help. You're the only person I can turn to, Cecily. I can't have Leta and Tate publicly humiliated for something that's basically my own damned fault. On the other hand, I can't let organized crime get a foothold on the reservation." His dark eyes met hers. "I think the key is what they're holding over Tom Black Knife. They've got something on him, too, maybe, and they're using it to dip into government allotments the tribe receives from grazing rights and leased land. Will you help me?"

"Do I have a choice?" she replied with a smile. "At least you had good taste in women," she added dryly.

"She didn't have good taste in men, though," he returned curtly. "I loved her, but I was willing to sacrifice her for a glorious career. I spent most of it married to a woman who drank like a fish, cursed like a sailor and hated me because I couldn't love her. I cheated both of us. Eventually she drank herself to death.''

"Some people are self-destructive," Cecily told him. "It's a fact of life. You do what you can to help, but they have to want to help themselves. Otherwise, no treatment will ever work."

His black eyes narrowed. "Tate practically raised you from what I hear. You love him, don't you?"

Her face closed up. "For all the good it will ever do me, yes," she said softly.

"He won't have the excuse of pure Lakota blood much longer," he advised.

"I'm not holding out for miracles anymore," she vowed. "I'm going to stop wanting what I can never have. From now on, I'll take what I can get from life and be satisfied with it. Tate will have to find his own way."

"That's sour grapes," he observed.

"You bet it is. What do you want me to do to help?"

"It's dangerous," he pointed out, hesitating as he considered her youth. "I don't know…"

"I'm a card-carrying archaeologist," she reminded him. "Haven't you ever watched an Indiana Jones movie? We're all like that," she told him with a wicked grin. "Mild-mannered on the outside and veritable world-tamers inside. I can get a whip and a fedora, too, if you like," she added.

He chuckled. "Okay. But only on the condition that you let me know if you find yourself in danger."

"I'll call Colby Lane if I do," she said. "He's not Tate, but he comes pretty close."

He searched her eyes. "Are you *sure* you want to take such a risk?"

She nodded. "So what's the plan?"

"I want you to find an excuse to go to Wapiti Ridge and keep an eye on Tom Black Knife. I want to know why he's cooperating with these people and exactly what they're trying to do out there. Try to find where those missing tribal funds are going while I try a few political maneuvers here. You stay with Leta from time to time, and everyone knows that you're involved with the new museum. You won't attract attention while you're snooping around. If I can discover exactly who these people are and where they are, I can get to them before they start publishing my past sins."

"Good thinking," she agreed. Then she hesitated. "What do I tell Leta?"

He studied his linked hands on the edge of her desk. "Good God, I haven't the slightest idea. She had my child, and she never told me." He closed his eyes, as if in anguish. "I had a son, and I didn't know. I guess I'd never have known if this hadn't come up. No wonder Jack Winthrop was so cruel to her, and to Tate." He drew in a steadying breath. For an instant he looked defeated. Then his head lifted. "The hell of it is that my son, my only child, has to turn out to be," he added with a return of his old spirit, black eyes flashing, "the one man in Washington, D.C. who hates my guts!"

"You weren't too fond of him, either, if you recall," she pointed out.

He glared at her. "He's hot-tempered and arrogant and stubborn!"

"Look who he gets it from," she said with a grin.

He unlinked his hands as he considered that. "Those can be desirable traits," he agreed with a faint smile. "Anyway, it's nice to know I won't die childless," he said after a minute. He lifted his eyes to her face. "Leta can't know any of this. When and if the time comes, I'll tell her."

"Who's going to tell him?" she ventured.

"You?" he suggested.

"In your dreams," she said with a sweet smile.

He stuffed his hands back into his pockets. "We'll cross that bridge when the river comes over it. You'll be careful, do you hear me? I've invested a lot of time and energy into hijacking you for my museum. Don't take the slightest risk. If you think you've been discovered, get out and take Leta with you."

"She's afraid to fly," she pointed out. "She won't get in an airplane unless it's an emergency."

"Then I'll come out and stuff her into a car and drive her to the airport and put her on a plane," he said firmly.

She pursed her lips. He was very like Tate. "I guess you would, at that."

He started back toward the door. He paused with his hand on the doorknob. "Since this is my fishing expedition, I'll have my secretary arrange for your tickets to be sent over."

"You'll be in front of an investigating committee for sure…"

"I'm paying for them, not my office," he interrupted. "I'm not about to take advantage of the travel budget. After all, I don't want to tarnish my halo."

"That'll be the day, when you wear a halo," she murmured dryly.

He chuckled with amusement. "I'll be in touch. See you."

"See you."

He closed the door and Cecily sat back in her chair and stared blankly at the mass of unfinished paperwork on her desk, sharing space with some of the cultural handiwork she was acquiring for the lifestyle exhibit.

Holden was taking it for granted that he could solve this problem without ever telling Tate the truth of his parentage, but Cecily wasn't sure he could. It would come out sooner or later, regardless of what happened with the syndicate, if the press got wind of even a hint of impropriety. That would hurt Tate, lower his mother in his estimation and give him another reason to hate Holden. It would, also, give him a reason to hate Cecily, because she knew the truth before he did, and she hadn't told him. He hated lies as much as she did.

She hoped she could live with the contempt he was going to feel for her. She'd share it, she was certain, with both his parents. Leta didn't even know that Holden knew. What a tangled web!

But meanwhile, she was going to help Senator Holden solve his little problem and she hoped she could do it before the nasties went to the media with their show-and-tell story. She'd spent enough time around spies to know the ropes, at least. Colby had told her plenty about covert ops. She wished he wasn't away. He'd be the very person to help ferret out the bad guys and discover the extent of their plans.

Senator Holden sent her tickets over the next day, following a staff meeting with the curator of the museum, Dr. Phillips.

Jock Phillips was a tall, balding man with Cherokee blood, a gentle personality and a genuine reverence for Native American culture. Everything they added to the collection fascinated him. He had to touch the objects, as if by making physical contact he could almost absorb them through his fingertips. He was an old bachelor with plenty of friends, and Cecily adored him.

"Matt says you're going out to South Dakota on another acquisition trip, but this time he's got something specific in mind," Phillips told her with wide, bright eyes. "Care to tell the old man what it is?"

"Something unusual," she said, hoping she could fill that order. "And you're going to love it."

He grinned from ear to ear. "How much is this unusual thing going to cost me?" he asked.

"Cheap at the price, I promise," she said with a smile. "I'll make the trip worthwhile."

"I know that. You're quite a bonus to us, you know. You have a knack for Paleo-Indian archaeology. You'd have been wasted in forensics, Cecily," he added solemnly. "That sort of thing kills the soul."

"Why, Dr. Phillips," she said, surprised, searching for words.

"I was a forensic scientist in my youth," he said in a grim tone. "I thought it would be like detective work. It was. But one of the first victims I had to identify turned out to be a missing friend. I gave it up and went into archaeology." He smiled sadly. "It's much more rewarding."

"Yes, it is to me, too," she assured him. "I love working here."

"So do I," he confided with a smile. "Go to South Dakota and bring me back something that will make us famous. We're very young, remember. We have to be able to compete with the big guys."

"I'll do my best," she promised.

She packed that evening after she finished dinner. She was sipping coffee when the doorbell rang. Perhaps Colby had come back early!

She was thinking what a godsend that would be

when she opened the door and found Tate on the other side.

He was wearing jeans and a black turtleneck sweater with a silk jacket. He looked very sophisticated, and she was very aware that she was barefooted in tattered jeans with a blouse that had been washed until the red had faded to a tie-died sort of pink. She stared up at him without speaking.

"Do I get to come in?" he asked.

She shrugged and stood aside. "I'm just packing."

"Moving again?" he asked with faint sarcasm. "You used to be easier to keep track of."

"Because I was living in a nest of spies!" she threw at him, having only recently gleaned that bit of information from Colby. "You got me an apartment surrounded by government agents!"

"It was the safest place for you," he said simply. "Someone was always watching you when I couldn't."

"I didn't need watching!"

"You did," he returned, perching on the arm of her big easy chair to stare at her intently. "You never realized it, but you were a constant target for anyone who had a grudge against me. In the end, it was why I gave up government work and got a job in the private sector." He folded his arms over his broad chest, watching surprise claim her features. "There was a communist agent with a high-powered rifle one day, and a South American gentleman with an automatic pistol the following week. You were never told about them. But you had two close calls. If you hadn't been living in a 'nest of spies,' I'd have buried you. Funerals are expensive,'' he added with a cold smile.

She stared at him blankly. "Why didn't you just send me back to South Dakota?" she asked.

"To your stepfather?" he drawled.

That was still a sore spot with her, and she was certain that he knew it. But she wouldn't give him the satisfaction of arguing. He seemed to be spoiling for a fight. She turned away to the kitchen. "Want a cup of coffee?"

He got up and took her by the shoulders. "I'm sorry," he said. "That was a low blow."

"Another in a long line of them lately," she said without meeting his eyes. "I seem to do nothing except rub you the wrong way."

"And you don't know why?" he asked curtly, letting her go.

She moved one shoulder as she went about the business of getting down a cup and saucer. "At a guess, you're mad at somebody you can't get to, and I'm the stand-in."

He chuckled. "How do you see through me so easily? Even my mother can't do that."

If he thought about it, he'd know, she thought miserably. "Who pulled your chain today?" she persisted.

"Holden," he bit off.

She was proud that she didn't flinch. "Oh?" she asked nonchalantly.

"He'd contracted with me to do a freelance security update on his offices. Today he phoned and said he'd reconsidered."

"You can't be missing the check," she mused, remembering that he drove a new Jaguar sports car, and frequently wore Armani suits. It hurt to remember that her college fees had probably been little more than pocket change to him. He not only had money from his job with Pierce Hutton, but he also had money everywhere from freelance covert work in his preintelligence service days.

"I'm not. It's the principle of the thing. He did it deliberately, even if he won't admit it. Holden is a guy who carries grudges. I suppose he was still steaming from the talk we had at his birthday party."

She bit her lower lip. Matt Holden had put her in a terrible position by swearing her to secrecy.

"You didn't talk at his birthday party," she pointed out. "You yelled at each other."

He changed the subject. "Just where are you going, if you're not moving again?" he asked abruptly.

She put the fresh cup of black coffee on the coffee table in front of the sofa. She knew that he didn't take milk or sugar. She curled up in the armchair as he moved to sit on the sofa. "Actually I'm going back out to see Leta," she told him, which was partially true. "I've got a line on an ancient artifact I want for the museum." Which wasn't true.

There was a long pause. "Ancient artifacts have a sacred meaning for our people," he told her irritably.

"They don't belong in museums. They're part of our culture."

He didn't know yet that he had only a partial claim to that culture. He was so proud of his ancestry. The truth was going to hurt him badly.

"It's not that sort of artifact," she lied. In fact, she had no idea what she was going to come up with that would satisfy Dr. Phillips and Tate both as well as justify her spying trip for Senator Holden.

"You were just in South Dakota a couple of weeks ago," he pointed out. "Why didn't you get it then?"

"It wasn't available then." She brushed back a tiny strand of loose hair. "Don't cross-examine me, okay? It's been a long day."

He ran a hand around the back of his neck, under his braid of hair, and stared at her own hair in the tight bun at her nape as she replaced the errant strand. "I thought you took it down at night."

"At bedtime," she corrected.

His eyes narrowed. "Lucky Colby," he said deliberately.

She wasn't going to give him any rope to hang her with. She just smiled.

He glared at her. "He won't change," he said flatly.

"I don't care," she said. "I appreciate all you've done for me, Tate, but my private life is my own business, not yours."

"That's a hell of a way to talk to me."

"That works both ways," she replied, eyes narrowing. "What gives you the right to ask questions about the men I date?"

Her words made him mad. His lips compressed until they made a straight line. He looked like his father when he was angry. He finished his coffee in a tense silence and got to his feet. He glanced at his watch. "I've got to go. I just wanted to see how you were."

"You just wanted to see if Colby was here," she corrected and smiled mirthlessly when he blinked.

"You know I don't approve of Colby," he told her.

"Like I care!" she said.

He took a step toward her. His black eyes glittered with conflicting emotions. She aroused him more lately than any woman he'd ever known. Just looking at her sent him over the edge.

On some level she recognized the tension in him, the need that he was denying. He was upset about Matt Holden pulling him out of the security work, not because of the money, but rather because it seemed nothing more than spite. Actually Holden was saving them both from a political upheaval because he could have been accused of nepotism. But deeper than that was a frustration because he wanted a woman he couldn't have. Cecily knew that at some level. He was trying to start a fight. She couldn't let him.

"Colby is a sweet man," she said gently. "He's good company and he doesn't drink around me, ever."

"He's an alcoholic," he said quietly, trying to control the anger.

"I told you before, he's in therapy," she said. "He's trying, Tate."

"So you expect me not to worry about you? After what my own father put me and my mother through?"

Chapter Five

She saw the hurt as if it were visible on his expressionless face. She got out of the chair and stood just in front of him. "People aren't basically cruel," she said in a soft, sympathetic tone. "Sometimes they just hurt so much inside that they can't bear the pain. They can't cope with the ordinary pressures of day-to-day life, and they turn to drugs or alcohol for comfort."

"What reason did my father have to hurt inside?" he demanded harshly.

That his son wasn't his son and his wife loved another man, she thought. She looked at him, seeing plainly how the years of torment and anguish had formed the man he'd become. His face was like granite, but every line, every furrow, concealed an emotional wound from years past. "Steel tempered by fire," she said aloud, without thinking.

"Am I?" he asked.

She smiled sadly. "Aren't you?"

He let out a long, slow breath and some of the tension drained out of him. He looked at her quizzically. "You give me peace," he said unexpectedly. "The only time I ever feel it is when I'm with you. God knows why, when you set me off like a bomb."

She searched his eyes. "Tate, Senator Holden has a reason for what he did," she told him seriously. "I don't pretend to know what it is, but I know him. He's not like some politicians who lie when the truth would suit better. He has integrity. He doesn't hold grudges and he doesn't backstab. You know that," she added with conviction.

He scowled. "Yes, I do." His narrow eyes searched hers. "What do you know, Cecily?"

"I know archaeology," she replied.

He reached out and touched her firm little chin with hard fingers. "You're keeping something from me," he said in a low, deep tone. "I'm not sure why I sense that, but I do."

"You think you know all about me," she replied, trying to draw back. "Don't...do that," she muttered, reaching up to catch his hair-roughened wrist in her warm fingers.

His breath caught. "Fatal error, Cecily," he said huskily, moving in, giving in to the hunger that had really brought him to her apartment at this hour of the night. "You shouldn't have touched me..."

Before she could ask what he meant, his mouth was

hard on her lips. He groaned and backed her up against the wall while his lips did unspeakably erotic things to her open mouth. She felt his powerful thigh parting her legs, felt his lean, fit body press itself hungrily to hers as he crushed her sensuously into the wall behind her.

She had no defense whatsoever. She was on fire for him. Her nails dug into the long, hard muscles of his back and she moaned harshly against his demanding mouth. There was a rhythm that she didn't recognize. It made little darts of pleasure run up into her body from some secret recess of joy. One lean hand was at her hip, teaching her the rhythm. His whole body was an instrument of delicious torture, taking her far beyond any small pleasure she'd had in her life. She sobbed under his mouth as her body began to swell with it. And at the same moment, she felt the change in him as well, a physical change that was all too noticeable given their proximity.

He knew they were getting in over their heads. He pulled back, despite the intense pain it caused him to stop. His eyes were dazed, ferocious as they met her own from a space of inches. He exhaled roughly, unsteadily, at her swollen mouth. He looked down to find her body so close that barely a breath could get between them. He was aroused and she knew. He'd let her know, for the first time.

He looked back up into her misty eyes. "You have to stop letting me do this," he bit off, half-angrily.

"If you'll stop leaning on me so that I can get my hands on a blunt object, I'll be happy to…!''

He kissed the words into oblivion. "It isn't a joke," he murmured into her mouth. His hips moved in a gentle, sensuous sweep against her hips. He felt her shiver.

"That's…new," she said with a strained attempt at humor.

"It isn't," he corrected. "I've just never let you feel it before." He kissed her slowly, savoring the submission of her soft, warm lips. His hands swept under the blouse and up under her breasts in their lacy covering. He was going over the edge. If he did, he was going to take her with him, and it would damage both of them. He had to stop it, now, while he could. "Is this what Colby gets when he comes to see you?" he whispered with deliberate sarcasm.

It worked. She stepped on his foot as hard as she could with her bare instep. It surprised him more than it hurt him, but while he recoiled, she pushed him and tore out of his arms. Her eyes were lividly green through her glasses, her hair in disarray. She glared at him like a female panther.

"What Colby gets is none of your business! You get out of my apartment!" she raged at him.

She was magnificent, he thought, watching her with helpless delight. There wasn't a man alive who could cow her, or bend her to his will. Even her drunken, brutal stepfather hadn't been able to force her to do something she didn't want to do.

"Oh, I hate that damned smug grin," she threw at him, swallowing her fury. "Man, the conqueror!"

"That isn't what I was thinking at all." He sobered little by little. "My mother was a meek little thing when she was younger," he recalled. "But she was forever throwing herself in front of me to keep my father from killing me. It was a long time until I grew big enough to protect her."

She stared at him curiously, still shaken. "I don't understand."

"You have a fierce spirit," he said quietly. "I admire it, even when it exasperates me. But it wouldn't be enough to save you from a man bent on hurting you."

He sighed heavily. "You've been...my responsibility...for a long time," he said, choosing his words carefully. "No matter how old you grow, I'll still feel protective about you. It's the way I'm made."

He meant to comfort, but the words hurt. She smiled anyway. "I can take care of myself."

"Can you?" he said softly. He searched her eyes. "In a weak moment..."

"I don't have too many of those. Mostly, you're responsible for them," she said with black humor. "Will you go away? I'm supposed to try to seduce you, not the reverse. You're breaking the rules."

His eyebrow lifted. Her sense of humor always seemed to mend what was wrong between them. "You stopped trying to seduce me."

"You kept turning me down," she pointed out. "A woman's ego can only take so much rejection."

His eyes ran over her hungrily. "I couldn't get it out of my mind," he said, almost to himself, "the way it felt, back at my mother's house. I was never so hungry for anyone, but it wasn't completely physical, even then." He frowned. "I want you, Cecily, and I hate myself for it."

"What else is new?" She gestured toward the door. "Go home. And I hope you don't sleep a wink."

"I probably won't," he said ruefully. He moved toward the door, hesitating.

"Good night," she said firmly, not moving.

He stood with his back to her, his spine very straight. "I can trace my ancestors back before the Mexican War in the early 1800s, pure Lakota blood, undiluted even by white settlement. There are so few of us left..."

She could have wept for what she knew, and he didn't know. "You don't have to explain it to me," she said solemnly. "I know how you feel."

"You don't," he bit off. He straightened again. "I'd die to have you, just once." He turned, and the fire was in his eyes as they met hers, glittering across the room. "It's like that for you, too."

"It's a corruption of the senses. You don't love me," she said quietly. "Without love, it's just sex."

He breathed deliberately, slowly. He didn't want to ask. He couldn't help it. "Something you know?"

"Yes. Something I know," she said, lying with a

straight face and a smile that she hoped was worldly. She was not going to settle for crumbs from him, stolen hours in his bed. Men were devious when desire rode them, even men like Tate. She couldn't afford for him to know that she was incapable of wanting any man except him.

The words stung. They were meant to. He hesitated, only for a minute, before he jerked open the door and went out. Cecily closed her eyes and thanked providence that she'd had the good sense to deny herself what she wanted most in the world. Tate had said once that sex alone wasn't enough. He was right. She repeated it, like a mantra, to her starving body until she finally fell asleep.

Cecily drove up to Leta's small house on the Wapiti Ridge reservation late the next afternoon. It had taken a change of planes in Denver to get a flight up to Rapid City, South Dakota, and she'd driven to the reservation from there.

Leta came out on the porch wiping her hands on an apron, grinning. "I barely had time to do a nice supper. You bad girl, you should have phoned yesterday, not from the airport!"

"I wanted to surprise you."

Leta grimaced at the word "surprise."

"What's wrong?" Cecily asked when she walked onto the porch with her bag.

"I forgot to give it to you."

"Give me what?"

"Tate gave me your birthday present when you were here before," she confessed. "I put it on top of the cabinet in the dining room and forgot to give it to you. Here, I'll fetch it!"

Cecily felt as if she'd had the wind knocked out of her just at the sound of his name. She could almost taste him on her mouth, feel the fierce hunger of his body as he pressed her into the wall...

"He remembered my birthday," she said faintly, touched.

"He always remembers it, but he said you weren't speaking then." She handed the small box to Cecily. "Go on," she said when the younger woman hesitated. "Open it."

Cecily's hands went cold and trembled as she tore off the wrappings. It was a jewelry box. It wasn't a ring, of course, she told herself as she forced up the hinged lid. He certainly wouldn't buy her a...

"The beast!" she exclaimed. "Oh, how could he?"

Leta looked over her shoulder at what was in the box and dissolved into gales of laughter.

Cecily glared at her. "It isn't funny."

"Oh, yes it is!"

Cecily looked back down at the silver crab with its ruby eyes and pearl claws, and one corner of her mouth tugged up. "He is pretty, isn't he?"

She took the pin out of the box and studied it. It wasn't silver. It was white gold. Those were real rubies and pearls, too. This hadn't been an impulse purchase. He'd had this custom-made for her. Tears stung her eyes. It was the sort of present you gave to someone who meant something to you. She remembered his passionate kisses, and wished with all her heart that he'd meant those, too.

She pinned the small crab onto the collar of her blouse and knew that she'd treasure it as long as she lived.

"Now. Why are you here?" Leta asked pointedly while they ate the supper she'd cooked and drank black coffee.

"I've got a line on an ancient artifact," she began glibly.

Leta looked at her. "There is no ancient artifact here, except the sacred bundle, and you know very well that it's never displayed except on ceremonial occasions. Nor would any member of the tribe allow you even to touch it, much less carry it off to a museum."

Cecily sighed and sipped coffee. "Leta, it would be so much easier if you'd just believe me when I lie."

Leta chuckled. "You don't do it well."

"I can't tell you everything," she said. "But I'll tell you what I can. I'm here to do some snooping."

Leta's eyes widened. "Covert ops," she said enthusiastically. "Oh, boy. What do we do?"

"Listen, this is serious stuff," came the reply. "There are some bad people running around here."

"Going back and forth in chauffeured limousines

with out-of-state license plates," Leta said. "And every time they come and go, Tom Black Knife goes down to his nephew's house and has several jiggers of whisky."

Cecily's mouth fell open.

Leta gave her a speaking look. "I know everything that goes on. I know when something's not right. Tribal funds are vanishing, and I can't believe Tom would steal. He's my cousin."

"He's also the good friend of a powerful man in Washington," Cecily said carefully, "who's going to blow the whistle on the whole operation if he can get enough evidence."

Leta silently picked at her food. "These people don't come at you head-on," she said. "They come from behind, or both sides. They prey on people with secrets."

"Not people like you," Cecily teased deliberately. "You don't have secrets."

Leta was silent again. "Have you seen Tate?"

Her heart jumped. "I saw him last night, in fact."

"Is he well?"

She grimaced. "Very well, thanks. He doesn't like it that I go out with Colby Lane."

Leta lifted an eyebrow expressively.

"It isn't like that, Leta. He's concerned for me. Colby used to drink a lot. He doesn't anymore, but Tate thinks he's a bad influence." She sipped coffee. "Big brother Tate, to the rescue."

"He cares about you a lot."

"Like he'd care about a kid sister, Leta, and we both know it," she said curtly. "Audrey is the woman in his life, and she shows no signs of going away. If it hadn't been for his obsession about not marrying into another race, she'd probably be wearing a ring right now. She's gloriously beautiful."

"She hates Native Americans," Leta said coldly. "Just like another socialite I once knew. I've heard it all before—we're dirty, ignorant, primitive savages who sit down and let the government support us...."

Cecily got up and put her arms around the woman who'd taken the place of her mother in her life. "You're a clean, intelligent, modern woman with many skills and a great big heart!" she said. "And I'll knock down the first person who says different!"

"You do a lot for us, Cecily," Leta said solemnly. "More than you know." She studied her adoptive child with a puzzling scrutiny. "How did your face get scratched, there on your cheek?"

She remembered the faint rasp of Tate's unshaven cheek against hers the night before with shocking clarity. She flushed.

Leta pursed her lips. "So that's what's been going on," she mused. "I thought so. I was making sandwiches and it got real quiet in the living room that night before Tate left..."

"Stop that," Cecily muttered, sitting back down. "It didn't mean anything to him."

Leta shook her head. "He wants you."

The younger woman took a sharp breath. "Wanting

isn't enough," she said firmly. "I'm not going to become a diversion."

The dark eyes that met hers were wise and sad, full of bitter wisdom. "You stick to your guns," she said unexpectedly. "It's easy to give in, Cecily. But then you pay the price. Sometimes it's very high."

As Leta had reason to know, left pregnant by an ambitious politician who married to advance his career. Cecily could feel Leta's pain.

She reached across the table and gently clasped Leta's hands. "Perhaps it is," she said. "But there are some rewards worth the price."

Leta frowned. She seemed to stop breathing.

"What do you know?" she asked Cecily. Faint horror claimed her features her hands went cold. "Cecily…"

Cecily's hands tightened. "I have no secrets from you," she said. "But I made a promise not to say anything. I have to keep it."

Leta was badly shaken. "This man who sent you out here…a senator?"

"I can't answer that."

"A senior senator from South Dakota?"

"Leta…"

"Matt Holden?"

Cecily's eyes closed. She couldn't. She *wouldn't*.

"My God," Leta whispered, letting go of Cecily's hands. "My God, he knows. He knows, doesn't he?"

Cecily bit her lower lip. "I'm sorry. Yes, he does. The people I came out here to help investigate know the whole story. And they're threatening to go to the media with it. Considering Holden's prestige in the Senate, it could destroy his career, to say nothing of what it would do to you and Tate to have the truth come out that way.''

Leta put her face in her hands and wept silently.

Once again, Cecily got out of her chair and went to comfort the older woman. ''It's going to be all right. Senator Holden thinks we can stop them in time, if we can find out exactly who they are and what they're holding over Tom Black Knife. We aren't beaten, Leta. We're going to get through this. Really we are!''

Leta clung to her. ''I wanted to tell them. I wanted to tell my son, and his real father. But I waited and then waited some more, for the right time, the right place. But Matt was married and Tate was so proud of his heritage…'' She sat up and dried her eyes. ''Jack knew that I was pregnant when I married him, but he didn't know who the father was. He said he loved me enough to take us both on.'' She lifted pained eyes to Cecily. ''But he didn't, Cecily. It ate him alive to know that some other man had fathered my child, especially when we discovered that I was unable to conceive again with him. He hated me, he hated Tate. He punished us for his own sterility. He started to drink and he turned from a kind man into a monster. I did that to him,'' she said simply. ''To make matters worse, I denied Matt the knowledge of his son, and I denied Tate the knowledge of his real father. And now he's going to find out about it in some newspaper or on some television station. He'll hate me.''

''He'll probably hate us all for a little while, when it comes out,'' Cecily said comfortingly. ''He'll get over it.''

Leta shook her head and wiped her red, swollen eyes again. ''He won't. He's like you about lies. He won't forgive us.''

Cecily felt sick to her soul at those words. It was probably the truth.

''We can't guess the future,'' Cecily said quietly. ''We can do something about it, if we try. You have to look at the positive side.''

''Is there one?'' Leta asked on a sob.

''Certainly. We're going to single-handedly foil a renegade gambling syndicate and save the tribal chief and the tribal funds from embezzlement. We'll make the evening news shows!''

''Again,'' Leta mused, remembering how Cecily had made it before.

Cecily's fingers touched the dainty little crab fixed to her collar. ''This time will be much more politically correct,'' she said.

''How does Matt look?'' Leta asked, when she'd never meant to ask the question.

''Wickedly handsome. Silver-haired and arrogant, stubborn and hot-tempered—just like someone else we know,'' she said with a smile. ''He speaks highly

of you. He regrets what he did, you know,'' she
added. ''He said that he made bad choices.''

''He hates me for not telling him about Tate,
doesn't he?''

''No! Not at all!'' Cecily met the older woman's
miserable gaze. ''Leta, he only feels guilty at what
you both suffered at Jack Winthrop's hands. He certainly understands why you kept the secret from him.
It's just that…well, he and Tate are bitter enemies. It
was a shock for him.''

''I loved him,'' Leta recalled, her eyes soft and
faraway. ''He and I grew up together. He was older
than me, but he was so centered on how he was going
to live his life, so dedicated to helping people here. I
was amazed when he started taking me places. I
would have done anything for him. Then he said he
was going to marry that rich society woman and run
for office. We argued. But after the election, before
he left for Washington, he came to see me one last
time. We'd been apart for so long, and I'd missed
him so much. We started kissing and couldn't stop.''
She colored, embarrassed. ''Then he told me he was
already married. He was ashamed and sorry, but I
wasn't. It was all I'd ever have, and I knew it. A few
weeks after he left, I knew I was pregnant.''

Leta smiled. ''You can't imagine the joy it gave
me. I knew I could never tell him, but I was happy.
Then Jack Winthrop offered me a home and I took
it.'' She shook her head sadly. ''I should have known
better. I paid, and Tate paid. I tried to run away once,

but Jack beat me so badly that I couldn't even walk. He threatened to hurt Tate if I tried again, so I stayed." She glanced at Cecily. "They say it's easy to leave an abusive husband, you just walk out. Cecily, if I'd walked out, he'd have come after me and killed us both. He said so, and he meant it. Drunk, he was capable of cold-blooded murder. In those days, there were no shelters for battered women, nobody to protect us. Now, things are different. But Tate has many scars, inside where they don't show. So do I."

"You don't regret having Tate," Cecily said.

Leta shook her head. "I'll never regret it. But it makes me sad that Matt had to find out like this. He hasn't told Tate?" she added worriedly.

"No. He said I could," she murmured dryly. "And I said for him not to hold his breath waiting."

"Tate won't like it that we kept the truth from him."

"I'm resigned to that," Cecily said half-truthfully. "He would never have turned to me, anyway, even if he knew he had mixed blood. I've been living on dreams too long already."

"If you go away from him, he'll follow you," Leta said unexpectedly. "There's a tie, a bond, between you that can't be broken."

"There's Audrey," Cecily pointed out.

"Honey, there have been other Audreys," she replied. "He never brought them home or talked about them. They were loose relationships, and not very many at all—never any who were innocent."

"Audrey's lasted a long time."

Leta searched her eyes. "If he's sleeping with Audrey, Cecily, why can't he keep his hands off you?"

Cecily's heart turned over twice. "Wh...what?"

"Simple question," came the droll reply. She grinned at the younger woman's embarrassment. "When you came in the kitchen that last time you were here, before Tate left, your mouth was swollen and you wouldn't look straight at him. He was badly shaken. It doesn't take a mind-reader to know what was going on in my living room. It isn't like Tate to play games with innocent girls."

"He doesn't think I am, anymore," she returned curtly. "I let him think that Colby and I are...very close."

"Uh-oh."

She scowled. "Uh-oh, what?"

"The only thing that's kept him away from you this long is that he didn't want to take advantage of you," Leta replied. "If he thinks you're even slightly experienced, he'll find a reason not to hold back anymore. You're playing a dangerous game. Your own love will be your downfall if he puts on the heat. I know. How I know!"

Cecily refused to think about it. She'd put Tate out of her mind, and she was going to keep him there for the time being.

"I'll worry about that when I have to," she said finally. "Now you dry up those tears and drink some more coffee. Then we have to plan strategy. We're going to take down the enemy by any means possible!"

Chapter Six

In the days that followed, Cecily was introduced to Tom Black Knife, an elderly man with twinkling dark eyes and a kind disposition, as well as to several members of the tribal council. None of them seemed shady or underhanded in any way. Cecily was almost certain that whatever was going on here, they weren't part of it.

She shared her thoughts with Leta one night.

"The problem is, they're not going to want to confide in me," Cecily replied, thinking hard. "I wish Colby had come back. He could get in, pose as someone in a different gambling syndicate and infiltrate. I can't do that."

"Don't look at me," Leta mused. "I can't even win at gin rummy!"

"I'm going to call Colby," she said, reaching for the telephone that Tate had ordered installed for his mother years ago and still paid for. "If he's home, he'll help us."

She dialed his number, direct, and waited while it rang several times. She was about to hang up when a deep voice came on the line.

"Lane," it said curtly.

"I was afraid you were still out of the country," Cecily said with relief. "Are you all right?"

"A few new scars," he said, with lightness in his tone. "How about a pizza? I'll pick you up…"

"I'm in South Dakota."

"What?"

"It's a long story. Leta has a comfortable sofa. Can you come out here right away?"

There was a pause. "If you miss me that much, maybe we'd better get married," he pointed out.

"I'm not marrying a man who shoots people for a living," she replied with a grin.

"I only shoot bad people," he protested. "Besides…I know what a foramen magnum is."

"Darling!" she exclaimed theatrically. "Get the license!"

He chuckled. "That'll be the day, when you take me on. What sort of mischief are you up to, Cecily?"

"No mischief. Just an artifact-buying trip. But I need you."

"In that case, I'm on the way. I'll rent a car at the airport. See you soon."

He hung up.

"You're not going to marry Colby Lane," Leta said like a disapproving parent.

"But he knows what a foramen magnum is," she said teasingly.

"A who?"

"It's the large opening at the back of the skull," Cecily said.

"Gory stuff."

"Not to an archaeologist," Cecily said. "Did you know that we can identify at least one race by the dentition of a skull? Native Americans are mongoloid and they have shovel-shaped incisors."

This caused Leta to feel her teeth and ask more questions, which kept her from thinking too much about Colby's mock proposal.

Colby arrived the next day, with stitches down one lean cheek and a new prosthesis. He held it up as Cecily came out to the car to greet him. "Nice, huh? Doesn't it look more realistic than the last one?"

"What happened to the last one?" she asked.

"Got blown off. Don't ask where," he added darkly.

"I know nothing," she assured him. "Come on in. Leta made sandwiches."

Leta had only seen Colby once, on a visit with Tate. She was polite, but a little remote, and it showed.

"She doesn't like me," Colby told Cecily when they were sitting on the steps later that evening.

"She thinks I'm sleeping with you," she said simply. "So does Tate."

"Why?"

"Because I let him think I was," she said bluntly. He gave her a hard look. "Bad move, Cecily."

"I won't let him think I'm waiting around for him to notice me," she said icily. "He's already convinced that I'm in love with him, and that's bad enough. I can't have him know that I'm…well, what I am. I do have a little pride."

"I'm perfectly willing, if you're serious," he said matter-of-factly. His face broke into a grin, belying the solemnity of the words. "Or are you worried that I might not be able to handle it with one arm?"

She burst out laughing and pressed affectionately against his side. "I adore you, I really do. But I had a bad experience in my teens. I've had therapy and all, but it's still sort of traumatic for me to think about real intimacy."

"Even with Tate?" he probed gently.

She wasn't touching that line with a pole. "Tate doesn't want me."

"You keep saying that, and he keeps making a liar of you."

"I don't understand."

"He came to see me last night. Just after I spoke to you." He ran his fingers down his damaged cheek.

She caught her breath. "I thought you got that overseas!"

"Tate wears a big silver turquoise ring on his middle right finger,'' he reminded her. ''It does a bit of damage when he hits people with it.''

''He hit you? Why?'' she exclaimed.

''Because you told him we were sleeping together,'' he said simply. ''Honest to God, Cecily, I wish you'd tell me first when you plan to play games. I was caught off guard.''

''What did he do after he hit you?''

''I hit him, and one thing led to another. I don't have a coffee table anymore. We won't even discuss what he did to my best ashtray.''

''I'm so sorry!''

''Tate and I are pretty much matched in a fight,'' he said. ''Not that we've ever been in many. He hits harder than Pierce Hutton does in a temper.'' He scowled down at her. ''Are you sure Tate doesn't want you? I can't think of another reason he'd try to hammer my floor with my head.''

''Big brother Tate, to the rescue,'' she said miserably. She laughed bitterly. ''He thinks you're a bad risk.''

''I am,'' he said easily.

''I like having you as my friend.''

He smiled. ''Me, too. There aren't many people who stuck by me over the years, you know. When Maureen left me, I went crazy. I couldn't live with the pain, so I found ways to numb it.'' He shook his head. ''I don't think I came to my senses until you sent me to that psychologist over in Baltimore.'' He glanced down at her. "Did you know she keeps snakes?" he added.

"We all have our little quirks."

"Anyway, she convinced me that you can't own people. Maureen couldn't live with what I was. She's happy now," he added with only a trace of bitterness. "Her new husband is a bank vice president with two children from his first marriage. Very settled. Not likely to get shot up in gun battles, either."

"I'm sorry, Colby."

He leaned forward with his forearms on his splayed thighs. "I loved her."

"I love Tate. But at least you had a marriage to remember. I'll never have that."

"You're better off without anything to remember," he said harshly. "Tate's a fool. He doesn't know who he is, Cecily," he said unexpectedly.

"Why do you say that?"

"He puts too much emphasis on the culture. He's defensive about it. He uses it to identify himself. Heritage is important, but it isn't the whole man. Tate lives in a white world, makes his living in a white world. Surely it's occurred to you that a man with such an obsession about his roots would logically live in that world?"

She wondered if Tate had ever thought of that. She hadn't. "You mean, he doesn't live with Leta, or near his own people."

"Exactly. Some of the people he's associated with have made him self-conscious about his background.

They've made him uncomfortable, reminded him that he's part of a minority culture, intimated that it's just not quite sophisticated or urbane enough to be proud of.''

"Colby…"

He looked down at her. "You're white. You have no idea what it's like to be a minority, be treated like a minority. You can never know, Cecily. Even though you work for native sovereignty, even though you understand and admire Tate's culture, you can never, never, be part of it!"

She was uneasy. Even Tate had never said such things to her. She ran a hand over her forehead absently, disturbed by the truth in those harsh words.

"You want to know how I know that." He nodded at her quick glance. "I'm Apache, Cecily," he said. "You can't see it plainly, because I'm light-skinned through the addition of a little Scotch and German blood a generation back, but I'm almost full-blooded. I qualify for Apache status. I could live on the White Mountain reservation if I wanted to."

"You never said that before," she murmured.

"I didn't know you well enough before. It's almost funny. Tate's a fanatic about his roots, and I'm ashamed of mine. I don't even visit my people. I hate having to see how they live."

The confession rocked her to the soles of her feet. She didn't know how to talk to him anymore. The Colby she thought she knew had vanished.

"That's why Maureen really left me," he said

through his teeth. "Not because of my job, or even because I took an occasional drink. She left me... because she didn't want half-breed children. You see, I didn't tell her that I was almost a full-blood until after we'd been married for a year. A little drop of Native American blood was exciting and unique. But a full-blooded Native American...she was horrified."

Cecily's opinion of the legendary Maureen dropped eighty points. She ground her teeth together. She couldn't imagine anyone being ashamed of such a proud heritage.

He looked down at her and laughed despite himself. "I can hear you boiling over. No, you wouldn't be ashamed of me. But you're unique. You help, however you can. You see the poverty around you, and you don't stick your nose up at it. You roll up your sleeves and do what you can to help alleviate it. You've made me ashamed, Cecily."

"Ashamed? But, why?"

"Because you see beauty and hope where I see hopelessness." He rubbed his artificial arm, as if it hurt him. "I've got about half as much as Tate has in foreign banks. I'm going to start using some of it for something besides exotic liquor. One person can make a difference. I didn't know that, until you came along."

She smiled and touched his arm gently. "I'm glad."

"You could marry me," he ventured, looking

down at her with a smile. "I'm no bargain, but I'd be good to you. I'd never even drink a beer again."

"You need someone to love you, Colby. I can't."

He grimaced. "I could say the same thing to you. But I could love you, I think, given time."

"You'd never be Tate."

He drew in a long breath. "Life is never simple. It's like a puzzle. Just when we think we've got it solved, pieces of it fly in all directions."

"When you get philosophical, it's time to go in. Tomorrow, we have to talk about what's going on around here. There's something very shady. Leta and I need you to help us find out what it is."

"What are friends for?" he asked affectionately.

"I'll do the same for you one day."

He didn't answer her. Cecily had no idea at all how strongly her pert remark about being intimate with Colby had affected Tate. The black-eyed, almost homicidal man who'd come to his door last night had hardly been recognizable as his friend and colleague of many years. Tate had barely been coherent, and both men were exhausted and bloody by the time the fight ended in a draw. Maybe Tate didn't want to marry Cecily, but Colby knew stark jealousy when he saw it. That hadn't been any outdated attempt to avenge Cecily's chastity. It had been revenge, because he thought Colby had slept with her and he wanted to make him pay. It had been jealousy, not protectiveness, the jealousy of a man who was passionately in love; and didn't even know it.

* * *

It was two days later that Tate Winthrop, still nursing a few bruises and a sore jaw, went to the museum to find out why Cecily had really gone to South Dakota. He knew it had nothing to do with artifacts. Something was going on, and she was acting oddly—just like her paramour, Colby Lane. He was going to find out why.

He talked to Dr. Phillips, who said blandly that Cecily had located some unusual artifact that would make the museum famous and she'd gone to South Dakota to acquire it. In fact, Senator Holden thought so highly of that project that he'd even paid her airfare!

Armed with that tidbit, Tate went storming into Matt Holden's office, past his affronted secretary.

"It's all right, Katy," Holden told the young woman. "Close the door, will you?"

She did, with obvious apprehension. Tate looked like a madman.

It was the first time they'd seen each other face-to-face since Matt Holden had learned that the man across the desk from him was his son. He studied Tate's face intently, seeing resemblances, seeing generations of his people in those black eyes, that firm jaw, the tall, elegant build of him. Tate wouldn't know that he had French blood as well as Lakota, that his grandfather had been a minor royal in Morocco, that his grandmother had been French aristocracy. Tate was the continuation of a proud line, and he couldn't tell him. If things worked out in South Dakota, Tate would never have to know at all. The thought saddened him. He'd made so many mistakes…

"Well?" Holden asked, trying to sound as antagonistic as he usually did, despite the faint crack in his heart.

"Why did you send Cecily to South Dakota?"

Holden caught his breath. He looked around the room, certain that the office had at least one bug, even if he'd had some agents search it with sophisticated electronic equipment. He didn't dare say anything here.

Tate intercepted that concerned look. With a curt laugh, he retrieved some complicated electronic device from his inside pocket, opened it, activated it and put it on the desk in front of him.

He leaned back. "Set a spy to catch a spy, Holden," he said easily. "You can talk. It's safe. That—" he nodded at the device "—will give anyone listening a hell of a headache."

Holden relaxed a little. "I can't tell you much," he said. "It's complicated, and there are innocent people involved." Certainly there were; Tate was one of them.

"Tell me what you can," Tate said after a minute. Odd, that hesitation in Holden, that utter lack of real hostility. He'd changed. Tate wondered why.

Holden sat back in his burgundy leather chair and stared at his son. "There's a little cloak and dagger stuff going on at the reservation. I promised someone I'd have a look around, so Cecily's asking a few questions for me.''

"That would be a tribal matter, so why are you sticking your nose in?'' Tate said with a scowl, looking so much like his father that, to the man across the desk, it was like looking in a youthful mirror. "You don't have any influence there.''

Holden's high cheekbones flushed ruddy. He averted his dark eyes. His jaw tautened so that the muscles moved involuntarily. "It's a personal matter. A delicate personal matter. Cecily is…finding out a few things for me. Watching some people, that's all. Nothing dangerous.''

Tate leaned forward abruptly, eyes flashing with anger. "If you wanted somebody watched, why didn't you come to me? I've got contacts everywhere! I could have done an investigation for you, without involving Cecily.''

Holden closed his eyes. "You don't understand. I couldn't…have you involved.''

This was getting stranger and stranger. "Why not?''

He stared at a portrait of Andrew Jackson on the wall of his office. Absently he thought of the scandal Jackson had endured over his beloved Rachel. "I can't tell you.'' He turned his attention back to his son. "You have to keep right out of this. You can't become involved in any way, not even casually!''

Tate's scowl grew blacker. "You aren't making sense."

"Damn it…!" He pushed back a stray strand of silver hair and ran his hands over his face. "All right, it's a political threat," he said slowly, choosing every word. "There's something in my past that I don't want known. It involves an innocent woman whose life would be destroyed. Some people are threatening to go public with it if I don't do…certain things for them."

"I can be discreet," Tate said, puzzled.

"I know that." He drew in a breath that sounded painful. He searched the face of the other man with concern in every line of his own. "But I can't involve you. I won't. If you have any respect for me at all, honor what I'm asking of you. I want you out of this. As far out as you can get!"

The oddest sensation washed over Tate. He felt a sudden strong bond to this man, this enemy. He didn't understand it. It was almost as if Holden were trying to protect him. But why would he need protection?

"I worked for the CIA," Tate pointed out. "I know how to take care of myself."

"I know that. It has nothing to do with survival skills." Holden put his broad face in his hands again. "I've never been in a situation like this, never had my hands tied like this. I deserve whatever I get. I brought it on myself. But I can't let her pay for my sins. I have to protect her, whatever the cost."

Tate had never thought of the terse senator as a

sensitive man. His voice was vibrant with pain, with loss. "You still love her."

"Of course I still love her!" he bit off, raising his worn face. "I've always loved her. But I was so damned ambitious. I had to be powerful, rich, a world-beater. I married money and sacrificed everything for this office. Now, here I sit, with my sins spread out before me, waiting for the ax to fall. And I've got nobody to blame for it except myself."

Tate stared at him for a long time. "Does this have something to do with the reason you backed out of the security upgrade you asked me to do for you?"

Holden didn't look at him, but he nodded, a quick jerk of his head.

"None of this makes sense."

"I hope it never will," Holden said solemnly. He leaned back wearily in his chair, his big hands gripping the arms until his knuckles went white. "I haven't sent Cecily into any danger, I promise you. I have friends she doesn't even know about who are watching out for her."

This was puzzling. "You have friends at Wapiti?"

Holden's eyes averted again. "My mother taught school there when I was a boy while my father was serving in the military, so she wouldn't have to drag me all over the world to be educated. I grew up on the reservation."

There was something. Tate could almost bring it out of his mind, but not quite. There was something he remembered hearing, something...

Holden got to his feet, interrupting the flow of thoughts. "Don't go to South Dakota," he said. "Don't get mixed up in this. You may do irreparable damage if you do. It's a...delicate situation."

Tate got up, but he didn't move toward the door. "It was a woman on the reservation," he said suddenly.

Holden didn't answer him.

"Were you ashamed of her, is that why you kept it secret?"

Holden's dark eyes met his. "She isn't the sort of woman a man could be ashamed of," he said softly. "Quite the contrary. But I made bad choices, and lost her."

Tate was surprised that the man would confide in him. It didn't make sense. Of course, nothing else Holden had said made sense, either.

Tate lifted a hand to his forehead. The big silver turquoise ring caught Holden's eye. Funny, it was almost as if the man recognized it.

"My mother gave it to me after my father died," Tate told the other man, who was obviously curious about the piece of jewelry. "She said it had been my father's. She gave it to him when they first started going together. I hated him. But I wear it to honor her. It was obviously something she cherished."

Holden remembered the ring. She'd given it to him, the day before he was forced to confess to her that there was no chance for them to be together. He'd given it back to her when he confessed. She'd given it to their son. Their son. He could hardly bear the pain.

Tate wondered at Holden's reaction to the story. His eyes narrowed. "Did you know my mother?"

Holden looked at him with determined blankness. "Cecily talks about her. Her name is Leta, isn't it?"

He nodded.

"I knew a lot of people on the reservation, but at my age, names don't connect with faces anymore," Holden said.

"Didn't you waste time campaigning at Wapiti Ridge?" Tate asked caustically.

Holden drew himself up to his full height. "No, I didn't," he confessed coldly. "You see, my wife didn't like Native Americans. She was ashamed for people to even know that my mother had once taught school there." Holden's eyes began to kindle with bad temper. "In case you don't recognize that attitude, you might ask your friend Audrey why she won't go out there with you. Or are you afraid of the answer?"

Tate stiffened and his eyes glittered at the older man. His fists balled at his lean hips. "Go to hell."

Holden didn't back down an inch. "I was a battalion commander in Vietnam," he said in a deceptively soft tone. "Special forces. Don't make the mistake of thinking I'd be a pushover in a fight with a younger man."

Tate stared at Holden curiously, not intimidated, but recognizing something about the stance of the man, about the look of him. Odd, these flashes of intuition. This man was the worst enemy he had on the Hill. But he respected him. No. There was something more than respect, but he couldn't grasp what it was. "Bring Cecily home," he said curtly. "I won't have her at risk, even in the slightest way."

"I'll take care of Cecily," came the terse reply. "She's better off without you in her life."

Tate's eyes widened. "I beg your pardon?" he asked, affronted.

"You know what I mean," Holden said. "Let her heal. She's too young to consign herself to spinsterhood over a man who doesn't even see her."

"Infatuation dies," Tate said.

Holden nodded. "Yes, it does. Goodbye."

"So does hero worship," he continued, laboring the point.

"And that's why after eight years, Cecily has had one raging affair after the other," he said facetiously.

The words had power. They wounded.

"You fool," Holden said in a soft tone. "Do you really think she'd let any man touch her except you?" He went to his office door and gestured toward the desk. "Don't forget your gadget," he added quietly.

"Wait!"

Holden paused with his hand on the doorknob and turned. "What?"

Tate held the device in his hands, watching the lights flicker on it. "Mixing two cultures when one of them is all but extinct is a selfish thing," he said after a minute. "It has nothing to do with personal feelings. It's a matter of necessity."

Holden let go of the doorknob and moved to stand directly in front of Tate. "If I had a son," he said, almost choking on the word, "I'd tell him that there are things even more important than lofty principles. I'd tell him...that love is a rare and precious thing, and that substitutes are notoriously unfulfilling."

Tate searched the older man's eyes. "You're a fine one to talk."

Holden's face fell. "Yes, that's true." He turned away.

Why should he feel guilty? But he did. "I didn't mean to say that," Tate said, irritated by his remorse and the other man's defeated posture. "I can't help the way I feel about my culture."

"If it weren't for the cultural difference, how would you feel about Cecily?"

Tate hesitated. "It wouldn't change anything. She's been my responsibility. I've taken care of her. It would be gratitude on her part, even a little hero worship, nothing more. I couldn't take advantage of that. Besides, she's involved with Colby."

"And you couldn't live with being the second man."

Tate's face hardened. His eyes flashed.

Holden shook his head. "You're just brimming over with excuses, aren't you? It isn't the race thing, it isn't the culture thing, it isn't even the guardian-ward thing. You're afraid."

Tate's mouth made a thin line. He didn't reply.

"When you love someone, you give up control of yourself," he continued quietly. "You have to consider the other person's needs, wants, fears. What you do affects the other person. There's a certain loss of freedom as well." He moved a step closer. "The point I'm making is that Cecily already fills that place in your life. You're still protecting her, and it doesn't matter that there's another man. Because you can't stop looking out for her. Everything you said in this office proves that." He searched Tate's turbulent eyes. "You don't like Colby Lane, and it isn't because you think Cecily's involved with him. It's because he's been tied to one woman so tight that he can't struggle free of his love for her, even after years of divorce. That's how you feel, isn't it, Tate? You can't get free of Cecily, either. But Colby's always around and she indulges him. She might marry him in an act of desperation. And then what will you do? Will your noble excuses matter a damn then?"

Tate flicked off the switch of his device and walked out the door without another word or a backward glance. It didn't occur to him until much later that Matt Holden had called him by his first name.

Matt Holden sat back down at his desk, considering what he'd said to his son. Well, it wouldn't make Cecily any more miserable for Tate to understand why he kept pushing her away. And it had accomplished one important thing—it had diverted his son from asking any more questions about what Cecily was really doing in South Dakota.

Chapter Seven

The autumn sun was bright, even if the day was cold. Colby had put on a stylish jacket with his shirt and slacks, and Leta and Cecily introduced him to Tom Black Knife.

"You have much company these days," the elderly, slight Tom said to Leta with a smile.

"Oh, these two are close," Leta said with a grin at the couple near her. "Colby is between jobs, you see, so he spends a little time with Cecily where my son won't see them together. Tate is very protective of her, like a big brother."

"I remember Tate," Tom said. He studied Colby. "What sort of a job do you do?"

"I'm a croupier," Colby lied glibly. "But I can deal faro and blackjack equally well. I worked for the Cherokee nation in their casino in North Carolina."

Tom looked uncomfortable. "I see."

"They're trying to get a casino here, I hear," Colby said carelessly. "I just thought I might throw my name in the hat. I might get lucky, having a job in a place where Cecily spends a lot of time."

Tom bit his lower lip. He moved close to Colby and took him by the arm. "The casino is…is not hiring outsiders. That is, if it even gets built. You should go away. You should not stay here. Nor should you," he added, glancing at Cecily. "You could be in danger?"

Colby's eyes narrowed. "What sort of danger?"

"I can say nothing more," the proud old man said miserably. He let go of Colby's arm. "I pray for guidance, but I am told nothing. It is as if everyone has deserted me."

Colby suddenly drew the old man away from the women and spoke to him in a Lakota dialect, softly, so that none of the neighbors could overhear.

Tom Black Knife's eyes widened with surprise. "You speak my tongue!" he said in Lakota.

"Yours and my own—Apache," Colby replied. "I will say nothing to Cecily, nor to Tate. You have my word. Tell me."

The story came tumbling out. The gambling people knew of a murder that had been committed on the reservation during the time of the militant uprising on the Sioux reservations in the seventies. They could connect Tom with one of the unsolved murders. He could go to prison. There was enough circumstantial evidence to convict him. Although it had been a fair

fight, he'd been drinking at the time and some of the
details escaped him. Those men had brought evidence
with them of his crime, gleaned from his own grandson who'd sold the casino idea to the syndicate as a
way to save his life. He owed the men a huge gambling debt. He told them about his grandfather's past
and the ideal location of the small reservation and the
old notion of the casino. Then he turned them loose
on the old man. They had dipped into the funds earmarked for the reservation and dared Tom to tell
about it. They had even hired a surveyer and a
builder, and they had started greasing political palms
to get the casino approved.

"Their names," Colby persisted.

"It is more than my life is worth to speak them,"
Tom said.

"All right. Then tell me when they come again."

"I cannot," came the reply in a dead tone. "And
you must not be here when they come. They are using
our money to hire surveyors and do marketing studies. When I tried to stop them, they threatened to call
the FBI."

Colby knew the terror those threats would strike in
the heart of an old man who'd lived free all his life.
He wanted to get these men. "Say nothing to anyone," he concluded. "I'll watch. I'll do something."

Tom Black Knife looked older than the very hills.
"You are not a gambler, I think," he speculated.

"No, I'm not."

"But you are a good man."

"Not anymore," Colby said grimly. "But I have friends who are." He thought of something else. "There must be something on paper, some record of these funds…"

The old man looked worried. "Yes, but I keep them locked in my office. I cannot show them to you. They would know."

Probably they would, Colby thought as the old man went on his way. But not until it was too late. He had a good idea of how to get his hands on the paperwork, without even Tom Black Knife knowing that he had.

"Tell me!" Cecily insisted later, shaking Colby by both arms.

"Cut it out, you'll dismember me," Colby said, chuckling.

She let go of the artificial arm and wrapped both hands around the good one. "I want to know. Listen, this is my covert operation. You're just a stand-in!"

"I promised I wouldn't tell."

"You promised in Lakota. Tell me in English what you promised in Lakota."

He gave in. He did tell her, but not Leta, what was said, but only about the men coming to the reservation soon.

"We'll need the license plate number," she said. "It can be traced."

"Oh, of course," he said facetiously. "They'll certainly come here with their own license plate on the car so that everyone knows who they are!"

"Damn!"

He chuckled at her irritation. He was about to tell her about his alternative method when a big sport utility vehicle came flying down the dirt road and pulled up right in front of Leta's small house.

Tate Winthrop got out, wearing jeans and a buckskin jacket and sunglasses. His thick hair fell around his shoulders and down his back like a straight black silk curtain. Cecily stared at it with curious fascination. In all the years she'd known him, she'd very rarely seen his hair down.

"All you need is the war paint," Colby said in a resigned tone. He turned the uninjured cheek toward the newcomer. "Go ahead. I like matching scars."

Tate took off the dark glasses and looked from Cecily to Colby without smiling. "Holden won't tell me a damned thing. I want answers."

"Come inside, then," Cecily replied. "We're attracting enough attention as it is."

She led the way into the house, which was empty.

"Where's my mother?" Tate asked at once.

"At her craft co-op, passing out new instruction sheets for the women to follow. They're making earrings and a buckskin dress for my exhibit."

He sat his hands on his hips and stared at her.

Colby cleared his throat. "I'm going to drive down to Red Elk's trading post and get some soft drinks and stuff. Anything you want?"

Tate shook his head.

"Cecily?"

She shook her head, too.

"I'll be back in an hour or so." He left.

"I want an answer," Tate told Cecily.

She moved into the living room, avoiding the thick armchair she'd once shared with him to sit on the edge of the sofa. "You'll have to ask Matt Holden. I only know a little part of what's going on here. I was trying to shake another part out of Colby when you drove up and saved him."

He put his sunglasses on the coffee table and sat down next to her. "What's he doing here?"

"I asked him to come. I needed someone who wasn't known on the reservation to pose as a...as a gambler and ask some questions. Why are you wearing your hair down?"

"Never mind my hair. Why a gambler?"

"Senator Holden was right about the gambling syndicate trying to move in here, I think. Tom Black Knife knows a lot about it, and he's scared. I can't speak Lakota, but I can read faces. Tom told Colby the whole story in Lakota."

"That's what you were trying to get out of Colby."

She nodded.

He looked at her in a way he never had before. "You asked him for help instead of me."

She lowered her eyes to her lap uncharacteristically. "Yes. I did."

He didn't say anything for a minute. He slid closer to her. His hands went up into the thick braid of her hair and began to unfasten it.

"Tate…!" she exclaimed, shocked and resisting.

"Don't fight me." He unwound the braid and took out the pins, letting her long, silky hair fall to below her waist, all around her face. He reached for her glasses and took them off, placing them beside his dark ones on the table.

He got up from the sofa, still staring down at her, and went to close and lock the front door. As an afterthought, he put on the chain latch.

"How long will my mother be away?" he asked.

She could hardly speak. Her heart was beating her to death. "She only left a few minutes ago. She's having lunch with her group."

He nodded and his eyes never left hers. "Colby won't be back for a while, either."

He moved toward her with an intent that even a blind virgin would have recognized. She got to her feet and tried to back away, but he pulled her to him gently and held her there.

"Cold feet, Cecily?" he asked at her lips. "Or genuine fear?"

"I…don't know." She rested her clammy, nervous hands on his chest.

He tilted her chin up so that he could see her eyes. "I would never try to force you," he said solemnly. "Not in any way."

Her breathing eased, but just a little. She dropped her eyes and stared at the top button of his shirt. A long strand of his black hair almost covered the pocket. She reached up and touched it, savoring its coolness.

He hadn't moved. Her posture, her skittishness, was giving away secrets. "You're afraid of me."

She had to wait until she could get words past her dry throat. "No. Of course I'm not."

His hand went hesitantly to her own loosened hair, weaving through it. He stared over her head, breathing deliberately, aware of her warmth against him, the soft, excited sigh of her breath at his throat.

"Why did you tell me Colby had had you?" he asked tightly.

"Now, listen here…!" she began heatedly.

He put a long, lean finger over her lips and met her angry gaze. "I beat the hell out of him over it. Did he tell you?"

"Not over me, you didn't," she said. "I'm not that important to you."

He laughed curtly. "You have no idea."

"How's Audrey?" she asked deliberately.

"How would I know?" He caught the thick hair on both sides of her neck and used it to lever her face up to his. "I haven't seen her lately. And I've never slept with her."

"That's a nice fairy tale," she bit off.

"I mean it."

"You never go around with anyone else," she said.

"Have you ever taken a good look at her?" he asked quietly. "She's slight. Blond. Light-eyed."

He was telling her something she couldn't believe. She lifted her eyes to his dark, intent ones.

"I thought I could have you," he said in a haunted tone. "I've dreamed about it, ached for it, since I kissed you. I came all the way out here bristling with sexual tension, so jealous of Colby Lane that I could have used him as a brush broom. But even so, if he'd had you, you wouldn't still be innocent. I could have had you, without complications, without…guilt." He sighed harshly and let her go. He moved away to the window and stood looking out it. "I must have been out of my mind. I should have realized that what happened to you would make intimacy a real obstacle, with any man."

She didn't move. Her eyes were glued to his long, broad back. "He always liked to try to fondle me, even when Mama was alive. After she died…" She lowered her eyes. "That wasn't the only time he tried to rape me. I guess I was just lucky, that last time. I don't know what I would have done without you. You saved me."

When he turned to stare at her, his eyes were terrible. He was almost shaking with rage. She'd never told him that.

"I wasn't sure what you would have done to my stepfather if I'd told you," she continued. "I didn't want you to hurt him and get in trouble with the law. I figured I got off lucky. Anyway, it taught me not to trust men. And later on, I had a very bad reaction to boys who tried to grab me or get too intimate with me." She managed a faint smile. "A couple of my dates in college got a little out of hand. I hurt one of them, with one of those defenses you taught me. After that, nobody wanted to go out with me. The therapist said that even with the sessions, it might take time for me to trust a man enough to let him make love to me completely. The memories I have of intimacy are warped and sickening, and there's still some guilt there. I should have run away sooner...."

"Don't."

She looked up at him. His voice was harsh, choked with anger. "You have to know this," she said firmly. "I can't talk to anyone else about it, least of all to your mother. When you kiss me, I get hot all over. I want you closer than I can get to you. I love it when your body swells against me and I know I caused it. But it's never been more than that between us." She smoothed back her loosened hair. "It was funny that you believed I'd slept with Colby, although I'm sorry it made you hit him for something he didn't do." She glanced at him with a rueful smile. "I don't know if I can function sexually. Not even with you."

He stuck his hands into the pockets of his slacks. In the silence of the room, she heard the faint jingle of loose coins as he touched them.

"I wish you'd told me this before."

"It wouldn't have changed anything."

"Maybe not. But talking about wounds can help heal them."

"You don't talk about yours," she pointed out.

He sat down on the sofa facing her and leaned forward. "But I do," he said seriously. "I talk to you. I've never told anyone else about the way my father treated us. That's a deeply personal thing. I don't share it. I can't share it with anyone but you."

"I'm part of your life," she said heavily, smoothing her hair back again. "Neither of us can help that. You were my comfort when Mama died, my very salvation when my stepfather hurt me. But I can't expect you to go on taking care of me. I'm twenty-five years old, Tate. I have to let go of you."

"No, you don't." He caught her wrists and pulled her closer. He was more solemn than she'd ever seen him. "I'm tired of fighting it. Let's find out how deep your scars go. Come to bed with me, Cecily. I know enough to make it easy for you."

She stared at him blankly. "Tate…" She touched his lean cheek hesitantly. He was offering her paradise, if she could face her own demons in bed with him. "This will only make things worse, whatever happens."

"You want me," he said gently. "And I want you. Let's get rid of the ghosts. If you can get past the fear, I won't have anyone else from now on except you. I'll come to you when I'm happy, when I'm sad, when the world falls on me. I'll lie in your arms and comfort you when you're sad, when you're frightened. You can come to me when you need to be held, when you need me. I'll cherish you."

"And you'll make sure I never get pregnant."

His face tautened. "You know how I feel about that. I've never made a secret of it. I won't compromise on that issue, ever."

She touched his long hair, thinking how beautiful he was, how beloved. Could she live with only a part of him, watch him leave her one day to marry another woman? If he never knew the truth about his father, he might do that. She couldn't tell him about Matt Holden, even to insure her own happiness.

He glanced at her, puzzled by the expression on her face. "I'll be careful," he said. "And very slow. I won't hurt you, in any way."

"Colby might come back...."

He shook his head. "No. He won't." He stood up, pulling her with him. He saw the faint indecision in her face. "I won't ask for more than you can give me," he said quietly. "If you only want to lie in my arms and be kissed, that's what we'll do."

She looked up into his dark eyes and an unsteady sigh passed her lips. "I would give...anything...to let you love me," she said huskily. "For eight long years...!"

His mouth covered the painful words, stilling them. He delighted in her immediate response. Even without knowing the whole truth of her traumatic experience, he'd wondered sometimes if she'd ever be capable of complete intimacy. He'd worried about it, because some men were insensitive with women. Such a man would have scarred her permanently. He wouldn't. Even if she wasn't capable of giving herself completely, he was going to make her first intimacy a joyful experience.

He smiled as he felt her mouth open under his, with more enthusiasm than experience. Yes, she wanted him. That was the first step.

She felt the smile and drew back, her wide eyes meeting his anxiously.

"We're all beginners once," he said gently. His lean hands framed her face and he searched her eyes warmly. His mouth brushed lightly, teasingly, over hers, nibbling at first her upper lip and then her lower one with lazy pleasure. His thumb drew over the corner of her mouth, feeling the kisses sensuously as he coaxed her to relax against him.

Her fingers had a tight grip on his shirtfront. She hung at his lips, feeding on the slow, sensual tracing of his mouth in the silence of the living room.

His hands left her face to smooth over her shoulders and down her back, bringing her slowly against his taut body. The touch of her hips against his had a predictable effect and his breath drew in at the impact of it.

She moved away to look at his face, seeing the new rigidity in it, the flare of his narrowed eyes. He didn't seem to be teasing now. She could feel a faint tremor in his powerful body as his head bent to hers again. His lean hands pulled a little roughly at her hips, dragging them against his while his mouth began to devour hers with kisses that were no longer playful. This, she thought dazedly, was pure seduction. Even if she'd never experienced it before, she recognized the skill that drove it. She moaned as new sensations began to ripple through her untouched body. Her hands contracted. She began to lift toward him, encouraging the fierce hands that were moving her hips sensually against the hard thrust of him.

She went on her toes to prolong the contact, shivering as she felt the first wave of desire send a tremor through her.

His hands pressed her closer while he deepened the kiss. He could hear her heartbeat. She was gasping, moaning, sobbing under the ardor of his mouth. He smoothed his hands under her blouse and around her, slowly tracing the slope of her breasts before he eased steadily toward the hard peaks with his thumbs.

She moaned again and her arms went up around his neck, pulling, pleading, her mouth answering his kisses with utter submission.

He bit her lower lip and lifted his mouth a fraction of an inch away to look into her eyes. She looked feverish, so completely yielded that he could have her where she stood. "If you want me to stop, tell me now."

She couldn't think, could barely breathe. The main thing, she thought dazedly, was that he mustn't stop. "Don't...stop," she choked. Her body trembled as she tried to drag his mouth back over her swollen lips. "I love you," she whimpered.

He groaned harshly as he kissed her again. He lifted her like priceless glass, and carried her down the hall to the guest room she occupied, pausing just long enough to kick the door shut and reach down to lock it.

She lay on the quilted coverlet in the tiny room, vibrating with sensations she'd never felt before while he stood over her and slowly stripped the clothing from his powerful body. Then he stood beside the bed, letting her look at him, indulging her curiosity about the raging arousal that even a virgin couldn't mistake.

"You've seen photographs like this, I imagine," he murmured as he bent to remove her own things.

"Not like you," she replied huskily, her eyes wide and curious.

He smiled. "No last-minute reservations?" he asked softly, moving the last flimsy piece of fabric from her warm, pretty body.

"No," she said. She watched him smooth a lean hand down her bare flesh, watched him smile tenderly as his dark eyes enjoyed her for the first time without clothing. It wasn't embarrassing at all. It was exciting.

He bent and pressed his mouth gently to her soft belly, moving lazily onto the bed with her as his lips traveled up and suddenly began to suckle hungrily at her breast. Her soft cry of pleasure made him ripple with delicious anticipation. Her hands caught in his long hair, tangled in it as she held his mouth to her body, frightened that he might stop.

He smiled against her damp body. It was going to

take a long time, but he wasn't worried about it anymore. She wanted him. It would be all right.

He slowed the rhythm of his caresses to suit her inexperience, teaching her how to touch him, how to give back the pleasure he was giving her. She clung to him, fascinated with the newness of physical pleasure, overwhelmed by the mastery of his lean hands as he gave her little tastes of fulfillment that lifted her completely off the bed in mindless delight.

Finally, when she was trembling with unexpected urgency, her eyes wide and dazed with the tiny bursts of pleasure he'd already coaxed from her taut body, he eased down against her. He saw her eyes widen more as he positioned her.

"This is a rite of passage," he whispered as he nibbled at her lips, moving his hips into stark contact with the threshold of her innocence. "Don't be afraid of it. If I have to hurt you, I'll make up for it. All right?" She nodded, and as his hips moved down tenderly, she looked straight into his eyes. Her hands contracted around his strong fingers where they pressed into hers at either side of her head. She tensed at the first tiny stab of pain. She'd never dreamed that he'd be looking into her eyes when it happened. Or that having his eyes on her face would excite her so much.

"Are you afraid?" he whispered softly.

"Oh, no," she whispered back lovingly, surprised that they could talk during such intimacy. Her legs trembled as he pushed against her once more. It was…incredible, the way it felt. She moved her legs to accommodate him, watching his face tauten as he eased closer and she felt the sting of his soft, slow invasion.

When she gasped and her fingers clutched wildly at his, he smiled. He moved sensually and felt her body lift toward his. "There? Right there?"

"Y…es!" she cried, gasping again.

He shifted with muted passion and laughed deep in his throat at her soft, throbbing moan, a predatory sort of delight that echoed in the rough kiss he pressed against her open mouth. His eyes glittered as he lifted above her and looked down the length of them as they joined.

She gasped again. She couldn't see him clearly, but she felt him move deeper with every sharp thrust of his hips. She felt him, deep and powerful and so… welcome…in the hungry emptiness of her body. She arched sensually as she felt the stab of ecstacy come again and again with each movement of his lean hips. She clung to him, sobbing. She hadn't dreamed that it would be so pleasurable.

"I've never enjoyed anything in my life so much," he whispered to her, clenching his teeth as the pleasure shot through him, too. His eyes met hers. He was breathing roughly, raggedly. His hand swept down, tracing her soft thigh as he increased the rhythm. Her eyes closed and she cried out as he touched her. His mouth ground into hers. His eyes closed too, finally, as the glory of their intimacy washed over him like fire. Deep, and soft, he thought, deep and soft and slow, like a river of molten lava flowing, flowing, flowing...!

His body began to shudder. He could feel her twisting under him, reaching for fulfillment, desperate for fulfillment, her gasping pleas lost in the fierce thunder of his own heartbeat. Her name pulsed out of his tight throat as he drove against her desperately in search of that hot, sweet, oblivion. "Cecily...Cecily... Cecily!"

She cried out and she didn't even recognize her own voice. The pleasure was unbelievable, unbearable! She couldn't let it go, not yet...oh, not yet! She arched up to him with failing strength, whispering to him, begging him. Her body was a roman candle with the fuse burning, burning, and there, yes, there, was...the...explosion!

"Tate!" She heard his name pulse out of her mouth in startled triumph as what her body had been searching for was suddenly, shockingly, found. Waves of pleasure throbbed in her legs, her belly, waves that lifted her, that convulsed her. She stared at his face above her with blind ecstasy, saw it contort and clench as if in a dream.

He cried out hoarsely as his lean body arched down violently into hers. It corded and stilled above her. A sound like a hoarse sob accompanied the harsh convulsion of him above her. He shuddered and shuddered. For a second his eyes opened, black as night, stabbing down into her own.

"Never…this intense…" he bit off, shivering over and over again. "Oh…God…never this deep, never…!"

He convulsed, as she had. She held him, comforted him, while the waves made him groan hoarsely, momentarily helpless in her soft arms. She whispered to him, kissed his face, his eyes, adored him with her mouth.

It was a long time before he was still. She felt his eyelashes, thick and soft, against her cheek. They could have made a baby, she thought suddenly. He hadn't asked if she was protected. She hadn't asked if he was protecting her. She wouldn't say a word. He would never have to know. Then she remembered Senator Holden who had a son that Leta had never told him about, and felt guilty to her soul.

He stirred slowly, moving against her in remembered pleasure, his body throbbing deliciously in the aftermath, every movement rekindling the delight.

His hand swept down the side of her, lingering on her soft skin, exploring lazily. He lifted his head and drew slowly away from her, watching the faint shock and embarrassment in her eyes, smiling at her fascination. For a first time, he thought, it had been fairly volcanic.

He rolled over onto his back and stretched a hand to catch her waist. "Come down here."

He drew her against him with possession, smoothing a hand down the length of her hair. He was satiated, and he wished he could feel guilty about what amounted to pure seduction, but he couldn't. She loved him. He'd enticed her in here and made beautiful love to her. Now he knew what it meant to love a woman physically, and he was shocked and awed and frightened by the ecstasy she'd given him. That he'd given it back was pleasing, but he felt as if he'd taken advantage of something she couldn't help. He hadn't used anything. He hoped that she was on the pill. He hadn't asked. He didn't want to ask. He'd been irresponsible and she was too green and far too aroused to realize it. Amazing, he thought, that he was such a fanatic about birth control, and he'd had this sudden lapse. With a virgin. *His* virgin. His woman. He drew in a long, slow breath, amazed at the pride he felt. Of all the men in the world, she'd chosen him. Considering her traumatic past, it humbled him to realize the magnitude of her gift.

"Guilt. Torment. Sorrow. Shock. Which?" she asked against his chest.

"I'm trying," he murmured on a weary chuckle. "But all I can manage is pride," he added softly. "I satisfied you completely, didn't I?"

"More than completely," she murmured against his damp shoulder. Her hand traced his chest, feeling the coolness of his skin, the ripple of muscle. "Hold me close."

He wrapped both arms around her and drew her on top of him, holding her hungrily to him, their legs lazily entwined. "I seduced you."

She pressed a soft kiss to his collarbone. "Mmm-hmm."

He caught his breath as the tiny, insignificant movement produced a sudden, raging arousal.

She lifted her head. "Did I do something wrong?"

He lifted an eyebrow and nodded toward his flat stomach. She followed his amused glance and caught her breath.

He drew her mouth down over his and kissed her ferociously before he sat up and moved off the bed.

"Where are you going?" she asked, startled.

He drew on his briefs and his slacks, glancing down at her with amused delight. "One of us has to be sensible," he told her. "Colby's probably on his way back right now."

"But he just left..."

"Almost an hour ago," he finished for her, nodding toward the clock on the bedside table.

She sat up, her eyes wide with surprise.

"I took a long time with you," he said gently. "Didn't you notice?"

She laughed self-consciously. "Well, yes, but I didn't realize it was that long."

He drew her off the bed and bent to kiss her tenderly, nuzzling her face with his. "Was I worth waiting for?" he asked.

She smiled. "What a silly question."

He kissed her again, but when he lifted his head he wasn't smiling. "I loved what we did together," he said quietly. "But I should have been more responsible."

She knew what he was thinking. He hadn't used anything, and he surely knew that she wasn't. She flattened her hand against his bare chest. "There's a morning-after pill. I'll drive into the city tomorrow and get one," she said, lying like a sailor. She had no intention of doing that, but it would comfort him.

He found that he didn't like that idea. It hurt something deeply primitive in him. He scowled. "That could be dangerous."

"No, it's not."

He traced her fingernails while he tried to think. It seemed like a fantasy, a dream. He'd never had such an experience with a woman in his life.

She closed her eyes and moved closer to him. "I could never have done that with anyone else," she whispered. "It was even more beautiful than my dreams."

His heart jumped. That was how it felt to him, too. He tilted her face so that he could search her soft eyes. She was radiant; she almost glowed. "Kiss me," he murmured softly.

She did. But he wasn't smiling. She could almost see the thoughts in his face. "You didn't force me, Tate," she said gently. "I made a conscious decision. I made a choice. I needed to know if what had happened to me had destroyed me as a woman. I found out in the most wonderful way that it hadn't. I'm not ashamed of what we did together."

"Neither am I." He turned, his face still tormented. "But it wasn't my right."

"To be the first?" She smiled gently. "It would have been you eight years ago or eight years from now. I don't want anyone else—not that way. I never did."

He actually winced. "Cecily…"

"I'm not asking for declarations of undying love. I won't cling. I'm not the type." She moved in front of him. "You have to go home," she told him.

He seemed puzzled. "I am home."

"You know what I mean. I'll dig whatever Colby's discovered out of him, and I'll tell the right people what they need to know." She reached up and tangled her hands in his long, thick hair, loving the feel of it in her fingers. She smiled and then touched his mouth gently. "You said that it would be the two of us from now on, if this happened. That there would be no more Audrey, no other woman. That you'd come to me to be comforted, to be cared for."

He took great handfuls of her own wonderfully soft hair and framed her face in his lean hands. He bent to kiss her with breathless tenderness, savoring her warm mouth. "I will. Even if I don't know that I can cope with that again," he said huskily.

"With lovemaking?"

He took a long, long look at her. "You don't know much about this," he said finally. "There are… degrees of pleasure. Sometimes it's good, sometimes it's even great. Once in a lifetime or so, it's sacred."

"I don't understand."

"You were a virgin," he whispered solemnly. "But we joined souls. I was inside you, but you were inside me, too." He nuzzled her nose with his. "I remember wondering if a man could die of pleasure, just at the last. It was so good that it was almost painful."

She smiled. "I know. I love you," she said softly.

He looked away from her. His hands on her shoulders were bruising.

"Sorry," she murmured, pulling away. "You don't want to hear that. But it's a fact of life, like middens and projectile points and horizons in archaeology. I can't help it, and it isn't as if you didn't already know. I couldn't have slept with you only because I wanted you. Not with my past."

He knew that. He knew it to the soles of his feet. He was confused and afraid and overwhelmed by the passion they'd shared. It was an addictive, narcotic experience that left him shaken and uncertain for the first time in his life.

She looked up at him, matter-of-fact now, even if she was shattered inside. "Listen to me, you have to go home," she said quietly. "There's a reason, a good one, that you shouldn't be here."

"That's what Holden said. Why? I know how to be discreet. If there's something going on here, I have every right to help find out what. You know how I feel about the casino. How can you be sure that Holden hasn't engineered this so-called renegade gambling syndicate idea to get support against gambling on the res?''

"I'm sure he hasn't," she replied. "But either way, it isn't my secret to tell," she lied. "Just by being here, you're jeopardizing an innocent person's future."

He frowned down at her, with both hands in his pockets. He looked as if he hadn't really heard her. "Cecily, I want you to move in with me when you come back to Washington," he said with sudden decisiveness.

Her heart turned over, but she shook her head.

"Why not?"

"I've already been your financial responsibility for too long. I'm my own woman now. I'm independent. I can take care of myself."

"And once with me, like that, was enough?" he asked in a soft, sensual tone.

She smiled. "It would never be enough if we did it four times a day for the rest of our lives, and you know it," she said. "But I won't be your mistress, Tate."

"Cecily…" he began hesitantly.

"Go home and stop feeling guilty about something we both wanted. I'm not going to intrude in your life. I haven't asked for anything, and I won't." She reached up and kissed him just below the jaw. "And you needn't worry about consequences. There won't be any. Okay?"

He felt those words right through the heart. He'd forced her into that decision with his fanaticism about not mixing blood. He knew that if she did anything, she'd never be able to live with it. She wasn't the type to put her own needs first, regardless of the trouble it caused. He finished dressing while she got her own things back on. He didn't speak, but he was thinking, worrying. When they were back in the living room, he hesitated. "Listen, you don't need to do anything," he said abruptly.

"What?"

"That pill," he said stiffly. "I don't like the idea of it."

She liked having him worry about her. She wondered if he usually made love like that, to other women. She wished she knew more about men. It had been an incredible experience for her, the most beautiful of her entire life. She felt whole. But she didn't want Tate to suspect that she had no intention of taking any sort of preventative measures.

Her voice was soothing. "Whatever you say. Go home." She caught his hand in hers, opened the front door and led him right out to the side of his rented sport utility vehicle. "Everything's fine. You have nothing to worry about."

"Stop pushing me toward the airport, damn it!" he said angrily.

"I'm not pushing. I'm coaxing."

"I don't want to go," he said, and whether or not she realized it, that statement came straight from his heart.

"Sometimes we all have to do things we don't want to," she reminded him. "I'm going to be all right. It's absolutely the wrong time of the month for anything unexpected to happen," she added firmly, lying through her teeth.

"It is?" he asked, with some vague sense of disappointment.

She smiled and nodded. "It is. Now have a nice trip."

He gave in. He got in under the wheel and slammed the door. "If it's the wrong time of month, then you won't need to put yourself at risk with some chemical, will you?"

"No, I won't," she assured him.

"Or any other way?" he persisted.

She smiled at him. "No," she promised.

He smiled back, framing her in his memory like that, with her glorious long blond hair loosened and blowing around her soft oval face. Her glasses were still off, and he wondered if she could see him clearly. "If you need me, I'll come back. All you have to do is call me."

"I know that." She moved closer so that she could search his black eyes. It was different, the way he looked at her now. It was…possessive, but not in the old way.

He reached out and touched the collar of her

blouse, the clean one she'd grabbed up from the chair in her room, the one that she'd put the crab pin on. "Do you like it?" he asked.

She smiled. "Yes. Thank you. He's beautiful. I'm, uh, sorry about the lapful of crab bisque," she said belatedly and with a helpless chuckle.

"As you saw in the bedroom," he said with a wicked glance, "it didn't do any lasting damage to the area it flooded."

She flushed and he laughed.

"I suppose I'm leaving," he murmured dryly. "Come here and kiss me goodbye and I'll go, if I must."

She stepped on the running board and let him kiss her, savoring the wealth of black hair in her hands and the slow, sweet hunger of his mouth. "Why did you take your hair down?" she asked breathlessly when his head lifted.

"You don't know? Ask my mother." He pursed his lips. "Or better yet, ask Colby. He knew the minute he saw me why I'd done it." His eyes began to darken. "If he touches you, I'll cost him more than a few stitches next time. You belong to me now."

He started the vehicle and she moved back. He waved one last time as he drove away before she could give him a speech about people not being possessions. She watched him go with vestiges of pleasure still rippling through her body. She wished she could go with him. He'd have time to think, and he'd convince himself that he'd taken advantage of her. Or maybe, she thought optimistically, he'd convince himself that he couldn't live without her. After all, he had asked her to move in. She turned with a sigh, troubled. She didn't want to live with him unless they were married. It might be a modern world, but Cecily wasn't modern. And he wouldn't marry her. She knew that for a fact. He wouldn't marry her because there weren't going to be any children; not any that he knew about, she amended.

As she started up the porch she recalled abruptly what loosened hair meant. In the old days, just before going to war, some Plains warriors unbound their hair even as they added war paint patterns to their faces, their own special "medicine" to protect them from wounds in battle. She laughed softly to herself as she realized the significance of what Tate had done. Without a word, he'd told Colby that he was in for a fight.

Chapter Eight

Cecily was very calm by the time Colby returned, despite the shattering events of the past hour.

"How did you get him to leave?" he asked amusedly.

"I gave him a quarter," she murmured dryly.

"That never worked for me."

"I wouldn't try it if I were you," she advised with a forced smile.

He grinned at her. "I can't help but agree, considering that unbound hair. Nice of him to make his intentions clear. I suppose you're off-limits now."

She chuckled. "That's what he meant. But I'll decide that for myself."

He smiled, but he could see the look in her eyes. There was never going to be anyone except Tate for her. He understood. He had his own ghosts. But it was nice that Tate had finally realized and accepted Cecily's importance in his life.

She motioned him to a seat on the couch. "I want to know, I have to know, what Tom told you."

"I promised I wouldn't," he said. "You'll have to trust that he's being threatened with something concrete. He stands to lose everything if he's exposed."

Tom, Senator Holden, Leta, Tate…everyone stood to lose something. She felt furiously impotent. "I hate blackmailers," she said through her teeth. "There must be something we can do!"

"There is," he assured her. "I'm going to do a black-bag job."

"A who?"

"You've been hanging around Tate long enough to know what I'm talking about. It's covert ops. And I'm not telling you anything more," he added firmly. "I'll have you a name by tomorrow. Maybe even a location. Will that do?"

She brightened. "Oh, yes. That will do."

Tate had a meeting with Pierce Hutton in Washington the day after he flew back from South Dakota. His head was still spinning, and he still felt guilty about taking advantage of Cecily's feelings for him—in between exquisite dreams of her that got worse by the hour.

"Your mind isn't on this," his broad-shouldered, dark-headed boss muttered when he kept staring into space.

"Sorry," Tate said at once. "I've had a...diversion lately."

"So I recall." His eyes narrowed. "I hear she's staying with your mother and looking for new exhibits for the museum."

Tate glowered at him.

"Why don't you take a few days off and go out there?"

"I did. She practically lifted me into my truck and sent me on my way."

"Amazing girl. Carried you there, did she?" Pierce mused.

Tate gave him a hard glare. "She's doing something risky. I don't know what. Nobody will tell me anything."

"It's probably an elaborate birthday celebration in the planning stages," he commented, stretching out his long legs in a deck chair. "Brianne did the same thing to me on my birthday." He grinned. "We had a major opera star and two famous baseball players, not to mention a string quartet and a French chef."

"Decadent, absolutely decadent," Tate scoffed.

"You can come to the next one. Bring Cecily."

The thought of going out with Cecily made him feel warm inside. They'd rarely gone anywhere together. As she'd once said, he ordered in food to her apartment and they watched television on his free days. His life had been unspeakably lonely without her. Now, it was worse. In the old days, he'd never had any intimate memories to torment him. He missed her badly, in every way there was. He thought ahead to a time when she might fit quite nicely into his life.

"I might do that," he mused absently.

Pierce leaned back. "Now, if you can spare the time to listen, I'll tell you what needs doing."

Tate leaned forward with a faintly apologetic smile. "Sorry. Go right ahead."

When he got back to his apartment, it was unlocked. Frowning, he opened it and walked inside. Audrey was in the small kitchen, taking food out of the oven.

"There you are," she said brightly, as if he'd never told her their relationship, superficial though it was, had ended.

"How did you get in?" he asked curtly. He was angry because she had a habit of invading his privacy and he'd just had the locks changed.

"The manager let me in, of course, just as he always does," she said. "Here, I fixed supper."

"I've had supper," he said flatly. "I had it with my boss. You can leave whenever you like."

She looked shocked and there was a strange glitter in her eyes. "Why? Tate, I'm cultured, I'm talented, I'm quite beautiful, and I'd be willing to do anything you liked in bed."

He just stared at her. His eyes were colder than they'd ever been. "We've been friends, Audrey. I hope we still are. But no one encroaches on my privacy without an invitation. That includes you."

She took off the oven mitt and turned off the oven. Seconds later, tears were running down her cheeks. "Oh, dear," she said. Her lower lip trembled and she managed a brave little smile. "Are you mad at little Audrey?"

He opened the door and stood holding it. He couldn't imagine touching her again, even innocently, after what he'd shared with Cecily. He was still reeling mentally from an experience that surpassed any interlude he'd ever had with a woman.

Seeing that the ruse wasn't working, Audrey wiped the crocodile tears off her cheek and shrugged. "Well, don't think I'm giving up," she said as she swept up her coat and started past him. Her blue eyes lifted to his and she smiled coquettishly. "Just imagine how many men would love to be in your shoes. I'm rich."

On her ex-husband's money, he thought, but he didn't say it. "So am I."

She laughed a little hollowly. "You're Native American," she said. "They aren't rich."

"This one is." Her belittling words wounded him, but it didn't show on his face. "Good night, Audrey."

"You aren't going to humiliate me with the brush-off," she said suddenly, staring at him with fixed eyes. "I won't be dumped by a man with your background! I'm not some pitiful little archaeology nerd that you can just cast off when you feel like it!"

He could have cursed his own stupidity at that moment. What had he ever seen in this woman that had made him let her into his life, even in a minor way?

"You'll never be half the woman that Cecily is," he said curtly.

She smiled coldly. He couldn't know that Cecily had phoned while he was out; that Audrey had answered the phone. He didn't know that she'd told Cecily all about the designer wedding dress she was having made, or the purring insinuation about how wonderful a lover Tate was. And he wouldn't know. Cecily's pride wouldn't let her mention it to him, and Audrey wasn't talking. Tate belonged to her. She wasn't going to lose him.

"I'll be around when you come to your senses, darling," Audrey purred. "But, of course, you don't really mean to throw me out of your life. You'll come back. They always do."

He gestured toward the hall. She went out and he closed the door. Tomorrow, he promised himself, he was changing the lock again and having a heart-to-heart with his soft-touch apartment manager. He wondered at the way Audrey had behaved, like someone with an almost psychotic fixation. He'd run into that sort of thing at least once when he was in covert operations. A woman had chased a friend of his until the man was forced to have her arrested. She'd actually tried to kill his wife. Of course, Audrey wasn't that unbalanced. She was just a poor loser. He started to telephone his mother's house and talk to Cecily, but he had a lot of work to do. There would be plenty of time to consider the problem of his relationship with her later, when he was less uncomfortable about what had happened.

Cecily was unusually quiet when she and Leta sat down alone to the supper table. Colby had gone out without saying where he'd be, or when he'd return.

Leta stared at her until she looked up. "Somebody said that Tate was here yesterday," she said. "You never mentioned it."

"I made him go home." Cecily tried to put the phone call she'd made out of her mind.

"Why couldn't he stay here?" Leta wanted to know.

"Because Senator Holden doesn't want him involved, in any way. He's afraid he might find out something if he started looking around."

"That's true enough," Leta said sadly. "But I would love to have seen him." She looked up. "You're very quiet tonight. Something's wrong."

She shrugged. "Nothing much. I phoned to make sure Tate was home safely and got Audrey."

"She must live with him. I'd hoped I was wrong."

"Apparently she does," Cecily said coldly. She remembered Tate denying that he was intimate with the woman at all. He'd lied. Audrey was cooking his supper, and they'd only just gotten out of bed. Cecily was so sick that she didn't think she could even eat. Why had Tate lied to her? Had it only been to get her into bed? She knew that he was almost obsessed with her physically, that it had driven him to find her, that he'd been jealous of Colby. But men were devious when they wanted a woman. Could he have been rationalizing? He said he felt guilty about it, and he probably did, but because he'd been unfaithful to Audrey. Nothing had ever hurt so much!

"What did Audrey have to say?" Leta persisted.

"That he got back safely and he's a wonderful lover and she's having a wedding gown made." She looked up. "Lucky you. What a beautiful daughter-in-law you're going to have."

"He won't marry her," Leta said firmly. "And you know why."

"She thinks he will. So do I, when he learns the truth." She met Leta's worried eyes. "I'm sorry, but you must know it's going to come out sooner or later. Even if the press doesn't get hold of the story, it's inevitable that he's going to find out."

"I don't like to think about it."

"I know."

"He'll hate me."

"He will not," Cecily said firmly. "He'll be upset, and angry, and he'll go away and sulk for a few days. Then he'll accept it and come home. You know him," she said sadly, and smiled.

"Yes, I do." She searched Cecily's wan face. "You should tell him how you feel."

"He knows how I feel," Cecily said. "But it doesn't change anything. He still says he doesn't want to marry a white woman. I guess Audrey's the exception.''

"Something fishy is going on here."

"I know. It involves a tribal chief."

"Cecily!"

Cecily smiled gently. "We don't have time to worry about my problems right now. We have to save Senator Holden." She sighed sadly. "He's going to be furious with me when he knows I've told you that he knows about Tate. He made me promise not to."

"We'll cross that bridge when we come to it. Eat your pudding. You're way too thin."

Cecily smiled and lifted her spoon.

It didn't take Colby long to riffle through Tom Black Knife's locked desk and find everything he needed. He photographed ledgers, vouchers and an unsigned letter with a New Jersey postmark. He photographed an address book with phone numbers. Then he closed the drawer and locked it back, with every paper exactly in its place. He let himself out and blended in with the night.

"Here," Colby told Cecily the next morning. It was a small roll of film. "Give that to your contact in D.C. with my blessings. It's everything you need to find the right people."

"You're a wonder, Colby. Are you coming back with me?"

"Not until Tate cools off. I think I'll go on out to Arizona for a couple of days and see my cousins."

She grinned at him. "Good for you! Thanks, Colby," she added sincerely. "We couldn't have done this without your help."

"It was a pleasure. I'll see you in D.C."

"You bet."

Cecily left Leta with a warm hug and started down the winding road to the highway when it dawned on her that she'd forgotten the valuable unusual relic that she'd promised to bring Dr. Phillips.

With a sinking heart she realized that she couldn't ask for anything from the tribe, because old things were sacred. It would be like asking for a person's living heart. But then something occurred to her. She turned the car in the direction of Red Elk's little trading post nearby. She knew the old man, who had no family. Perhaps he could suggest something for the museum that she hadn't even thought about.

Red Elk was an elderly Sioux, so elderly that nobody liked asking his age. They shook hands like old friends, which they were.

"I need something unusual," Cecily told him, glancing at a couple who were just getting out of their dusty van at the steps. "I need a relic for our museum. We're making a display of Lakota handicrafts and artifacts, but I can't ask the tribe for anything sacred. What can you sell me that won't give offense?"

He smiled at her with a gap in his teeth. "I have the very thing, Cecily."

He went into the back of the shop and came out

with a parfleche bag, very old and stained, with discolored fringe all around it and a hole in it. He handed it to her with great ceremony. The couple from the van, a man and a woman, middle-aged and dressed like tourists, hovered nearby. The man was staring curiously at what the old man had in his hands.

"This belonged to my grandfather," Red Elk told Cecily. "I have no family left to hand it down to, and my small band had no connection to Tom Black Knife's tribe. I would like it to have a safe place. I would like people to see it. It saved my grandfather's life at the Greasy Grass. He had placed a stone pipe in it, a ceremonial pipe of great power. A soldier's bullet shattered the stone, but did not penetrate the chest of my grandfather who was holding it over his shoulder in preparation for battle." He laid it in Cecily's hands.

She touched it with awe. "May I open it?" she asked.

He nodded.

She opened the flap with excited hands. Inside were remnants of a pipe carved from red pipestone, along with small pieces of wood, some with old pigments clinging to it. "This is…beyond my wildest expectations. You can name any price for it."

He waved her away. "I would not sell it," he said. "It would cheapen it. You take it for your museum. I would like you to put my grandfather's name, Crow Shield, below it, in a placard, and say that he was one of the Waist and Skirt Indians who fought at the Greasy Grass.''

"I will do that," she promised. "Is there something I can give you in return, something you would like to have?" she added, because it was custom to give a gift of equal value in return for one received.

"Yes," the old man said with a reminiscent smile. "I would like a German pipe. I saw a man come through here with one. It had an enormous big bole and a curved stem. It was magnificent."

She knew exactly what he was talking about. "I live near a tobacconist in D.C.," she said. "I know the kind you mean. I'll send it to Leta Warwoman Winthrop and she will bring it to you."

"I know Leta. A brave woman. A daughter of a brave family."

She shook hands with him. *"Pilamaya yelo."*

He chuckled. *"Pilamaya ye,"* he corrected. "I would say *pilamaya yelo,* for I am male. You forget that a woman speaks one way and a man another."

"I'm still learning," she told him.

"And very well." He gave her the Lakota for *you're welcome.* "Have a good journey," he added.

She took his gnarled hand in hers. "And you keep well. Thank you for this." She indicated the parfleche bag held respectfully in both her hands.

As she left, he turned to speak to the female tourist who had come in and stood, listening to what the old man had said to Cecily. The other tourist, the man, stopped her as she went out onto the porch.

"I didn't understand what he was saying," he said with a polite smile, nodding toward Red Elk. "I'd like to know what it meant. He said his grandfather fought at the Greasy Grass. I never heard of such a place, or of Waist and Skirt Indians. Can you explain? I'm a history buff, but I guess I haven't been reading the right books."

She smiled. "I'm an anthropologist," she told him. "A lot of people haven't heard these expressions unless they're very deep into Native American history. The Greasy Grass is what the Sioux called the Little Bighorn River. Waist and Skirt Indians are Santee Sioux. Sioux is actually a misnomer, because the people call themselves Lakota in this region. There are various bands of Lakota, like Minneconjou and Hunkpapa and Oglala. What I said to Red Elk was "thank you," in Lakota, but I used the wrong personal pronoun," she said with a grin. "I'm still a student. He replied that I was welcome."

"Do you teach?" he asked curiously.

She shook her head. "I'm assistant curator in charge of acquisitions for a new museum in Washington. It's a museum of the indiginous peoples of the United States. I hope that you'll stop by if you come to the nation's capitol. We're very proud of our facility."

"We'll do that." He glanced at the parfleche held so lovingly in her hands. "History," he murmured. "History you can see and touch. You're very lucky. I got to read a sixteenth century illuminated manuscript wearing gloves and a mask. It isn't the same thing."

She smiled at him. "I know. But protecting the legacy of the past is a huge responsibility. If everyone got to touch things, they wouldn't last long. Oil in the fingertips, you see."

He chuckled self-consciously. "I do now."

She wished them a safe trip, climbed in the car with her precious cargo, and drove to the airport.

She showed her acquisition to Dr. Phillips, who was beside himself with delight. "Our first real artifact, Cecily," he said breathlessly. "And what an artifact! Perhaps we can have Red Elk flown up here to speak about it when we open our doors to the public!"

"What a marvelous idea," she agreed. "And I have another one. Why not have a similar parfleche made that people can touch, so that they have a tactile idea of how one feels?"

"Another great idea," he said at once. "Can you have one made for us?"

"I'll get my adopted mama right on it."

But before she phoned Leta, she took that spool of film to Senator Holden's office and handed it to him without a word.

He smiled from ear to ear. "Pictures of the reservation, hmm?"

"Of an ancient artifact," she lied glibly. "A parfleche bag that contained a sacred pipe. It saved its owner from a cavalry bullet at the Little Big Horn.''

"I've got to see the real thing," Holden said at once.

"Come over whenever you like. We'll be delighted to show it to you."

He held up the film, and his face was solemn. He nodded, and smiled. She smiled back. At least something good had come out of her trip.

Inevitably Tate phoned her at her office when she'd returned. "Leta said you and Colby left suddenly," he said softly. "What did you find out?"

"This isn't a secure line," she told him without expression in her voice. It hurt to hear him talking to her in that almost intimate tone after what Audrey had told her.

"Stop talking like a secret agent," he teased.

"You start thinking like one again," she told him. "I'll meet you for coffee in the usual place."

"What usual place?"

"Where you and Audrey go, of course."

That hadn't been a teasing tone in her voice. "I only took her there once, Cecily, the day you ran into us…"

"Ten minutes." She hung up, got her jacket and went out, telling her secretary that she had a meeting and would be back in an hour. She dreaded seeing him again. But if she could just keep her head, perhaps she could bluff her way through. She felt betrayed.

* * *

Tate was sitting impatiently at a small table near the window with a cup of black coffee. He looked up, watching her get coffee at the counter. She paid for it and came to sit down beside him. It was difficult to pretend that they hadn't been intimate. She looked at him now and felt the weight of him in her arms, the heat of his body, the fierce passion as it moved on her. He'd said that there wouldn't be anyone else afterward, but Audrey had been in his apartment, right at home. She swallowed some coffee that was too hot and burned her tongue trying to forget.

"Why here?" he asked at once.

She studied him covertly over her cup. His hair was back in its braid. He was wearing a gray Armani silk suit with a turtleneck shirt. He looked as elegant as he always had. He was like the man she remembered from her teens today, because he didn't smile.

"I thought you liked good coffee," she replied finally, staring down into hers. "They have Jamaican Blue Mountain coffee here. It's wonderful."

"I like coffee that a spoon will stand in. I'm not particular about the brand." He sipped his own, wondering at the change in Cecily. They'd been intimate and they sat here like polite acquaintances. She was as remote as he'd once been. Her behavior puzzled him, made him uneasy. They were lovers, but she was pushing him away as certainly as if she'd done it physically.

"I want to know what's going on, Cecily."

"You do know."

He shook his head. "Insinuations, gossip, rumors. Nobody will talk to me. It's like a code of silence."

He was frustrated. She could hear it in his voice. "Colby found out some things," she said finally. "I've given the information to the appropriate person. Now we sit back and hope that what we've got is enough to prevent a humdinger of a political scandal."

"Involving Holden."

Her face lifted. Her pale green eyes in their big lenses were very intent. "How did you know that?"

"Do you know what they've got on him?"

"Oh, sure, I'm going to tell his worst enemy that," she said curtly.

"You might not believe this, but he told me himself," he said.

She was even more still than before. She looked apprehensive. "He told you...everything?"

Fishing, he thought, was an enjoyable sport. He carefully looked at the coffee cup she was holding in her neatly manicured hands. "How is it that you know?" he asked.

She put down her cup carefully. She looked at the white linen tablecloth instead of him. Softly a Viennese waltz played in the background from speakers over their heads. "Senator Holden had to tell me everything to get me to help him," she said after a minute. She looked up into his lean face. "You're very calm about it," she said. "And you aren't angry with me?"

He smiled carelessly. "Why would I be?"

"I thought it would be more traumatic than this," she ventured. He looked puzzled, and she wondered if she'd been deliberately led. "Suppose you tell me what Matt Holden told you?"

"Holden says he's being blackmailed because of a woman in his past," he said. "They had an affair while he was married, and the woman lives on the reservation."

She nodded, reassured. "Yes. And?"

He scowled. "And what?"

He didn't know! She hadn't thought he'd take the news of his true parentage so calmly. Now she'd almost given it away.

"The senator will have to tell you the rest," she said flatly. "I've said all I'm going to. Why did you want to see me?"

He studied her face curiously. "Why do I always want to see you?" he countered. His voice was like velvet. "You're part of me now, Cecily."

She colored. She couldn't meet his eyes. Did he think she didn't know about Audrey?

"And you wouldn't lie to me," she said.

"Any more than you'd lie to me," he replied softly.

So they were both liars. She stared at the big silver-

and-turquoise ring on his lean finger. Leta wore a matching one, smaller of course.

She sipped her coffee without speaking. It was hard to talk to him. She couldn't make the transition that he'd made so easily, from affection to intimacy. That must be the difference between experience and naiveté, she thought glumly.

They drank the rest of their coffee in silence. She smiled politely and got to her feet. "I have to get back. I'm working on a new display, and I have a lot of phone calls to make."

He stood up with her, scowling. His expression was uneasy. "What's gone wrong between us?" he asked abruptly.

She searched his eyes with sadness in her own. "Not a thing."

"Talk to me!"

She drew in a breath. "Audrey was cooking supper for you," she said, unable to hide the pain of it that showed in her voice. "She said she'd picked out a wedding gown. And that you're terrific in bed, of course."

"Damn Audrey!" he said under his breath.

She moved one shoulder. "I have to go." She noticed that he wasn't denying anything.

He could barely get his mind to work. He fell into step beside her as they reached the sidewalk, reluctant to let her go until they'd smoothed things out.

"You're going the wrong way," she pointed out. "Pierce Hutton's offices are that way."

"Your office is this way," he reflected. "I'm not going away until you finish that accusation."

She turned to him, pulling her jacket closer against the chill in the air. "You went back to her."

"I did not."

"I called you. She was there, in your apartment...!"

"She got the apartment manager to open the door for her. She was waiting for me when I got home. I threw her out." He looked completely inflexible. "I've only lied to you about one thing—who was paying your bills. Other than that, I've always been truthful to you. But if you don't believe me, you don't."

It reminded her that she'd lied to him, by omission, about the threat to him and his real father.

"Audrey is beautiful," she said.

"So is a rattlesnake, in the right light."

She smiled in spite of herself.

He sighed. "We've still got a long way to go. Are you sure you won't move in with me?"

She shook her head.

His eyes narrowed. "How about dinner tonight. Maybe a play."

She stared at his chest. "It isn't a good idea."

"I want you!"

"I want you, too, desperately." She looked up at him hungrily, but with eyes that held sadness. "But you don't want me permanently, Tate. Sooner or later, you'd tire of me and find someone else. Isn't that how it's done? You live with someone until they bore you and then you just find another lover.''

His face tautened. She made him sound like a rounder, which he never had been. ''What are you going to do, Cecily, walk away from me and pretend that nothing happened in my mother's guest room?''

''That's exactly what I'm going to do,'' she replied quietly. ''Because I can't bear the thought of living day by day with a man who doesn't share my dream for the future.''

He dug his hands into his pockets. ''You could give it a chance.''

''I'll live with a man when I get married,'' she said abruptly. ''That's the only way I ever will.''

And he never would. ''It's the twentieth century,'' he said coldly. ''Marriage is no longer a necessity for people to be together. I've told you that I have no plans whatsoever to marry, now or ever. And what the hell is the difference when you've already slept with me?''

''If you can't see the difference, I could never explain it to you.'' She turned away.

''Cecily.''

She glanced at him over her shoulder.

''Did you go to the clinic?'' he asked.

He wanted to know if there was any risk of her getting pregnant. Actually there was a terrific chance, and she hadn't gone to any clinic. But if there was a baby, she was going to have it and love it. She wasn't going to present him with a child who wasn't Lakota. Presumably that was what frightened him most.

"You have absolutely nothing to worry about," she lied. "See you around, Tate."

She walked away. He stood and watched her with his hands still in his pockets. He couldn't remember a time when he'd ever felt so alone. He didn't want her out of his life, but she was making demands he couldn't meet. Marriage was simply out of the question; so were children. She knew that already. So what was wrong with two consenting adults living together? Especially two adults who could share such a passion, such a feast of the senses. Why was she being so stubborn?

He wondered exactly what she and Colby had found in South Dakota. He wanted to phone his mother and try to dig it out of her, but if Colby hadn't told Cecily, he wasn't likely to tell Leta.

Tate was frustrated. But he was feeling something else as well: curiosity. Cecily knew something more about Holden's past that she wasn't telling him, something that would apparently make him angry with her. He wondered what it was. He was going to do some digging of his own. As for his future with Cecily, that would have to wait. She was as stubborn as he was, but perhaps she'd come around yet when she became lonely enough. His job, his heritage, his love of freedom combined to make marriage a distasteful prospect, but he loved the feel of Cecily in his arms. Even if his conscience was killing him by degrees for seducing her, he couldn't stop wanting her. And he wasn't giving up until she came to her senses.

Chapter Nine

Two weeks later, Matt Holden came to see Cecily at her apartment.

"Sorry about this," he said as she led him into the small living room and offered him her easy chair. "I think my office is bugged. I had to get a stranger to upgrade my security and now I think it may be worse than it was before. At least Tate would know if there were bugs here in your apartment."

"Only if he's psychic," she said darkly. "He doesn't come here anymore," she added in a subdued tone.

He sighed. "I gather you've seen the ring Audrey's flashing around."

She swallowed hard. "Ring?"

"A copy of the turquoise one that he wears." He leaned back in the chair and crossed his long legs, looking unspeakably irritated. "Everyone in town knows that she's a man-eater. As soon as she's sure of Tate, she'll be off looking for new men to conquer. She won't really marry him." He leaned forward. "He's Native American!"

She grimaced and curled up on the sofa. "He told me flatly that they were no longer involved and that her being in his apartment the last time I called was innocent. But there was a photo in the tabloid yesterday of them together at some gala benefit."

"I know. I saw it."

"Don't take this the wrong way, but why are you here?" she asked.

"I've got names and dates and ledger sheets and places," he said. "I handed them over to a member of my staff that I trust with my life. He has a brother with a detective agency. It's taken a little more investigation, but I have everything I need. The fire is about to hit the fan. There's a risk that the media may get hold of it in spite of everything I do. When I expose these rats, they're bound to retaliate. I can't stand between them and every reporter in the country."

"You're worried about how it will affect Tate and Leta."

He nodded. "Leta will manage. She's tough. But Tate is going to learn some things that will hurt him badly. I think he should hear it from his mother." He sighed angrily. "So I called her up on a pay phone and told her I knew everything, and that she should tell Tate the truth before he hears it on the evening news. After thirty-six years of silence, she suddenly became very vocal. She called me a name I won't repeat, told me what she thought of me and my career and hung up. When I rang back, she wouldn't pick up the phone.'' He ran his hands through his hair. ''What do I do?''

''Suppose I invite her here to stay with me, for a visit,'' she suggested. ''Then you can talk to her again…''

''There's no time, Cecily.'' He spread his hands on his thighs and a look of torment lined his broad, strong face. ''I'm going to have to tell him myself.''

She winced. ''I'm sorry.''

He sighed. ''I'm sorry, too. He's going to hate all of us for a little while, even Leta. I told her that. It made her furious, but it's the truth. We're going to have a bad thunderstorm that will last for a few weeks, and then there will be a ray of sunshine.''

She smiled. ''We may have a tornado instead.''

He got up. ''I just wanted to keep you updated. I thought for a while that I might be able to stick my head in the sand. I thought I could take the heat off Tom Black Knife, get the gambling syndicate off the reservation, and Tate would never have to know the truth. I was daydreaming. You can't keep a lie forever.''

''It's going to hurt him.''

''It's going to hurt you, too, you know that, don't you?'' he said gently. ''You knew the truth and you didn't tell him. He holds grudges. He isn't particularly forgiving, either. Like his mother," he added darkly.

"Leta isn't like that."

"Not to you, of course. She hates my guts," he said, and looked as if it had wounded him deeply to know it. "I don't blame her. I hate myself. Tate will really have something in common with her when he knows the whole story. I hope I can find the right words to minimize the damage. It will hurt her terribly to have Tate turn his back on her."

"You'll do the right thing. What about Tom?" Matt Holden had filled Cecily in on Tom's story.

"I've got the best investigators I can find looking for a loophole for him. There are still two witnesses living who saw what happened back in the seventies. One of them is in prison, and we may be able to cook a deal to get him to tell what he knows. It's the best I can do. I spoke to Tom. He understands. A brave man."

"Yes. And a sad story."

"Well, here goes nothing." He moved to the door. "Since nobody else has the guts to do the dirty work, I'm going to see Tate tomorrow and tell him who his father is."

"Good luck."

He shrugged. His glance at her was wry and full of self-contempt. "It will take more than luck, I'm afraid."

Tate was having a beer. He didn't drink as a rule, but lately he was morose and broody. He couldn't go to a party without finding Audrey nearby, ready to launch herself at him every time a camera flashed. She denied even talking to Cecily, but he knew better. Cecily didn't lie. He wished he could bring himself to go and see Cecily, but she was adamant. She wanted nothing to do with him since he'd put marriage out of reach. It made him mad that she was willing to deny them both fulfillment of a perfectly normal desire because he wasn't willing to stand in front of a minister with her. She might come around eventually, but meanwhile his enforced abstinence was making him hostile to everyone around him.

The sharp ring of the doorbell diverted him from his thoughts. He put down the beer and padded across the carpeted floor in his socks. He was wearing jeans and a sweatshirt, hardly the garb for visitors. If it was Audrey, he wasn't even going to open the damned door. He'd had the lock changed and threatened the apartment manager with homicide if he ever let her in the apartment again.

But the sight that met his eyes was a surprise. It was Senator Matt Holden, who was also wearing jeans and a sweatshirt. Well, it was Sunday afternoon. Maybe the man didn't live in suits on the weekend.

He opened the door with obvious reluctance and more than a little hostility.

"Lost your way?" he asked Holden. "The Senate Office Building is a few blocks east."

Holden studied the taller man quietly. "I need to talk to you. My office has bugs. The security guy I hired added a few more to the one that was already there.''

"Not my fault," Tate told him. "I would have found them all."

"I know that." He averted his eyes to the wall. Mandelas and dream catchers, a parfleche bag and a medicine shield adorned one dark-paneled wall. "Nice decor," he added.

"The medicine shield is supposed to ward off evil," Tate said, standing aside to let Holden in. "Doesn't work, does it?" he added with a speaking glance at the man.

"I'm not evil. I'm caught up in something that I can't avoid. I want to tell you about it before you see it on CNN."

"What business is it of mine?" Tate wanted to know. "And I seem to remember that you thrive on publicity. You got plenty out of Brauer's capture, not to mention Cecily's sleight of hand with the crab bisque at your fund-raiser."

Holden went to the window instead of taking the chair he was offered. He stuck his thumbs in the back pockets of his jeans and stared at the city skyline. The capitol building was visible in the distance.

"This won't be beneficial publicity."

"Cecily said she and Colby found something at Wapiti Ridge."

He nodded. "They found hard evidence of embezzled funds and mob-related gambling ties to plans for a casino." He turned. "I've contacted the state attorney general back home and given her the details. I've also spoken to Tom Black Knife and the tribal council. They all know the story and I have evidence that can put the perpetrators away. But they're going to retaliate. Tom Black Knife may go to prison despite my best efforts to save him, not because he did anything willingly, but because of something he did during the uprisings of the seventies that got covered up.''

Tate perched himself on the edge of the desk he used at home and frowned. ''So that's how they got him to cooperate.''

Holden nodded. ''They blackmailed him. Just as they threatened to blackmail me.'' He turned toward his son. ''I tried to get your mother to tell you, but she hung up and refused to even discuss coming here. She won't talk to you about it. Cecily won't, either. Since I'm the only member of the family with the balls to do it, I'm going to tell you what you should have been told years ago.''

''That the woman you had the affair with was my mother,'' Tate said, having worked that out for himself.

Holden blinked. ''Well, yes. How did you know?''

''It was the only reason you could have wanted me out of it, to protect my mother. Not that I think much of you for the way you treated her,'' he added coldly. ''Even you couldn't have been a worse husband than my father was. Of course, you wouldn't have wanted to marry beneath you, would you? A Lakota Indian in your bloodlines would have—"

"You're making this harder!" Holden interrupted. He ran a hand through his hair, disarranging it.

"You can tell my mother not to worry," Tate said shortly. "Anyone can make a mistake. I won't blame her. And I'll do what I can to protect her from the media."

"You're the one who's going to need protecting, damn it!" Holden snapped. His eyes were blazing, as fierce as Tate's had ever been. "There's more to this than a thirty-six-year-old affair! There was a child! Leta was pregnant when she married Jack Winthrop!"

Tate didn't move. He didn't breathe. He didn't blink. All the flyaway pieces of the puzzle of his life suddenly converged. Why Jack Winthrop had put away so much whiskey. Why he beat Leta. Why he hated Tate.

"Jack Winthrop wasn't my father." Tate said it in an unnaturally matter-of-fact, calm voice.

"No. The son of a bitch wasn't your father." He clenched his jaw. It was harder than he'd ever dreamed it would be. "I went my whole life thinking that Leta married the man because she really loved him. When she had a child a little later, it seemed that she'd found a good life for herself. She never blamed me for marrying money, for putting my career above her own happiness. She let me go and never told me, never, that she was…pregnant!"

His voice broke. He turned away from his son, unable to look at the man, even to speak until he got control of himself. Which was just as well, because Tate's face had gone white under its tan.

"What a hell of a way to learn that I had a child," Holden said finally. "What a hell of a way! A member of the gambling syndicate came and sat down in my office and told me that he was going to make me a political scandal poster-boy with my Lakota mistress and my bastard son."

Tate still hadn't said a word. He was trying to cope with what the older man was saying, and not managing very well at all. He noted idly the stance of the man, the way his hair grew, the nose that was his nose, the black eyes that were his eyes. The resemblance had always been there, and at some level, he'd known that. But not consciously. Not until now...

"You aren't Lakota," Tate said after a tense silence.

"My mother was French," Holden said heavily. "My father was Moroccan. They came to this country when I was three years old and became naturalized citizens."

"Which makes me a half-breed," Tate said, his voice choked with anger.

Holden turned. "Oh, it's a little worse than that," he said, nettled. "It makes you the illegitimate son of the senior Republican senator from South Dakota. And the press will eat you alive when it comes out. You, Leta, me, everyone our lives touch. Including

Cecily. She'll make a damned great sidebar, with her anthropology degree!''

"You'll lose face with your constituents," Tate said coldly.

"Oh, to hell with that! Maybe I'll lose my job, so what?" Holden said, glaring at him. "It wouldn't matter if your mother would speak to me! She cut me off before I got two complete sentences out. She wouldn't come out here and help me tell you the truth. She hung up on me!''

"Good for her! What a pity she didn't try that thirty-six years ago.''

The older man's eyes darkened. "I loved her," he said very quietly. "I still love her. I made the mistake of my life when I thought money and power would be worth marrying a vicious damned socialite who could help me politically. Your mother was worth ten of my late wife. I never knew what hell was until I tried to live with the devil's deal I made to get my office." He turned away again and sat down on the sofa wearily, glancing at the beer. "You shouldn't drink," he said absently.

Tate ignored him. He picked up the beer, finished it with pure spite and crushed the empty can.

"Aren't you leaving now?" he asked the other man with biting contempt.

Holden let out a long breath. "Where would I go? I live in a big empty house with a Jacuzzi and two Siamese cats. Until a few weeks ago, I thought I had no family left alive.''

Tate wouldn't have mentioned to save himself that he wanted to know more about his real background, his grandparents. He stood scowling at the man who'd just destroyed his life.

Holden stared at him with helpless pride. "One of your great-grandfathers was a Berber," he recalled. "He rode with the Rizouli, who was a revolutionary in Morocco about the turn of the century. There's a painting of him over the mantel in my study. I've actually been to see the Rizouli's palace, in Asilah, down the coast from Tangier. It's a beautiful little town."

Tate was quiet. He stuck his hands in his pockets. His mind was working again. "This is why you went back on the security contract," he said. "It would have been nepotism."

Holden nodded.

"And it's why you didn't want me at Wapiti."

Holden nodded again.

"But Cecily knew. She's known from the beginning, hasn't she?" he demanded, remembering tidbits of conversation that had puzzled him until now.

Holden got up from his seat, looking every year of his age. Things would only deteriorate from now on. He had to go, he had to give Tate time to work through it. It must have come as the worst kind of shock. He remembered how he'd felt when a complete stranger had confided that the senator had a son. Holden hadn't taken his word for it, of course. He'd dug into the records of Tate's birth for his whole name, which was Tate Rene Winthrop. Holden's father whom he adored was called Rene, and Leta knew it. His blood type, a rare one, was also shared with Tate. There wasn't much guesswork after that.

"I wanted you to know the truth before you heard it on the evening news," he said curtly as he paused at the door, meeting his son's hostile gaze evenly. "You'll never know how I felt when I learned about you. I hated your mother for a while. I had a child I'd never seen. I missed his first steps, his first words, I missed his whole damned life! And while I was sitting up here on my nice white cloud, Jack Winthrop was playing hell with the family I didn't have. While you're hating me, think about that. I could have spared you, and her, if I'd only known the truth!"

He opened the door and went out, closing it sharply behind him.

Tate opened another beer. He was glad he had several. He held up the beer to his image in the mirror. "To bastards everywhere!" he said sarcastically, and chugged it down.

Later, when he was calm enough to use the telephone, he called his mother.

"Guess who just paid me a visit?" he asked her with a faint slur in his angry voice. "My dad."

There was a long, heavy pause. "Your father…he did?" she stammered, shocked. She'd never dreamed when Matt Holden called her that he might be willing to tell Tate the truth himself. She was sick to her soul, to have her child know that his whole life was a lie. She felt guilty, as she had when she'd heard Matt's deep, beloved voice after thirty-odd years. She'd been too flustered to say much to him, and in the end, regretfully, she'd hung up on him out of sheer embarrassment.

"Why didn't you tell me?" he demanded. "Why?"

There was another pause. "I can't tell you how sorry I am, but now's not the time to discuss this. We'll talk about it one day, when you're ready to listen. Call me back after the shock's worn off. Please forgive me. I love you!"

She hung up.

He dialed the number again. She didn't answer. He tore the telephone cord out of the wall and threw the phone. It shattered with a nice noise. He wondered a little dimly if that had been his father's reaction when Leta had hung up on him.

His father. His *father!* He put his head in his hands, fighting the sickness that welled up in his belly. He'd been unique, a member of a vanishing race, a vanishing tribe, an individual in an ancient society. Now he was one of thousands with mixed blood, not unique anymore, not even Lakota. He was part Moroccan, part Berber if he believed the senator. The illegitimate son of a senator, how was that for a shocker? And if it hadn't been for a renegade gambling syndicate trying to get a casino on Sioux land that they could siphon off profits from, he'd have gone the rest of his life without ever knowing the truth. His mother had kept her secret for thirty-six years. His whole life.

He remembered Jack Winthrop's temper, the vicious attacks, the hateful attitude. No wonder the man hated him. It made sense now, when it was too late to matter. Leta's fault. His mother's fault. Not that she hadn't suffered, too.

He leaned his head against the wall. He didn't want it to clear. He didn't want to think about what he'd learned. Not now. It was too much. He needed to sleep.

He fell into his bed and all but passed out on a single six-pack of beer, which had hit him hard because he didn't ordinarily drink. The next morning he woke with a headache and a renewed burst of bad temper. Cecily had lied to him. She'd lied to him. Well, she wasn't going to get away with it. He was going to her office and he was going to tell her a thing or two!

It was midday of an otherwise unremarkable day when Cecily's head lifted with surprise at the force with which her office door was pushed open and then closed. Her secretary was at lunch. The office was deserted. And a furious black-eyed man stood over her desk looking as if he planned to come right across it after her. She knew what had happened, even before a weeping Leta had phoned her the night before to give her the latest news. She'd coaxed Leta into getting on a plane Tuesday and coming to stay with her before the news media ran the scandal and destroyed her privacy at Wapiti.

"Did you think I wouldn't find out eventually?" Tate asked in a bitter tone.

She wasn't sure how to handle him. He looked completely out of control. "Find out what?" she asked, even though she had a pretty good idea.

"Matt Holden finally got around to telling me who my father was," he said with an unpleasant smile. His calm voice belied the storms in his eyes.

It was no use pretending innocence anymore. She sighed heavily. "We were all trying to protect you," she began. "If we could have gotten enough on the syndicate, they'd never have dared print what they knew. But we didn't count on them doing it for revenge because Matt threw a spanner into their nasty plan. Matt decided that you had to be told, and there was only him to do it. Your mother wouldn't."

"My mother had no right to keep such a secret from me. Neither did he. Neither did you!" He pointed at her. "You had no right, Cecily!"

"I gave my word to Senator Holden, and to your mother, that I wouldn't say anything," she said softly, rising from her desk. She walked around it slowly, approached him cautiously as if he were completely wild. In fact, he was. He was vibrating with frustration, shock, hurt, fury. "I knew it was going to be impossible to keep the secret, but they wanted to try, to spare you the truth."

"All my life, I knew who I was," he told her. "I

knew what I was, where I belonged, where I was going in life. In the space of a day, I've been set adrift. Suddenly I'm an outsider among my own people. My ancestry is a lie. My life...is a lie!''

"That isn't true," she replied gently. "Your mother didn't dare tell your father the truth. His wife hated Native Americans. She could have hurt your mother. She could have hurt you. Even the knowledge of you could have cost him his career."

"Jack Winthrop knew the truth," he said huskily. "It's why he hated us so much—her for loving another man, me for not being his child. He made us pay every day we lived, and until yesterday, I never knew why!''

She winced, feeling his pain. She started to reach out to him. He backed up a step.

"Don't," he warned softly, his eyes glittering with conflicting emotions. "So help me God, if you touch me," he breathed, "I'll have you right here on the carpet!''

He made it sound like a threat, but in fact, it was what he needed, perhaps why he'd come here. He needed comfort and he'd come to her for it, bristling with bad temper to disguise the need. She wasn't afraid of him. She loved him too much to be bothered by sizzling black eyes and a straight line of a mouth. He had every reason to be angry, to be hurt. But what he needed from her wasn't words. She could give him what he really yearned for. It might be the last time he ever would touch her, now, when he was out of control and not thinking clearly. He wasn't a particularly forgiving man, and she'd betrayed him.

She went to lock the door before she went back to him. She reached up and pulled his mouth down over hers without a word.

He actually trembled before his arms caught her, held her, lifted her into the viciously aroused contours of his body. His mouth was devouring on her lips. He was bruising her a little with the ferocity of the embrace, but it was oh, so sweet, to be needed like that. She sighed into his lips. It seemed like forever since he'd kissed her.

It seemed that way to him as well. He was losing himself in her and she was seducing him deliberately. He didn't want to do this. It wasn't right. But he wanted her to the point of madness, needed her, ached to have her. He'd come to her for comfort, even if he couldn't admit it. All the long weeks he'd denied himself were over. Feast after the famine, even if he was angry. Somehow, the anger was translated into the hottest, fiercest passion he'd ever expressed to a woman.

Inevitably kisses weren't enough. Oblivious to the time, the place, their surroundings, he carried her down with him to the floor. Fastenings were loosened, obstacles moved aside, hands searching for bare skin in a frenzy of heat.

Then she lay under the slow, hard thrust of his body on the imported Persian rug with her eyes closed, her mouth answering the deep, hungry kisses, smiling under the ferocity of his lips. It was feverish and rough and even a little dangerous, here in her own office, even with the door locked. The danger made it even more passionate. She pulled him closer, dimly aware that they were still almost fully clothed. It didn't matter. Nothing mattered except the...pleasure!

He covered her mouth quickly to stifle the surprised sob of joy that prefaced the violent tremor of her body under him. He held her to him with a lean hand at her hip, jerking her up to him as the rhythm grew more violent, more demanding. He groaned into her welcoming mouth as the fever rose high and bright and suddenly exploded into fiery particles of pleasure that shot through his body like cellular fireworks. He stiffened helplessly as the spasms shook him and felt her eyes on him. He groaned harshly at the over-whelming pleasure it provoked to know that she was watching him.

When he could breathe again, he lifted his face from her throat and looked down into her eyes, his own eyes strange and turbulent.

"You watched," he said coldly.

"Yes." She opened the buttons of his shirt and slid her hand over his smooth muscles to where she could feel his heart beating. She could feel him intimately and she moved deliberately, knowing that he was still fiercely aroused and that her movements would renew the passion. She lifted her hips, gasped at the sensation. "Are you...going to watch...this time?" she whispered, pulling his head back down to her.

He went right over the edge. His eyes were as hostile as the look on his face when he pushed down with a fierce surge, impaling her further. It aroused him even more than her restless movements had. He did it again. His eyes blazed. His body shuddered.

"Yes, that's it," she whispered feverishly. Her hands slid down his back, under his slacks. "Yes. Do it again. Make it last. Make it last forever! You can watch me, too...!"

"Damn you, Cecily," he bit off with helpless desire, trembling with new urgency as he found her mouth and his taut body moved helplessly on hers all over again. It shouldn't even have been possible. She was demanding this time, fiercely enjoying everything he did to her, and he'd never been so aroused.

He lifted his head, and he did watch. She laughed with shocked pleasure, looked up at him with love blazing out of her green eyes.

When she lifted into his body with a sharp, funny little cry, he saw her eyes dilate until they were almost black. She clung to him, sobbing.

Her face was beautiful, like that, he thought while he could. She was completely uninhibited, as if the past had never happened, as if she were a whole woman. In the back of his mind he knew that there wasn't another man in the world she could give that response to, and it humbled him. Her contorted features and those pulsing little sobs took him over the precipice so that he could fall with her, into that exquisite hot void that beckoned so seductively. He heard himself cry out huskily with ecstasy before he finally collapsed in an exhausted, beloved weight over her.

"Why did you do that?" he asked roughly, when he was able to speak. "Why did you knock me off balance like that?"

"You know why," she said softly, brushing back a strand of loose dark hair from his broad forehead. "You needed me."

He lifted his head and looked down at them. "It was supposed to be a punishment!"

She lifted both eyebrows and smiled a little wickedly. "Was it really? I didn't notice. Do it again," she whispered boldly, "and I'll try to look chastised."

She always could knock him off balance when no one else could touch him. But this was too solemn for humor. He was still bristling with what he'd learned and her part in it. Besides that, he hated having her know how helpless he was with her. He'd come to tell her he didn't want such a woman in his life, a woman who'd lie to him. It had been pure fantasy to think he could get within five feet of her after weeks of abstinence and talk rationally. He ached for her even now, when he was satiated.

His pride gnawed at him. He pulled away from her without meeting her eyes and got to his feet. He didn't even look at her while he rearranged his clothing with vague shame and a lot of guilt.

She got up from the floor gracefully, glad that the

cleaning woman had done such a good job, and rearranged and dusted off her own clothing. It had been an exciting little interlude, and if he'd known that she suspected that she was pregnant—which she did—she supposed it would have been the last straw for him. He'd had quite enough shocks already.

"I can't believe I did that," he said almost to himself. He turned on her, furious. "I can't believe you *let* me do that! On the damned rug! Have you no pride, no shame?"

She leaned back against her desk with a weary but satisfied sigh. "I guess not. We both know I'd crawl to you over broken glass to do anything you liked," she said simply. "Why should you be shocked at what just happened?"

He glared at her. "You wouldn't move in with me because I wouldn't marry you. But now that I know I'm half white, you think I might be in the market for a white wife. So you seduce me on your office floor to show me what I could have if I gave you a ring. Is that how you see it?"

She shook her head. The mention of a ring hurt. She remembered what Holden had said about Audrey wearing a copy of Tate's. She remembered the tabloid photo of Audrey with Tate as well. It wasn't too hard to guess that he was probably going to marry the horrid woman out of sheer spite. There wasn't anything she could do about that. Although, she mused sadly, he certainly didn't act like a man who was getting what he needed in anybody's bedroom. "You're in no condition to think at all," she said. "Matt said you'd feel betrayed and hate us all for a while. I understand. It's all right."

"I wish the three of you would stop trying to guess what the hell I will or won't do." He glared at her. "My mother hung up on me. She hung up on him, too. I don't guess you've spoken to her?"

"Yes, I have," she said. "She's very worried and miserable. I asked her to come and stay with me before the media decides to break the story. I'm meeting her at the airport tomorrow."

"I don't want to see either of them," he said shortly. "I don't want to see you again, either."

"Okay." She nodded. She raised her eyebrows. "What comes next, the hair shirt or the leather flail?"

He wasn't going to give an inch. He was still furious with her, and it showed.

"Why didn't you tell me, Cecily?"

"It wasn't my secret to tell," she replied solemnly. "I'm sorry you had to learn it like this. But it could have been much worse. You could have learned it on the evening news. That was the plan, if your father hadn't given in to the syndicate's demands. That's why I went to Wapiti. That's why Colby was there."

He stared at her. "You're sorry. And you think an apology will make everything all right?"

Her eyes were quiet, and very sad. "I don't," she said wearily, searching his face. "We don't always get the things we want most in life. You know that it wasn't really for a racial reason that you didn't want to marry me,'' she added unexpectedly. ''It was because you want to be self-sufficient. You don't want to have to depend on people, because people have let you down so many times. The work you did for the government made you cynical, distanced you from normal ordinary folk. Now you feel that your own mother has betrayed you with your worst enemy. And, of course, there's me. I've let you down, too.''

He didn't speak. He just glared at her.

''I will love you,'' she said softly, ''for the rest of my life. But I can't live alone, work alone, die alone. I'm not going to grieve for you until my hair turns gray. You like being alone. I don't. I want a home of my own and children to raise. You can't give me those things. It took me a long time to realize why you went around with Audrey, but I think I understand now. It was because she didn't make any inroads into your privacy. She could marry you and she'd never want closeness except maybe in bed. That's not much of a relationship, but then, you don't want a real one. You have nothing to give. You only take.''

The words went through him with the force of a hammer. He turned away. His hand resting on the doorknob, he turned and glared back at her. ''I won't be able to forget that you betrayed me,'' he said. ''I won't be able to forgive it, either.''

''I know that, Tate,'' she said with deliberate calmness. Inside, she was screaming. ''You don't forgive people. It was inevitable that you'd find something eventually that you couldn't forgive me for. It's as good an excuse as any to cut me out of your life before you find yourself addicted to me."

"Don't flatter yourself," he said with a faint mocking smile. "You weren't my first woman. You won't be my last," he added with pure venom.

"And I know that, too," she agreed, holding on to the remnants of her smile as she absorbed the emotional blow that she was already expecting. But her face didn't show her grief.

It irritated him that he couldn't hurt her. He knew he was acting out of character. He couldn't help it. He'd lost everything he valued. She'd betrayed him. She'd lied to him. Nothing had hurt as much, not even his mother's silence for thirty-six years.

His black eyes searched over her one last time before they met hers. "Goodbye, Cecily," he said curtly.

She kept smiling. "Goodbye, Tate."

He closed the door behind him. The artificial smile went away, leaving her drained of energy and emotion. She sat down wearily behind her desk and caught her breath. The skirt was so tight that she couldn't fasten the button, so she let the zipper down under her overblouse and breathed in fresh air. She put a hand on her slightly swollen belly and smiled tenderly. It didn't take much imagination to understand why her waistline had increased. Here was another secret that Tate didn't know. But this was her own precious secret. She wouldn't share it. Even if he never forgave her, she had a tiny part of him that would last her all her life. She had his child.

"It's okay," she thought to the tiny creature under her heart. "I want you and I'll love you. We'll be fine...just the two of us."

Chapter Ten

Cecily bought two new skirts and some sweaters that were oversize to wear with them. She couldn't afford to let Leta find out what she suspected about the cause of her widening waistline. This was one secret she didn't dare share.

Leta was subdued when she arrived. "My son hates me," she said sadly when they were in the kitchen fixing a light supper in Cecily's apartment. It was Tuesday, and Cecily was going in late the next morning to work. "He was furious when he called me on the phone."

"He hates all of us," Cecily reminded her with a warm smile. "He'll get over it."

"I've done nothing right in my life," came the grim reply.

"There are erasers on pencils because people aren't perfect," Cecily commented.

"Yes, well, you haven't messed up your family the way I have."

Cecily could have argued that point. She sliced onion and tomato and radishes into the lettuce in the salad she was making and prayed that the queasiness she'd felt lately wouldn't reappear at an inopportune time. People who called it "morning sickness" must be normal, she mused, because hers came more often at night and in the evenings. She was tired a lot, too. She'd bought one of those home-pregnancy tests and was trying to work up enough nerve to use it. She wanted a child so badly...

"Cecily!" Leta exclaimed suddenly, gaping at her. "Cecily, you've cut your beautiful long hair off!"

She'd wondered when Leta would notice. She'd had her long locks snipped the day after Tate walked out of her life. It was like a new beginning. She felt the pixie haircut with a rueful smile. Actually the beautician had said that it suited her, and it did. It gave her oval face a new maturity and the makeup she'd learned to use had highlighted the attractive features in her face. She'd made one last concession: a new kind of contact lenses that she could actually wear without getting eye infections. She was so different that Leta had to have been really devastated and withdrawn not to have noticed it before now.

"I've made some minor improvements," Cecily said with a grin. She took the fettuccine Alfredo out of the oven, along with some apple pastries she'd made. "By the way, I didn't mention that we're having another dinner guest. You don't mind?"

Leta shook her head. "I like Colby."

That was a nice assumption, and it was going to save Cecily's life for the time being. She glanced at Leta in her pretty autumn-leaf patterned skirt with the cream sweater over it. Her hair was done in a complicated topknot. She did look her age, but she had traces of beauty in her high-cheekboned face and her dark eyes were full of life, even when she was sad.

"Do I look okay?" Leta asked worriedly.

"You look lovely."

The doorbell rang. Cecily turned back to the stove deliberately. "Could you let him in?" she asked innocently. "I can't leave the Alfredo."

"Sure."

Leta walked to the door and opened it with a ready smile for Colby Lane. And found herself looking straight into the eyes of a man she hadn't seen face-to-face in thirty-six years.

Matt Holden matched her face against his memories of a young, slight, beautiful woman whose eyes loved him every time they looked at him. His heart spun like a cartwheel in his chest.

"Cecily said it was Colby," Leta said unsteadily.

"Strange. She phoned me and asked if I was free this evening." His broad shoulders shrugged and he smiled faintly. "I'm free every evening."

"That doesn't sound like the life of a playboy widower," Leta said caustically.

"My wife was a vampire," he said. "She sucked me dry of life and hope. Her drinking wore me down. Her death was a relief for both of us. Do I get to come in?" he added, glancing down the hall. "I'm going to collect dust if I stand out here much longer, and I'm hungry. A sack of McDonald's hamburgers and fries doesn't do a lot for me."

"I hear it's a presidential favorite," Cecily mused, joining them. "Come in, Senator Holden."

"It was Matt before," he pointed out. "Or are you trying to butter me up for a bigger donation to the museum?"

She shrugged. "Pick a reason."

He looked at Leta, who was uncomfortable. "Well, at least you can't hang up on me here. You'll be glad to know that our son isn't speaking to me. He isn't speaking to you, either, or so he said," he added. "I suppose he won't talk to you?" he added to Cecily.

"He said goodbye very finally, after telling me that I was an idiot to think he'd change his mind and want to marry me just because he turned out to have mixed blood," she said, not relating the shocking intimacy that had prefaced his remarks.

"I'll punch him for that," Matt said darkly.

"Ex-special forces," Leta spoke up with a faint attempt at humor, nodding toward Matt. "He was in uniform when we went on our first date."

"You wore a white cotton dress with a tiered skirt," he recalled, "and let your hair down. Hair..."

He turned back to Cecily and grimaced. "Good God, what did you do that for?"

"Tate likes long hair, that's what I did it for," she said, venom in her whole look. "I can't wait for him to see it, even if I have to settle for sending him a photo!"

"I hope you never get mad at me," Matt said.

"Fat chance. You two come on into the dining room. I've got supper on the table."

Matt was a little awkward. So was Leta. But after a few minutes, the food and the nice bottle of wine Cecily had bought to go with supper had loosened them up a little bit.

"You aren't drinking?" Matt asked.

"Irritable stomach," she said, which was the truth. "I can't handle acids these days, whether they're in wine or citrus fruits."

"Tough," he said. He looked at Leta with soft, dark eyes. "Remember the oranges that Red Elk used to sell at the trading post? They were always the sweetest ones, especially around the holidays."

"I remember."

He sighed with sadness. "I'm sorry for the wasted years. I'm sorry that I cheated you—and myself.

"I'd just come home from the war with medals and aspirations, and she had a rich daddy," he said with bitter cynicism. "I married her in a small ceremony and started planning my senate campaign. Then I met you again and realized what a fool I'd been. I meant to tell you I was married, but I put it off too late. Like now."

"It's history," Leta said with genuine sorrow. "We can't go back and change things."

"Will you believe me if I tell you I wish I could?" he asked gently.

She smiled a little more warmly. "Yes, but it does no good."

He picked up her hand and saw the ring that he'd given her so long ago, still on her finger.

"I never take it off," she said self-consciously.

He lifted it to his chiseled mouth and kissed it softly. "You gave mine to Tate."

"Yes. His hands are the same size yours are. He doesn't know about the ring," she added. "Any more than he knew about you. I'm sorry. I was doing what I thought was best."

He let go of her hand. "I realize that. Funny, there was always a sort of pleasure in having Tate around, even when he irritated the hell out of me. We argued, but I always knew where I stood with him. And the one time he really needed help, he came to me," he recalled. "He and Pierce Hutton and Brianne, the girl Hutton married, came to me with an Arab refugee who was able to blow the horn on a wicked little insurrection that could have dragged this country into a war. I called a friend at the television station and pulled their irons out of the fire." He smiled a little with memory. "Imagine that. I'd never thought of it before. There were other avenues he could have taken. But he came to me.''

"He may not like you," Cecily murmured dryly, "but he's always respected you. He thinks you're arrogant and stubborn," she added wickedly.

"We all know who he gets that from, don't we?" he asked, and there was a note of pride in his deep voice.

Nobody argued with him. He stayed a long time, sitting on the sofa with Leta while they discussed people they'd known, places they'd seen together. They behaved as if the past thirty-odd years hadn't even happened. Minutes later, they were holding hands. They talked about Tate, but sadly. Cecily, observing, could only imagine how hard it was for them to have had to tell their son their secret. She touched her abdomen lightly and worried about her own secret. History was likely to repeat itself with her.

"He made her mad," Leta ventured when Matt had tried and failed to get Cecily's attention. "She's in a snit."

"Nice choice of words," he agreed, smiling at Cecily, who came out of her trance with a laugh.

"I'm not mad at him," she said. "Well, I'm not terribly mad. He's had a blow. It will take time for him to get over it."

"More time than we may have left, I'm afraid." He glanced at his Rolex, grimaced and got to his feet. "I've got to give a colleague hell about a stand he's taking on the new budget. Sorry, but he's a hard guy to reach except late at night.''

Cecily shook hands. ''I'm glad you came. We'll have to do it again.''

''You can both come to my place tomorrow night. I can't cook, but I have a chef who's wonderful with chicken. How about it? I'll even send the car for you.''

''Isn't it risky right now?'' Cecily asked worriedly.

''It's all out in the open,'' he told her. ''They can do what the hell they like with the information. I've got people working for Tom Black Knife and his thieving grandson is already behind bars. Tate knows the truth. Leta and I can take the heat. Can't we?'' he asked the older woman with a smile that wrapped her up in cotton.

Years of taking all sorts of punishment were in the lines of her face, but she smiled back with her heart in her eyes. ''I can take anything.''

He nodded, the same pride in his eyes when he looked at her that he felt about his son. ''Yes.''

''We'll come.''

''Bring Colby if he shows up,'' he added.

''I don't know where Colby is,'' she said, frowning, because he'd been away a long time. ''He said he was going to Arizona, but that was just before I left Wapiti. He wouldn't have been there this long, surely.''

''He's probably out of the country,'' came the reply, which was just a little too careless, but Cecily didn't notice. "But if he shows up, he's welcome."

"Thanks." Cecily started clearing the table, a signal that Leta should see their guest out.

Holden opened the door and impulsively pulled Leta out into the deserted hall with him, closing the door behind them.

"Matt..." she protested.

He jerked her into his arms and bent to kiss her with the pent-up hunger he'd felt for years. She felt just as she had all those years ago, she tasted like nectar. His arms enveloped her, his mouth demanded. She stiffened just for a minute and then sighed, and pushed closer, reaching around him to bring him near.

Finally he lifted his head. His heartbeat was as audible as hers. He searched her misty eyes hungrily.

"You gave me a child. You gave me a son." He framed her face in his big, lean hands. "It wasn't an affair, Leta. I loved you!"

"I know that." Tears stung her eyelids. "I loved you, too. But you were married. What could I say? She would have made you pay for Tate."

"And you. And Tate. But I've lost so much, honey, so many years." He brushed away the tears. "Don't cry. It's all right. We lost each other for a little while, but we're through being miserable. Neither of us will be alone now, and nothing will ever hurt you again, as long as there's a breath in my body!"

She couldn't stop. It was funny, she hadn't cried at all until now, bravely pressing back the pain of her son's anger. But Matt was holding her and she wasn't alone anymore. She laid her cheek against his jacket and gave in to the agony of all the lonely years without him, of Tate's hostility.

He dabbed at her eyes with a handkerchief. His own eyes were suspiciously bright. "You gave him my father's name. Rene."

She smiled wetly. "Yes. I remember meeting him just once. I thought Tate should have his name."

"He moved back to Morocco after I got into the Senate. My mother was dead by then. He said he couldn't stay in the house with Mavis when we moved to Maryland," he said ruefully. "He hated her. He never really forgave me for letting you get away."

"Regrets," she said, "do no good."

"I know. But you have to cauterize a wound before it will heal." He smiled down at her. "I'll expect you tomorrow night."

"Did you ever love her?" she had to know.

"I grew fond of her, and I pitied her. She wasn't lovable. Love was never the reason I married her. I made a huge mistake, Leta, and we've both suffered for it. Now our son is suffering, too. But I wouldn't have known about him if this situation hadn't arisen, would I?"

She drew in a steadying breath. "I wanted to tell you. I was afraid. It had been too long. I thought you might hate me."

He shook his head. "I could never hate you. I have

a pale idea of what you went through with your husband," he returned. "Did you ever love him?"

"I couldn't," she confessed. "He wasn't lovable, either. He knew I was pregnant, although not who the father was, and he said he loved me enough to accept the child and me. He thought his love was strong enough to make up for Tate, but it wasn't. And when he learned that he couldn't father a child of his own, it made him cruel. He hated both of us in the end. Tate had a hard childhood."

Matt's face had hardened. "I'm sorry for that. But it's made him the man he is," he said. "We're all products of our hard times. Fire tempers steel."

"So they say." She traced the lines of his face with her fingertips, relearning him by touch. "I thought of you while I lay alone in the darkness, with only Tate to console me when I felt lost and afraid."

"I thought of you," he said. His eyes were blazing with feeling as they searched hers. "I've been alone, too. While she was alive. Since she died."

She nodded. "What a curse, to want only one person."

He drew her into his arms and kissed her again, hungrily. "What a glorious blessing, to want only one person and be wanted back, even after thirty-six long years," he whispered.

Eventually he left. Leta came back into the apartment with a swollen mouth and bright eyes.

"So that's how you knew," Cecily said with pursed lips and twinkling eyes, remembering Leta's knowing look after Cecily and Tate had been alone together in the living room that day at her house.

"Huh?" Leta murmured, dazed.

"Never mind. I'll just finish up in the kitchen. We need an early night."

"Yes," Leta said, her eyes full of dreams. "Tomorrow is going to be lovely."

It was. Leta and Matt went over every inch of the house together while Cecily was given coffee on a silver tray in the living room. She begged off the tour, knowing that the two older people would enjoy having a little time together.

What she didn't know was that the first room they entered happened to be Matt's, and that they barely had the presence of mind to lock the door before they fell across his big, king-size bed in a tangle of arms and legs and mouths.

"In here...did you...with her?" she gasped as his mouth worked its way down her body.

"Never in here," he bit off. "Never with her. Never with...anyone!"

While he was speaking, barely able to get words past his tight throat, he was stripping her. Her body was as soft and pretty and welcoming as it had been all those years ago. Her hands were working, too, moving fabric, tugging at fastenings.

They kissed and touched and then laughed as stiff joints couldn't quite cope with remembered positions. But he loved her as sweetly as he had in her teens, taking his time, coaxing her body into need, then hunger, then uninhibited passion.

He kissed her as he possessed her, hearing her soft gasp as her body yielded to a man's for the first time in years. He lifted his head and looked into her loving eyes and smiled.

"Old people don't make love, did you know?" he whispered as he began to move again, more gently. "I read it in a book."

Her fingers threaded through his thick, cool hair. "Stop reading books."

He had her hair down around her shoulders. He gathered it in one hand and brought it to his mouth as his body moved warmly, sensuously, on hers.

She kissed his throat, letting her tongue slip against it. She felt his heartbeat stop and then accelerate. "I thought I remembered that you liked that," she whispered. "And this…"

He groaned.

"Oh, yes." She arched up to him, feeling his body surge down into hers in a fast, hard rhythm that very quickly lifted her right up off the bed. She gasped at the sensations that she'd forgotten she could feel.

"At…my age…!" she choked, gritting her teeth as the ecstasy swept through her in hot waves. "Matt!"

His name was a long, sweet little sob against his throat, which he barely heard through the mad pounding of his own heart. He'd barely been able to hold back long enough to satisfy her. She had no idea how many years had passed since he'd been with a woman. And being with Leta, whom he loved, whom he'd always loved...

He sobbed against her mouth as convulsion after convulsion racked him. He couldn't breathe. It was like dying, being born, sailing through fire. He choked her name and stiffened, wondering dimly if he was going to live through it.

She laughed. He heard the tinkling chimes of it from a long way away. He opened his eyes. He was lying on his back, his big body completely nude, open to her soft gaze.

"You're as beautiful as you were the night we made our son," she whispered, bending to kiss him tenderly.

His fingers traced her dark eyebrows, her cheeks, her mouth. "I wish we could have another baby," he said heavily.

"So do I. But I'm too old," she said sadly. She lay her cheek against his broad, damp chest and stroked the silver-tipped hair that covered it. "We'll have to hope for grandchildren, if he ever forgives us."

He held her tightly, as if by holding her he could keep her safe. What he felt for her was ferociously protective.

She misunderstood the tightening of his arms. She smiled and sighed. "We can't, again. Cecily will think we've deserted her."

His hand smoothed her long hair. "She probably

knows exactly what we're doing," he said on a chuckle. "She loves you."

"She likes you. Maybe we could adopt her."

"Better if our son marries her."

She grinned. "We can hope." She sat up and stretched, liking the way he watched her still-firm breasts. "The last time I felt like this was thirty-six years ago," she confided.

"The same is true for me," he replied.

She searched his eyes, already facing her departure. She would have to go back to the reservation, home. He could still read her better than she knew. He drew her hand to his mouth. "It's too late, but I want to marry you. This week. As soon as possible."

She was surprised. She didn't know what to say.

"I love you," he said. "I never stopped. Forgive me and say yes."

She considered the enormity of what she would be agreeing to do. Be his hostess. Meet his friends. Go to fund-raising events. Wear fancy clothes. Act sophisticated.

"Your life is so different from mine," she began.

"Don't you start," he murmured. "I've seen what it did to Cecily when Tate used that same argument with her about all the differences. It won't work with me. We love each other too much to worry about trivial things. Say yes. We'll work out all the details later."

"There will be parties, benefits..."

He pulled her down into his arms and kissed her tenderly.

"I don't know much about etiquette," she tried again.

He rolled her over, pinning her gently. One long leg inserted itself between both of hers as he kissed her.

"Oh, what the hell," she murmured, and wrapped her legs around his, groaning as the joints protested.

"Arthritis?" he asked.

"Osteoarthritis."

"Me, too." He shifted, groaning a little himself as he eased down. "We'll work on new positions one day. But it's...too late...now. Leta...!" he gasped.

She didn't have enough breath to answer him. He didn't seem to notice that she hadn't. Bad joints notwithstanding, they managed to do quite a few things that weren't recommended for people their ages. And some that weren't in the book at all.

Cecily knew before they told her that they were going to be married. It was in the way they looked at each other, with fascinated awe. They couldn't seem to bear being out of each others' sight. She envied them with all her heart.

Leta didn't go home with her, and she hadn't expected her to. She was well and truly Matt Holden's greatest treasure now, and she was going to stay locked away in his arms until he could get a ring on her finger. It was touching.

The doorbell rang just as Cecily came out of the shower the following morning. She had on her slip and a thick bathrobe, and she was expecting Leta. It was Colby instead, looking more battered than ever.

"Come in!" she said enthusiastically, dragging him into the apartment. "I've got so much to tell you!"

"I've got something to tell you, too," he said heavily and without smiling. "And I'm afraid you're not going to like it."

She gave him a hard stare as he came in. He looked completely out of sorts.

"Where have you been?" she asked.

"Most recently, over at Matt Holden's house," he said.

"Why?"

"I've been doing some work for him on the QT, trying to help our friend Tom. I managed to get an eyewitness to talk. Tom's going to be okay." He grimaced as he looked at Cecily. "I let myself get persuaded to stay for coffee, or I wouldn't have ended up in the middle."

"Middle of what?"

"The senator and one boiling mad Tate Winthrop."

Chapter Eleven

Cecily pulled her robe tighter around herself and sat down. "Go ahead. Tell me."

"Just a minute." He took out the same sort of device she'd seen used before, activated it, and put it on the table. "Just in case," he said. "You may have eavesdroppers, and I can't be too careful."

"Thanks," she said. "The senator had a man come over and sweep my office at work. It's the only other place I feel safe." She hesitated. "How is Tate?"

He dropped into the chair across from her with an irritated sound. "Well, he isn't the man I used to know."

Her eyes held a soft sadness. "You don't know why, Colby."

"Like to bet?" he asked with a wry grin. "He called Matt Holden everything except a man, and then he started on his mother. He was livid that she'd kept the truth about his real father from him all those years, and that she hung up on him when he called to get the truth out of her. But he was even madder when he found out that she'd moved into Holden's house and was living with him. He called her a name I won't repeat."

"What happened?" Cecily prompted impatiently when he paused.

"Senator Holden knocked him over the sofa. Leta got in the way and broke it up, but Tate left in a red rage, swearing that he'd never speak to either of them again."

It was no less than she'd expected, having known Tate for so many years. But she felt sorry for Leta and Matt. "Do you know where he went?" she asked.

"He didn't say. I wasn't willing to risk asking him, either," he added ruefully. "Tate and I have had our differences lately."

"What a mess."

"It'll blow over," he said. "People get mad, they get over it."

"Tate doesn't."

"Well, he can work on joining the human race, can't he?" He scowled. "What are you doing at home? It's Monday morning."

She picked at a thread on the robe. "Just a little morning sickness. It'll pass eventually and I'll go to work."

"Morning...sickness?"

She met his shocked gaze. "That's right." She

cocked her head. "Go ahead. Ask me who the father is."

He only smiled. "Do I look that stupid to you?"

She pushed back her short hair with a sigh. "He doesn't know, and you're not to tell him. In English, Apache or Lakota," she emphasized, covering all her bases.

He nodded. "What are you going to do?"

"I haven't the slightest idea," she confessed. "I only used the home-pregnancy test this morning, but I was pretty sure before then. I've got to find a place to live where Leta won't see me for a while. I can't risk having her tell Tate." She glanced at him. "Where were you all this time?" she wanted to know.

"Sitting calmly in a wing chair sipping coffee and trying to look invisible." He lifted his eyebrows at her disbelieving expression. "Somebody had to keep his head."

"There's an old saying that, if you can keep your head when everyone around you is losing theirs, you don't have a clue what's going on," she misquoted.

"Could be. But I'm not sporting a bruised face, like some I could name." He leaned forward. "Want to marry me?"

"Thanks, Colby," she said softly. "I really mean it. But it wouldn't be fair to any of us. Especially you."

He folded his arms and leaned back. "The offer doesn't have a time limit. I really do love children."

"So do I," she said dreamily. "Boys and girls. I'll be happy with whatever I get."

"And you're not going to tell Tate."

Her face reflected the turmoil the question caused. "Well, not anytime soon. He isn't speaking to me, actually. He said he'd never forget or forgive that I knew about his father and wouldn't tell him. I'm sure he meant it."

Her expression said more than that calm tone. Colby's face tautened a little as he considered Tate's inflexibility. "A man who can't forgive isn't human."

"Go tell him that, if you can find him. I've talked myself hoarse. He doesn't hear what he doesn't like." She got up. "I'm going to change and make some toast. Want some?"

"I'll make it." He went into the kitchen while she pulled on a loose dress and her mules.

She went into the kitchen after him, feeling oddly numb. He was using the toaster to make toast, and coffee was steaming fragrantly in the coffeemaker.

"I hope that's strong," she murmured. "It's the only thing that settles my stomach."

"I made decaf," he said. "Caffeine isn't good for you."

"Thank you, Mama Lane."

He made a face at her. "Tate and I used to share everything. Let him go off in a snit. I'll share his baby. If he doesn't come back, I'll appropriate it, and you."

"That's one area where all your commando skills

will fail, dear man,'' she said affectionately. ''I like you very much, and you can be baby's godfather. But I'm raising this child myself.''

''Godfather.'' He was savoring the word when the toast popped up.

''Bad choice of words,'' she murmured. ''I wouldn't want to give you any bad ideas. I don't want my child outfitted in a fedora and a machine gun.''

''Commando godfathers are a different breed.''

''Black bags and camo gear aren't much better,'' she informed him.

''Spoilsport. Where's your sense of adventure?''

''Hanging in the shower trying to dry out.'' She poured coffee and they sat down, with the plate of toast he'd buttered between them. ''No idea where he might be?'' she asked in spite of her resolution not to.

''Sorry.''

''Poor Leta.''

''Matt will take care of her.''

''And vice versa.'' She stared over her coffee cup at him. ''You can see how they feel about each other a room away from them. Imagine that, after thirty-six years.''

''Yes.'' He nibbled toast, still looking worried.

''What is it now?''

''I haven't told you what I really came here to say.''

''Well?'' she prompted.

''The story broke this morning. It was on the seven

o'clock news. I suppose by now it's in most of the newspapers, too."

"About Senator Holden?" she asked tautly.

"Yes. And his illegitimate son. That's what set Tate off, unless I miss my guess. You of all people should know how he hates publicity."

She groaned aloud, dropping the toast. "Damn!"

"They'll find you, too, sooner or later. You can move or go to a hotel, but you have to go to work and they'll find you there. We'd better have a few sessions to prepare you for the questions you're going to get." His face was grim. "It isn't going to be pleasant."

"Good thing I didn't go to a doctor yet, I suppose," she added uneasily.

"Good thing, indeed. A baby, if they found out about it, would certainly add a nice touch to the scandal. How would you guess Tate would take finding out about *that* on the morning news?"

She shivered. "Bite your tongue." She put down the last little bit of her toast and took a sip of coffee. "How do you think the senator and Leta are taking it?"

"As you'd expect—badly." His eyes were compassionate as they met hers. "That was the other thing that set Tate off, having to find out on the morning news that his mother had moved in with his real father. He had blood in his eye when he went for Holden."

"Pity Matt didn't help him through a window instead of over a sofa,'' she grumbled. ''He needs an attitude adjustment.''

''You can't blame him, Cecily. His whole world is upside down.''

''So is mine,'' she said miserably. ''So is his parents'. And all because of one little lie, actually one little omission, thirty-six years ago. It's true, isn't it, about our past indiscretions coming back to haunt us? I suppose it's always best to tell the truth in the first place, however painful. Look at how he hurt me by not telling me that he was my benefactor. I guess he forgot about that.''

''Few people can see far enough ahead to anticipate the consequences of what they do,'' he reminded her.

That statement reminded her of something. Tate had never thought about precautions when they were together. Neither had she; but, then, she loved him and she would have loved a baby. He was a fanatic about no mixed bloodlines, and their first time together, he hadn't known his blood was mixed. Curious, that a man who kept saying he didn't want to risk fathering a child was so careless about prevention. Perhaps he thought she was taking something. That, she mused, would have required industrial-strength optimism on his part. He wasn't a stupid man. Had he simply lost his head, or could there be a reason he wasn't admitting for that lack of forethought? It was an intriguing possibility. What if he did want a child with her, subconsciously? Then she remembered the coldness of his eyes as he said goodbye to her, with such finality. He'd said that he wouldn't forgive her. She had to believe he'd meant it.

"Are you listening?" Colby asked. "I have to be on a plane out of here at six o'clock this evening and I won't be back for two or three weeks."

"Oh. Sorry. Away?"

"Yes, and I can't tell you where." He finished his coffee. "Leta asked me to tell you that she and the senator are having a small wedding service at that pretty little Catholic church near the White House at ten next Friday morning. She'd have called you, but she's afraid your phone might be bugged."

"It wouldn't surprise me," she said darkly.

"I'll sweep the room before I leave," he promised. "For now, that—" he indicated the device on the coffee table in the living room "—will do the job. Now, how about another cup of coffee, and I'll be on my way!"

There was one bug. Colby disposed of it and warned her about letting repair people into the apartment unless she confirmed their identities. He couldn't tell her who'd put the listening device there. The media wouldn't be quite that rash, he was fairly certain. That left the gambling syndicate or whichever agency would be responsible for Matt Holden's safety after the story broke. Either way, it disturbed him to know that people could be watching or listening to everything she said. He didn't make heavy weather of it, but he cautioned her not to go anywhere deserted by herself. And she'd also have to be very careful about mentioning her condition to anyone who came to visit.

The story was on the front page of all the morning dailies when she went in to her office later in the morning. It was more sedate in some than in others, but there was no getting around the fact that the senior Republican senator from South Dakota had an illegitimate son.

Pierce Hutton was, apparently, able to take some of the heat off Tate by sending him out of the country on assignment for the first few days after the story broke. Matt Holden, Leta and Cecily weren't so fortunate. Neither was Audrey, but she seemed to be enjoying the publicity, and she exaggerated her relationship with the senator's son with the tabloid press.

And then the media descended on Cecily, and she learned how terrifying it could be to find herself in the public eye. Reporters wanted to know about her connection to Tate and her connection to Matt Holden and Leta. When they learned that Tate had paid her bills, they assumed she'd been his lover. It was the truth, in a sense, but not in the sense they were trying to portray. She found herself on the front page of one of the tabloids, as Tate's former teenage love slave.

Audrey phoned her office in a rage, to condemn her for giving out false information. "You needn't think Tate will appreciate it, either," the woman said scathingly. "I phoned him in Nassau and told him what you'd done. He's furious with you for making him look like some sort of cradle robber! What a pathetic attempt to get his attention!''

''I told them nothing,'' Cecily said through her teeth. ''Which is more than I can say for you, Miss Gannon.''

''I hardly need to stretch the truth, since Tate is marrying me,'' she said in a smooth as silk tone. ''Poor little Cecily. Did you really think you had a chance with him? He feels sorry for you, but he loves me. He'll never give me up now. The fact that he isn't a full-blooded Sioux means that he doesn't have to be concerned about marrying a white woman anymore. He's mostly white himself.''

Cecily could have strangled her. ''You'd like to think so, wouldn't you? But whatever he may be, his mother is a full-blooded Lakota!''

''His mother is an embarrassment,'' Audrey said, ''but since he isn't speaking to her anymore, she doesn't count. You stay away from Tate or I'll make you sorry,'' she added in a husky-toned fury. ''Don't phone him, don't come to see him. And don't expect an invitation to our wedding, either! We're planning a Christmas wedding and that's one story the newspapers got right!''

She hung up the phone before Cecily could get the words past her tight throat. So he'd gone that far. He was actually going to marry the horrible woman. She ground her teeth together and slammed the receiver down so hard that it hurt her hand.

"You're a worse punishment than even he deserves, lady," she bit off as she turned away from the phone. "I wouldn't wish you on my worst enemy!"

The phone rang again and she picked it up, ready to give Audrey a fierce piece of her mind. But it was a journalist wanting to know if the story in the tabloids was true, about Tate and Cecily being lovers when she was still in school.

"It most certainly is not," she said curtly. "But I'll tell you what is. Tate Winthrop is marrying Washington socialite Miss Audrey Gannon at Christmas. You can print that, with my blessing!" And she hung up again.

The story hit the papers with the force of a bomb blast, and Cecily had to fight tears every time she saw Audrey's lovely face on the front page of the paper. The only blessing was that it took the heat off herself. The media, having decided that Audrey was much more photogenic and willing to talk, dumped Cecily like old news. Audrey revealed intimate details of their relationship that made Cecily sick. She refused to read anything else about the forthcoming wedding. Tate had made his choice. He could live with it.

Matt and Leta's wedding took place a week later. Colby had heard and phoned Cecily to offer to come back for the event in case Tate showed up, but she wouldn't let him.

"I'm not afraid of him, Colby," she said curtly. "I doubt very seriously if he'll even show up. You don't have to rush back on my account, although it's sweet of you to offer.''

''You be careful,'' he said coolly. ''I don't like the idea that someone planted a bug in your apartment. I still don't think it was anybody from the media. It worries me.''

''I'm fine,'' she assured him. ''I have dead bolts on the doors and I do know how to call the police if I have any problems.''

He was silent. ''Just watch your step. Promise me.''

''I will.'' She hesitated. ''Colby, do you know something that you aren't telling me?''

There was another pause. ''Let's just say that if you expect trouble, you're better off. And that's all I can say for now. Be careful. Be extra careful.''

''I will. You do the same,'' she added with a chuckle.

''I'm a tough old bird,'' he told her. ''Otherwise, I wouldn't still be alive in the first place,'' he assured her. ''You eat properly and take your prenatal vitamins.''

''Stop mothering me,'' she muttered.

He grinned. ''Somebody has to. See you, kid.''

''Sure.'' She hung up. It was going to be lonely without Colby for company, but she had plenty of work to keep her busy. She wondered where Tate was, and how he was handling the shock waves that had reverberated through his life. Eventually he'd have to accept the truth and get over it. But judging by the condition he'd been in the day he came to her office, he was a long way from acceptance.

She did go to the wedding, in a pretty blue sheath dress a size larger than she usually wore. It was cold, too, so she could wear her leather coat and a neat little hat over her pixie hairdo. The coat, a trench style that was bulky, made a good disguise for her growing waistline. She entered the church trying to turn a blind eye to the cameras and journalists making a human gate outside.

Since she wasn't directly related to anyone involved in the scandal, and especially since Audrey's engagement to Tate had been announced, the media hadn't been quite as persistent as she'd been afraid of at first. But she did get phone calls at her office, and at her apartment. She was polite, but firm. She wasn't telling anybody anything else.

She'd seen on the evening news how fiercely the media had chased the senator, though. He finally gave in and told the story exclusively to one of the more conservative newspapers. After that, it was a little easier for him to go out with Leta in public. Leta used the publicity to focus on the problems back at the Wapiti Ridge reservation. It was a prime example of turning bad publicity to good, and Cecily was proud of the way Leta used the incident to benefit the reservation. So was Matt, judging by the wide grin on his face as he watched her at the microphones.

The church was sparsely occupied, mostly by

friends of Matt's from Congress who'd braved the press to support him. Cecily hesitated just inside the door, and Leta and Matt Holden came forward to greet her. Matt still had a mark on his cheek from the fight with his son, but he almost glowed with happiness in his formal suit, and he was holding Leta's hand as if he thought she might escape. Leta herself wore an oyster-colored suit and a fancy hairdo. She looked elegant. Cecily told her so as they embraced.

"He won't come," Leta said sadly. "We sent him an invitation, but he'll ignore it."

Cecily knew she meant her son. She patted the older woman's shoulder reassuringly. "Well, I came."

Matt studied her, looking so much like his son that Cecily felt her heart jump. "Are you okay?"

"As good as can be expected," she said wryly. "I had hoped that Tate might show up and I could talk to him."

"Fat chance," Matt said gruffly. "I guess you heard what happened?"

She nodded. "Good for you," she replied with a smile.

He grimaced. "I never meant to lose my temper like that." He slid a protective arm around Leta. "I just made things worse."

"They couldn't get worse," Leta murmured. "Look out the door and you'll see what I mean."

"At least we've got police officers keeping them out of here," Matt inserted. He turned toward the altar, saw the priest in place and smiled. "Here goes," he added, smiling gently at Leta. "Come on."

She clung to his hand, pausing to smile at Cecily. "Wish us luck."

"You don't need it," Cecily returned warmly. "I'm glad things worked out for both of you."

"We're not out of the woods, yet," Matt said. "But we'll have to talk about that later. We're going over to the Carlton for lunch with a few senior members of Congress who came to lend support," he added, waving a hand in the general direction of several dignified-looking men in the front pews. "Want to come?"

She shook her head. "Thanks, but I begged off just long enough to come to the ceremony. Dr. Phillips is out of town and I'm expecting a delegation at the museum to talk about future exhibits."

"Don't let them talk you into anything you don't like, and tell Phillips I said so," Matt instructed. "As a major private contributor to the museum, I think I have a little say over the direction it takes."

"Okay."

She sat down in the back pew while they went to the altar and the small, tasteful ceremony began.

She wasn't sure when she realized that she wasn't alone. She'd heard a louder murmur from the crowd outside, but she hadn't connected it with the door opening. She looked over her shoulder and saw Tate standing against the back wall. He was wearing one of those Armani suits that looked so splendid on his lithe build, and he had his trenchcoat over one arm. He was leaning back, glaring at the ceremony. Something was different about him, but Cecily couldn't think what. It wasn't the vivid bruise high up on his cheek where Matt had hit him. But it was something… Then it dawned on her. His hair was cut short, like her own. He glared at her.

Cecily wasn't going to cower in her seat and let him think she was afraid to face him. Mindful of the solemnity of the occasion, she got up and joined Tate by the door.

''So you actually came. Bruises and all,'' she whispered with a faintly mocking smile, eyeing the very prominent green-and-yellow patch on his jaw that Matt Holden had put there.

He looked down at her from turbulent black eyes. He didn't reply for a minute while he studied her, taking in the differences in her appearance, too. His eyes narrowed on her short hair. She thought his eyelids flinched, but it might have been the light.

His eyes went back to the ceremony. He didn't say another word. He didn't really need to. He'd cut his hair. In his culture—the one that part of him still belonged to—cutting the hair was a sign of grief.

She could feel the way it was hurting him to know that the people he loved most in the world had lied to him. She wanted to tell him that the pain would ease day by day, that it was better to know the truth than go through life living a lie. She wanted to tell him that having a foot in two cultures wasn't the end of the world. But he stood there like a painted stone statue, his jaw so tense that the muscles in it were noticeable. He refused to acknowledge her presence at all.

"Congratulations on your engagement, by the way," she said without a trace of bitterness in her tone. "I'm very happy for you."

His eyes met hers evenly. "That isn't what you told the press," he said in a cold undertone. "I'm amazed that you'd go to such lengths to get back at me."

"What lengths?" she asked.

"Planting that story in the tabloids," he returned. "I could hate you for that."

The teenage sex slave story, she guessed. She glared back at him. "And I could hate you, for believing I would do something so underhanded," she returned.

He scowled down at her. The anger he felt was almost tangible. She'd sold him out in every way possible and now she'd embarrassed him publicly, again, first by confessing to the media that she'd been his teenage lover—a load of bull if ever there was one. Then she'd compounded it by adding that he was marrying Audrey at Christmas. He wondered how she could be so vindictive. Audrey was sticking to him like glue and she'd told everyone about the wedding. Not that many people hadn't read it already in the papers. He felt sick all over. He wouldn't have Audrey at any price. Not that he was about to confess that to Cecily now, after she'd sold him out.

He started to speak, but he thought better of it, and turned his angry eyes back toward the couple at the altar.

After a minute, Cecily turned and went back to her seat. She didn't look at him again.

He stood alone in the back of the church, with his resentments making a cocoon around him. He hated the man who was his real father, he hated his mother for lying to him his whole life, he hated Cecily for being a party to it. He didn't know why he was here at all, except that it had seemed the right thing to do, despite his fury.

He glanced at Cecily with narrowed eyes. He'd noticed immediately that she'd cut her hair, just as he'd cut his own. He wondered why. His excuse was grief, but he doubted she had similar feelings. She was spending plenty of time with Colby. Maybe he liked it short. The thought of Cecily with another man, after what they'd shared, hurt. Lately everything did. Something inside him was glad to know the truth of his parentage at last, but it couldn't get through the rage of betrayal. He glanced down at the floor while the murmur of voices buzzed around his ears like bees. He wondered if the pain would ever stop.

Minutes later, when the priest pronounced Leta and Matt Holden man and wife, Cecily was careful not to look toward the back of the church as she drifted down to the front of the altar to congratulate them.

Matt hugged her, too, before he looked over her

shoulder and his eyes began to darken. "Just what I need," he muttered. "That!"

Cecily's eyes followed his disgusted stare and her heart jumped as she saw Audrey clinging to Tate's arm. So that was why he'd been so uncommunicative. He was waiting for Audrey. Cecily felt loss to the soles of her shoes. Now she knew that Audrey had been telling the truth about their relationship. They gave one last look toward Leta and Matt before leaving the church. Tate didn't even look back. Audrey did, with a smug little smile on her lips that Cecily was meant to see.

"At least he came," Leta said, trying to sound cheerful. "It was nice of him, under the circumstances."

Matt looked as if he wanted to say something, but he didn't. He caught Leta's hand in his and ignored the back of the church.

Three weeks passed with incredible slowness. Tate had apparently gone out of the country again and Cecily didn't hear from Colby, either. One Friday afternoon, as she was fielding complaints from a group of indigenous people from Montana, sleet began to pepper the grass outside her office window. She was tired already as her pregnancy advanced. But after lunch this Native American delegation from Montana had gathered in her office, protesting an exhibit that had been given to the museum by the elders of their tribe. They weren't members of the tribal council, and they had militant connections. But Cecily was able to reason with them by promising some much-needed publicity when the exhibit formally opened. This surprised them. Having had dealings with other bureaucrats, they were expecting excuses and dismissal. But Cecily spoke with intimate knowledge of their problems.

One positive thing that had occurred in the past few decades was the renewed pride of the Native American people in their heritage and its legacy of stewardship of the land. The resurgence of pride had resulted in native peoples speaking out in favor of sovereignty, demanding change, demanding accountability from the agencies that had jurisdiction over them. Things were getting better, little by little. More Native Americans were studying law as well, and at least one organization was quite active in the defense of indigenous people who ran afoul of the courts.

Cecily was proud that she understood enough about their problems to speak with authority about the methods which might be used to improve conditions on their reservation. She even made suggestions that delighted them.

One of the older members of the tribe actually grinned at her on the way out of her office.

"You're not half-bad," he murmured.

She grinned back, recognizing this as a compliment. "Thank you."

The sleet kept coming down. It wasn't such an odd thing for November in Washington, but Cecily hadn't listened to the weather reports and now she was sorry. She was wearing slick-soled little stacked-heel shoes and it was going to be the very devil to get to her car in the parking lot.

She wondered if Tate had gotten the message she'd left on his answering machine, about the stories in the paper. She wanted him to know that she hadn't given such a sensational lie to the press, but she also wanted him to know that Audrey had told her about the wedding. She'd only passed along what she'd heard from the woman. It probably wouldn't make any difference, but she wanted to clear her name. She wasn't vicious enough to do something like that to him, knowing how sacred his privacy was to him.

She never saw the dark car that had been sitting in the parking lot for several minutes before she came out the door. She didn't know that its driver had been studying her movements all week.

When she started toward her car, the vehicle with its engine idling suddenly shot into gear and sped toward her, its chains holding it in the ruts made by other departing cars.

Cecily, her mind on the pleasant end to the meeting in her office, was watching her feet. She heard the car, but only when the noise became disturbing did she look up, just in time to see it heading straight for her, with its headlights blinding her.

She threw up an arm and gasped, leaping to one side just in the nick of time to avoid being hit head-on. Her feet, predictably, went right out from under her on the slick ice coating the pavement. She cried out as she fell over the concrete bar of an empty parking spot and went careening down the small rise that bordered the parking lot and right into the path of an oncoming car. The last thing she remembered was the horrible squeal of tires on slick pavement.

She came to in the emergency room. Her hands went immediately to her belly and she looked around for a doctor, a nurse, anyone who could reassure her.

A nurse caught her eyes and smiled. "It's all right," she said gently. "The baby's fine."

Cecily let out the breath she'd been holding. Thank God for miracles!

"But you've got some nasty bruises and a sprained wrist," the nurse continued. "The doctor wants you admitted so that we can observe you overnight. You were concussed, you know."

"I've got a dreadful headache," Cecily murmured, shaken.

"He'll give you something for that presently. Slipped on the ice, did you?"

Cecily hesitated. "Sort of." She didn't want to say what had really happened, not until she had a chance to talk to Matt Holden. The car had deliberately tried to hit her. If she hadn't jumped in time, she might have been killed. As it was, falling into the path of traffic had almost cost her her life anyway. She was too upset to discuss it now.

The nurse smiled. "Is there someone we can notify for you? Any family?"

Cecily's eyes closed as the drugs they'd given her began to work. "I have no family," she mumbled drowsily. "None at all."

It was true, although Leta would have been astonished to hear her say it. Leta would have come right over, but Cecily wasn't doing that to her, not on her honeymoon. She and Matt had slipped off to Nassau for a few days, and Cecily wasn't going to be the cause of bringing them back. Besides, she thought, the baby was her family now. She placed her hands over her thickened waist with a dreamy smile, pushing to the back of her mind the reality of what had almost happened.

Two days later, they let her out, after a battery of tests and with a bandage on her wrist to keep it straight while it healed. Fortunately it was her left hand, not her right one, so she would be able to get on with her work.

The reporters hadn't come looking for her in the hospital, thank God. But then, there was a juicy new scandal going on in Washington, and Matt Holden's wicked past had just been relegated to history.

Cecily did wonder where Tate had gone. Probably he'd taken Audrey off to some hideaway. It was something of a statement of intent that he'd brought her to his parents' wedding. Every time she thought about that, for the rest of her life, Cecily was going to see Tate turning away from her. Nothing had ever hurt quite as much.

Not that she'd forgotten what had happened in the parking lot at work. She didn't know what to do. She should probably tell someone, because if the driver had meant to kill her, he'd probably try again. The only people she could think of who had a reason to hurt her were the gambling people whose leader was in jail pending trial. It was a scary thought that someone out there might want her dead.

She dressed into loose sweatpants and a matching blue sweatshirt and made herself a pot of decaf in the kitchen. She fixed herself half a bagel with some nofat cream cheese and nibbled it halfheartedly at the kitchen table while she waited for the scalding coffee to cool. She wasn't really hungry, but she had to eat for the baby's sake.

"Sorry, little guy," she murmured, staring at the unappetizing bagel. She put it down. "It should be vegetables and fruits and fish and high-protein dried beans, huh? I'll go shopping tomorrow…"

The doorbell rang. Surely that would be Colby. He was already overdue back from his trip. She could tell him what had happened, and he'd take care of it. She felt a burst of relief as she opened the door with a smile that went into immediate eclipse. And found Tate there.

He stared at her, taking in her wan complexion, her short hair, her glasses perched back on her nose because she wasn't able to manage the contacts with the bandage on her wrist. He was wearing a black turtleneck with black slacks. He looked very sophisticated. With his hair short, he didn't look very much like a Lakota at all.

"What do you want?" Cecily asked quietly, and without welcome.

His chest expanded and fell. "I need to talk to you."

"We don't have anything to talk about," she said stiffly, remembering his harsh words at their last meeting, at Leta's wedding.

"Like hell we don't. You've been in the hospital," he said sharply. "They took you off in an ambulance two days ago."

How had he known that? "I fell on the ice," she said, quickly averting her eyes. "I'm fine."

He just stared at her, looking disturbed and worried. "You told the staff at the hospital that you had no family to notify."

"I haven't," she said matter-of-factly and glared up at him. "Except maybe Leta. She and Matt are in Nassau on a belated honeymoon, and I wasn't about to have them bothered."

That seemed to bother him. He leaned against the doorjamb, frowning. "No matter what disagreements we have, you'll always be family to me."

She wondered how he'd felt about her phone message. She almost asked, but there wasn't much point.

She lifted her chin. She didn't smile. "I'm very tired," she said. "If that's all you wanted to say…"

He was oddly hesitant. "Well, no, it isn't. Cecily, it would be more comfortable if we talked sitting down. Wouldn't it?"

She didn't want him in her apartment. She was worn and sore and half sick, and the sight of him hurt her. Her eyes told him so.

"Please go away, Tate," she said wearily. "We've already said everything that needs saying. You get on with your life, and let me try to find some peace in mine."

"I can't do that," he said, his voice even more strained. He propelled her gently back into the apartment and closed the door with a snap. His expression wasn't easily read. It ran the gamut from concern to wounded curiosity. "I've had a man watching you since the story broke. You didn't take a fall on the ice, Cecily. A car tried to run you down, and damned near succeeded. You're going to tell me what's going on. Right now!"

Chapter Twelve

Cecily glared at Tate, but she gave in. She led him into the small living room and offered him a seat on the sofa. She curled up in her armchair, full of resentment and hurt and trying not to let it show. If only her heartbeat would slow down. If only she could forget how it felt to be close to him, held by him. But he was only concerned about her for old time's sake.

"Anytime today," he prompted tersely, tossing his overcoat onto the seat beside him.

"I was walking to my car when I looked up and a dark-colored sedan seemed to be aiming itself right at me. I jumped out of the way, slid on the ice, rolled down a small grassy embankment and, apparently, right into the path of an oncoming car. It must have had chains and good brakes, because it barely brushed me. I had a concussion and I sprained my wrist from the way I landed.'' She held it up to show him the bandage. "They kept me for observation, and bandaged my wrist. I'm all right."

She was giving him only the bare bones. She looked paler than ever, drawn, worried. He hated knowing that she could have been killed. "Did you tell the doctor not to release the information on your chart to anyone?" he asked.

She blinked. "Yes." She had, because she was afraid Tate might find out about the accident and start digging. She didn't want him to know about the child.

"Why?" he asked curtly.

She met his eyes, trying not to let the uneasiness she felt show. "Because it's nobody's business but mine," she replied emphatically. His expression was so grim that she added, "I don't have anything fatal, if that's why you look so worried."

He seemed to relax a little. Not much. He leaned forward to study her. The bruise high up on his cheek where Matt had hit him had gone away. "Who has a reason to want to kill you?"

She linked her hands together in her lap. "I can't imagine that I have enemies myself. Maybe somebody was after Colby," she added, voicing one fear she hadn't been able to shake. "He does some freelance work, and people know that he spends a lot of time here," she added matter-of-factly.

"Yes. He spends a lot of time here," he said icily. "So, in other words, maybe they were trying to get at Colby through you."

She nodded. "It's rather far-fetched, though."

"Not so far-fetched. It could even have been someone trying to settle a score with me," he said irritably, running a restless hand through his short hair. He glanced at her. "Then there's Matt Holden."

She nodded. "That's what I thought. A lot of shady people lost a lot of their ill-gotten gains because of him, and several of them are facing jail terms over what happened at Wapiti." She shifted her legs. "They want revenge. They can't get to Matt or Leta. He has around-the-clock protection. It's highly unlikely that they'd target Tom Black Knife again. And only an idiot would go after you," she mused. "I seem to be the one weak link in the chain, and Leta and Matt are fond of me. Maybe they decided to go after someone they could get. At least, that's how it seems to me."

He nodded solemnly. "That's the same conclusion the man who's watching your apartment and I came to."

She shifted again, trying to get more comfortable. "What are the odds of getting me in the witness protection program?" she jibed.

"About as good as my odds of getting the lead in the next Batman movie. You didn't see anything that you could testify to."

She sighed. "Then if you've got someone watching me, can I assume that he can use a gun if he needs to?" she asked uneasily.

"Yes. But you're my responsibility..."

"I am not." Her voice was much calmer than her turbulent eyes. "I've been your responsibility for the past eight years. That's over. I live alone. On any normal day, I can take care of myself. All I need is someone to watch out for me until this blows over and the ringleaders of the plot go to prison."

His expression wasn't reassuring. "Cecily, people escape prison terms all the time through technicalities or well-meaning jurors. There's no guarantee of a conviction. Even if there is, these people have plenty of clout on the outside. They can pay someone to get to you, or have someone on the outside do it for them."

She felt sickness whirl in the pit of her stomach. He was outlining a nightmare. It was worse than he could imagine, too, because he didn't know about the baby she was carrying. She looked at him hungrily, wishing she could tell him. But the news wouldn't be welcome. She didn't dare tell him about the child.

"I'm not leaving you alone, even with a good shadow," he said firmly. "So either you move in with me, or I sleep on the couch here. Your choice."

"Where will Audrey sleep?" she asked coldly.

He looked outraged. "At her own apartment," he said flatly.

She was really in the fire now. She couldn't stay with him; she had morning sickness. Tate wasn't stupid. It wouldn't take him long to connect her continual nausea and fatigue with pregnancy. She couldn't have that.

"I can stay with Matt and Leta when they come home," she lied. Leta would see her pregnancy long before she was told about it. She didn't dare go and stay with Leta, but she wasn't telling him that.

Tate knew she'd be safe with his parents. But it wounded him that she was so determined not to let him protect her. He and Audrey had gone together to the wedding because he didn't want to face it alone. Perhaps he'd done it deliberately to wound Cecily, too, for hiding the truth from him and telling lies to the press. But Audrey had become so possessive and insanely jealous that he hadn't seen the woman since the wedding. He wanted to tell Cecily that, but her expression told him she wasn't going to believe him. He couldn't blame her. He'd traded on his relationship, such as it was, with Audrey for too long already. He'd played hell, and his lack of foresight was coming back to haunt him.

"Or I can stay with Colby when he comes back," she added deliberately. She even smiled. "He'll take care of me."

His black eyes narrowed. "He can barely take care of himself," he said flatly. "He's a lost soul. He can't escape the past or face the future without Maureen. He isn't ready for a relationship with anyone else, even if he thinks he is!"

She didn't rise to the bait. "I can count on Colby. He'll help me if I need it."

He looked frustrated. "But you won't let me help you."

"Colby isn't involved with anyone who'd be jealous of the time he spent looking out for me. That's the difference."

He let out an angry breath and his eyes began to glitter. "You have to beat the subject to death, I guess."

She managed to look indifferent. "You have your own life to live, Tate. I'm not part of it anymore. You've made that quite clear."

His teeth clenched. "Is it really that easy for you to throw the past away?" he asked.

"That's what you want," she reminded him. There was a perverse pleasure in watching his eyes narrow. "You said you'd never forget or forgive me," she added evenly. "I took you at your word. I'll always have fond memories of you and Leta. But I'm a grown woman. I have a career, a future. I've dragged you down financially for years, without knowing it. Now that I do..."

"For God's sake!" he burst out, rising to pace with his hands clenched in his pockets. "I could have sent you to Harvard if you'd wanted to go there, and never felt the cost!"

"You're missing the point," she said, feeling nausea rise in her throat and praying it wouldn't overflow. "I could have worked my way through school, paid for my own apartment and expenses. I wouldn't have minded. But you made me beholden to you in a way I can never repay."

He stopped pacing and glared at her. "Have I asked for repayment?"

She smiled in spite of herself. "You look just like Matt when you glower that way."

The glare got worse.

She held up a hand. "I know. You don't want to talk about that. Sorry."

"Everyone else wants to talk about it," he said irritably. "I've done nothing but dodge reporters ever since the story broke. What a hell of a way to do it, on national television!"

"Matt didn't have much choice," she stated. "If he'd tried to keep it under wraps, the media frenzy would have been even worse. He's a powerful member of the Senate. He had to think about damage control or kiss his career goodbye."

Tate knew that, but it didn't make him feel much better. "They need to go back to news four times a day instead of around-the-clock," he said. "They've got too much time to fill and not enough real stories to fill it with."

"Don't tell me," she said. "Tell them."

He studied her thin, wan face. "Are you sick?" he asked suddenly.

"No. Why?"

He moved closer. "Your face is like rice-paper."

"I had a bad fall. It shook me up, but I'm fine," she assured him.

He wasn't buying it. There was something different

about her. It wasn't just the fall, or the scare she'd had. He couldn't quite decide what it was.

"You're staring," she pointed out with growing uneasiness.

"Something's changed," he replied slowly. "There's a difference in you."

She forced herself not to react to his suspicions. "I've grown up. I have a responsible job and constant disagreements with various groups of people over exhibits," she said. "Plus the very real competition of another Native American museum that has more contributors, more exhibits and more space than we do. We're almost redundant."

"You're unique," he disagreed. "It may be a small museum, but it has a real feel for native issues. It isn't as full of bureaucrats as some of the others."

"Thank you," she said, surprised.

He shrugged. He stopped just in front of her, his eyes narrowed in thought. "You're hiding something, Cecily," he said, and her heart jumped because there was conviction in it. There had always been a bond between them, but he felt it more now than ever before. And it wasn't just because they'd been intimate. There was something…more.

She folded her hands on her pants and tried to look nonchalant. "I can't hide anything from you," she said. "You'd see right through a lie."

"I didn't see through you when you kept the truth about my father from me."

She grimaced. That would always be a sore spot

with him, she knew, and there was nothing she could say that would make a good defense. "You seem to forget that you did your own bit of lying, Tate," she replied, lifting her eyes to his. "You were keeping me from the time I was seventeen, and I had to find it out from Audrey."

His lips made a thin line. "I kept it from you for your own good."

She held out a hand, palm up. "Exactly. What good would it have done you to know that Matt was your father until you had to be told?"

He didn't speak. His hand jiggled the loose change in his pocket.

"He agonized over how to tell you, you know," she said, her voice a little softer. "If he could have, he'd have kept the knowledge from you for the rest of your life. So would Leta."

"Why?" he demanded.

"Because you were so proud of being a full-blooded Lakota," she said evenly. "Nothing mattered more to you. They knew how badly it was going to hurt you, and Leta was afraid that you might hate her when you knew the truth."

"Jack Winthrop hated me," he said coldly.

"Yes. Because he couldn't have children of his own. You were a constant reminder of it. He loved Leta and she loved someone else. You were a reminder of that, too."

He looked away. "One lie. And it still makes ripples."

She nodded. "Even good lies do damage," she said introspectively.

He stared at the wall for a minute before he turned back to her. "All right," he said decisively. "If you're determined to stay here, I'll put two men nearby and have you watched around-the-clock." He held up a hand when she started to protest. "Colby hasn't contacted any of us, so I assume he's still undercover somewhere out of the country. This is the only workable solution. I'm not going to let you get killed over this."

"Thanks," she murmured.

"But I'd like a straight answer to one question."

She pondered that. "If I can," she said finally.

He moved closer. "Why don't you want me here?"

That was a complicated question and she didn't dare give him a truthful answer. She searched his lean, beloved face. "You don't belong to me," she said finally, choosing her reply carefully. "You're engaged to another woman."

He frowned. That wasn't the answer he'd expected.

He was going to tell her the truth about Audrey when the doorbell rang. He turned, his hand smoothly going under his jacket to the .45 holstered there. He motioned Cecily back into her chair and moved toward the door.

She realized at once that he expected trouble and that he was used to handling deadly situations. It was the first time she'd actually seen him do it, despite their long history. It gave her a new, adult perspective on his lifestyle. No wonder he couldn't settle down and become a family man. She'd been crazy to expect it, even in her fantasies. He was used to danger and he enjoyed the challenges it presented. It would be like housing a tiger in an apartment. She sighed as she saw the last tattered dream of a future with him going up in smoke.

Tate looked through the tiny peephole and took his hand away from the pistol. He glanced at Cecily with an expression she couldn't define before he abruptly opened the door.

Colby Lane walked in, eyebrows raised, new scars on his face and bone weariness making new lines in it.

"Colby!" Cecily exclaimed with exaggerated delight. "Welcome home!"

Tate's face contracted as if he'd been hit.

Colby noticed that, and smiled at Cecily. "Am I interrupting something?" he asked, looking from one tense face to the other.

"No," Tate said coolly as he reholstered his pistol. "We were discussing security options, but if you're going to be around, they won't be necessary."

"What?"

"I'm fairly certain that the gambling syndicate tried to kill her," Tate said somberly, nodding toward Cecily. "A car almost ran her down in her own parking lot. She ended up in the hospital. And decided not to tell anyone about it," he added with a vicious glare in her direction.

"Way to go, Cecily," Colby said glumly. "You could have ended up floating in the Potomac. I told you before I left to be careful. Didn't you listen?"

She shot him a glare. "I'm not an idiot. I can call 911," she said, insulted.

Colby was still staring at Tate. "You've cut your hair."

"I got tired of braids," came the short reply. "I have to get back to work. If you need me, I'll be around." He paused at the doorway. "Keep an eye on her," Tate told Colby. "She takes risks."

"I don't need a big strong man to look out for me. I can keep myself out of trouble, thank you very much," she informed Tate.

He gave her a long, pained last look and closed the door behind him.

As he walked down the staircase from her apartment, he couldn't shake off the way she looked and acted. Something was definitely wrong with her, and he was going to find out what.

Cecily had made more coffee and Colby brought the tray into the living room before he sat down across from Cecily, scowling. He put the electronic jammer in place with a wry smile. "He still doesn't know, I gather?" he asked at once.

She shook her head, lifting her mug from the tray and adding cream and sugar to it. "He won't ever know if I have my way." She leaned her head back against the seat. "Maybe I should just find a job somewhere away from here, in a small town."

"I don't think you should leave." He shifted on the sofa as if it hurt him to move.

"What happened to you?" she asked.

"Bullets hurt," he said. "It missed the artificial arm by two inches, damn the marksman. I hate people who can't shoot straight."

"How many this time?" she asked with a smile.

"Just one," he said. "In the shoulder. It's much better now." He shook his head. "I'm getting too old for this. I've got so many broken bones that I can't move fast enough anymore."

She smiled wider. "Someday you'll find a woman who's worth giving up the danger for." The smile faded. "You're like Tate. He loves his work. He probably lives on adrenaline. Funny. I never understood that before. Now suddenly everything is clear. I was living on pipe dreams."

He sighed. "It was more than his heritage that kept him away from you," he said. "I knew, but I couldn't explain it to you. Work like ours demands sacrifice. Any loved one can become a hostage. Any relationship can take away the edge we need when we're under fire. A man with something to lose isn't a man to send on a potential suicide mission. Take your mind off the objective for one minute, and you're dead."

"I understand that now," she said.

He let his gaze drop to her waistline, "What are you going to do?"

"Go away," she said with determination. "You're going to have to help me. I don't want Leta or Matt to find out about the baby, either. I have to have a new job in a remote location, so far from a city that reporters would have to hunt me with pack animals."

He grimaced. "That isn't the best place for a pregnant woman alone."

"Neither is here," she said earnestly. "At least if I'm inaccessible, I stand a better chance of not getting killed!"

"Oh, boy." He put his face in his hands. "Cecily, this is a no-win situation."

"Don't I know it?" she muttered. "All those lectures Tate used to give me in my teens about prevention, and look at me!"

He grinned in spite of the gravity of the situation. "It suits you," he said. "You have a radiance about you."

"It's just morning sickness," she assured him dryly, "and a touch of heartburn."

"You look healthy enough."

"I'm living on decaf, strawberry milkshakes and crushed ice, actually. Come on, Colby. You have to help me find a place to hibernate until this blows over."

"The best place would be with Tate," he said.

Her heart jumped. "We don't have a future together."

He let out the breath he'd been keeping back. "I do understand how you feel, believe me. But running is the worst thing you can do. I saw one of Tate's men by the entrance when I came up. You're watched constantly now. I won't be responsible for helping you move someplace where you're at risk. For one thing, Tate would kill me if anything happened to you."

"He might maim you a little…"

"I'm not joking," Colby said quietly. "You don't understand how he is about you. He isn't normal when you're threatened, in any way."

He studied her for a long moment. "Cecily, how do you think it would affect him if he knew you were carrying his child?"

Her heart almost jumped out of her chest. She put a hand over her slightly swollen waistline and sighed. "I don't know. He…loves little things," she said after a minute, smiling as she recalled Tate with a succession of her pets over the years. "He likes children, too. We always had a Christmas party at the school on the Wapiti reservation every year, and Tate would help pass out presents. The kids were crazy about him."

"He loves children," Colby agreed. "He'd want his own child."

She lowered her eyes to the carpet with a sigh. "Maybe. Or maybe it would just make him feel trapped all over again." She put her head in her hands. "It's all such a mess," she murmured. "I don't know what to do."

"In which case, you should do nothing," Colby said firmly.

She didn't quite meet his eyes as she smiled. "Good advice."

Which didn't mean she was willing to take it, she thought an hour later as she packed a suitcase. She couldn't tell Colby her plans for fear he might tell Tate. She couldn't tell Matt or Leta for the same reason. Her only logical solution was to get on a bus or a train or an airplane and just...vanish. So that's what she did.

Chapter Thirteen

An airplane would have been a better choice, but Cecily had applied to and been hired by a small community museum in Tennessee. The town in which it was located had no airport. She'd have had to fly into Nashville and hire a car to drive to Cullenville. It was easier to get on the bus line that went through the little town.

She'd put most of her things in storage and had all her utilities disconnected before she left Washington. She had only the clothes she'd need and some of her most important papers and books to carry. It was a little awkward to use her luggage carrier with a sprained wrist, but fellow travelers had been kind to her.

It had been a wrench to leave her job at the museum, and before Leta and Matt came home, too. But it was for the best. Tate had been suspicious about her reason for swearing her doctor to secrecy. He didn't like mysteries, and he had a good track record for solving them. She wasn't about to throw a spanner into the works by letting him find out about the baby. Not now, when he and Audrey were planning a Christmas wedding.

It was nice that he'd been concerned for her safety, but then, that was just an old habit. In the long run, this move was for the best. She could never get over him so long as they were living in the same city. Eventually he'd make up with Leta, if not with Matt, and Cecily would have to hear about him and Audrey secondhand for the rest of her life. Running was better than that, if cowardly.

Colby had been furious at her when she phoned him from the bus station in Washington—without saying where she was—and informed him that she was on her way out of town. He pleaded with her to let him know where she was going, but she wouldn't tell him a thing. She hung up the phone.

The bus trip was long and difficult, because of the nausea that seemed to be her constant companion now. The first thing she'd have to do was to find an obstetrician. The museum had guaranteed her a nice little rental house to live in, with utilities included. It as only two blocks from the museum, which was dedicated to Paleo-Indian artifacts in the Tennessee Valley. It wasn't big, nor was the salary, but it would suit her, and fit right into her area of expertise. She'd been lucky to find a job so quickly.

In the back of her mind, she worried that she might be placing her child, not to mention herself, in danger. But if she covered her tracks well enough that Colby couldn't find her—and she knew he was going to try—then hopefully the gambling syndicate couldn't find her, either. As for Tate, well, he'd more than likely find her disappearance a relief. He could get on with his life with no further distractions.

Tate Winthrop was having a long, and reluctant, telephone conversation with Audrey, who'd convinced herself that she and Tate were getting married at Christmas.

"We aren't getting married," he said shortly. "I've told you that."

"Cecily put it in the paper," she said huskily. "You must have told her. And about that dreadful episode when she was a teenager, too. Goodness, she must hate you, to embarrass you so badly in public."

Tate was thinking the same thing. It infuriated him that Cecily wouldn't answer her phone or her door to him since the day they'd talked. He found that he missed her enough to affect his job as well as his sleep. He was worried for her safety, despite the man he had watching her apartment now. He shouldn't have argued with her. He should have told her the truth about Audrey. But, of course, Cecily had dug her own grave there, embarrassing him in print with news of a wedding that wasn't going to take place. She denied it, of course.

"I've given Cecily a hard time," Tate said in her defense. "But despite that story in the tabloids, I don't have any plans to get married. You know that. We were friends, Audrey, and we dated. It was never anything more."

There was another pause. "Don't think she'll take you back now," Audrey said in a venomous tone. "I told her you didn't want her. I told her you were never going to marry her, and that she needed to get out of your life and leave you alone."

His caught breath was audible. "You told her what?"

"She knows you hate her," she purred. "She didn't even argue. She's such a fool. So besotted with you that she'll do anything to make you happy, even stand aside to let you marry someone else. When I told her we were getting married, that I even had the wedding gown, she never questioned it. When I told her I was living with you, after you came back from South Dakota, she never questioned that, either."

He was only beginning to realize how much damage Audrey was responsible for. No wonder Cecily was barely civil to him. And he hadn't even explained…!

"If you don't marry me," Audrey continued, her voice slightly slurred, "your reputation will be ruined. I'll give the tabloids a much better story about you and Cecily when she was in her teens. I can find out things about her. I'm rich. I can pay a private detective," she added, threatening.

"If you hurt her, in any way," he said in a deceptively soft tone, "you'll pay for it. You might remember what I did for a living before I worked for Pierce Hutton. If you have one skeleton in your closet, Audrey, you'll read about it in the same tabloids you used to embarrass me."

"You wouldn't!"

"Try me."

He hung up, barely able to contain his fury, and phoned a reporter he knew. It was payback time. Audrey could read about their "cancelled wedding" in all the morning papers, along with the lies about Cecily. It wasn't much in the way of damage control, but perhaps it would help Cecily keep her job at the museum.

He tried calling her again, but there was nothing, only a message that the phone had been disconnected. He slammed the receiver down furiously. She'd unplugged the damned thing.

He ran a hand through his hair and thought about the turmoil of his life since Cecily had dumped crab bisque in his lap. He'd lost his heritage, discovered that he had a father he didn't even know about, seduced Cecily, turned against his own mother, been crucified by Audrey in the tabloids...and on top of that, Cecily didn't want anything to do with him. Tate couldn't find one single reason for her to want him, especially after his smug certainty that she'd be willing to live with him after they'd been intimate. He'd treated her very shabbily over the past two years, especially over the past two months.

He looked around his high-tech apartment with dead eyes. He had his work and somehow he would come to terms with his parentage and make peace with his mother. But he'd done irreparable damage to his relationship with Cecily. It was the fear of love that had kept Cecily out of his life. He hadn't wanted to let her that close, for fear that it wouldn't last. He'd had so little love in his life, except from his mother. He didn't trust it to last, mainly from seeing his mother's misery with Jack Winthrop and remembering his own tormented childhood at the man's hands. If that was love, he wanted no part of it.

But then he remembered Cecily's soft arms pulling him closer in his office, her loving generosity at a time when he'd needed comfort so desperately. He groaned. Cecily had wanted to love him for years, and he kept pushing her away. Even when he'd seduced her, his motives had been selfish. He'd even blamed the tabloid stories on her, when somewhere in the back of his mind he'd known that Audrey was obsessed with keeping Cecily out of his life.

He'd made so damned many mistakes. Now he was faced with a life that didn't contain Cecily or his mother, the only two women in the world that he really loved. His father hated him, too. Well, he couldn't blame his father for punching him, not after what he'd said to Leta. He smiled sadly. The man had a vicious temper. He was pretty good with his fists, too. He remembered what Holden had said about Morocco. Impulsively he turned on his computer and connected to the Internet to do some searching.

While he was surfing the Internet for tidbits of information about Morocco and Berbers, and hating himself for being so interested in his father's native land, the phone started ringing. Thinking it might be Audrey, he ignored it. Morocco was a fascinating country, he had to admit, and he wasn't keen on being interrupted. Fortunately his computer modem was on a separate phone line, or that call would have knocked him right out of the connection.

It didn't quit, even after ten rings. It could be Pierce Hutton, he thought. Maybe he should answer it. Irritably he got up and lifted the receiver. "Yes?" he said impatiently.

There was a pause. "You wouldn't believe how many people I had to bribe to get this new number of yours. But I didn't think past getting you to answer the phone," Colby said reluctantly. "I don't know how to tell you this."

"You and Cecily are getting married," Tate drawled sarcastically, hating the very idea of it and trying not to let it show. "I can't say it's any big surprise. Was there anything else?"

There was another pause. "Cecily won't marry me."

"Tough." Tate wasn't going to admit how much that admission pleased him, even if she wouldn't answer her damned phone when he tried to call her. "So?"

Colby laughed mirthlessly. "I thought this was the right thing to do. Now, I'm not sure if it is."

"I'm not pleading your case for you," Tate replied. His voice was icy. Then he hesitated. His heart skipped a beat as another reason for this call occurred and chilled his blood. "Has something happened to her?" he asked immediately.

"She's not hurt or anything," the other man replied. "It's just that I can't find her. Maybe they can't find her, either," he continued, sounding as if he was talking to himself.

Tate had a terrible sinking feeling in his stomach. He broke the Internet connection on the other line and turned off the computer. "What's up?" he asked, sounding the way he used to, when he and Colby were colleagues in the old days.

"Cecily's done a flit," Colby told him. "She's gone and I can't find her. Believe me, I've used every contact I could find or buy. She didn't leave a trail."

Tate's abrupt intake of breath was electric. "She's gone?"

"Apparently. Her phone's been disconnected and her apartment manager says she's paid the lease for the next two months until she can get her stuff moved."

"For God's sake!" Tate burst out. "We don't know where she is and the gambling syndicate is most likely still after her. Did you tell her that?"

"Yes, I did, Then she talked about getting out of town and I didn't take her seriously. I thought she was just talking. I told her how dangerous it would be for her to go where she wasn't protected, that if the syndicate had threatened her once they might do it again. She didn't listen."

"Oh, God," Tate said in a strangled tone. He thought immediately of all the dangers. Coming on the heels of her near-miss, it was devastating to think of her all alone in some strange town. Why hadn't it occurred to him that her phone might have been disconnected instead of unplugged? "Maybe she went to Nassau to see Leta."

"Nope. I checked the airport—every flight."

He tried to think. "Wapiti," he said.

"No luck there, either. She's quit her job and given up her apartment. She didn't leave a forwarding address."

A string of vicious curses came over the line. "How long has she been gone?"

"That's the thing, I don't know," Colby said through his teeth. "I had a quick job that took me out of town. Hell, Tate, I thought you were having her watched...!"

"I was! I've had a man watching her apartment for over a week."

"Then why didn't your man notice that she was gone?"

"I'll get back to you. Are you at home?"

"Yes."

The line went dead.

Tate wasted no time in dialing the number of the man he'd had watching Cecily. There was no answer. That was disturbing. He tried another number and got another of his former associates.

"Where's Wallace?" he asked without preamble.

"Wait a minute. I'll ask. Anybody heard from Wallace?"

There was a muffled reply. "Damn. You don't say! And nobody bothered to tell us?"

"What is it?" Tate demanded impatiently.

"Sorry. Wallace had a heart attack and died on the spot. I can't believe none of us knew it! Three days ago, apparently...hello?"

Tate was off the phone. He spent the next ten minutes in a cold sweat, calling in markers, talking to old colleagues, doing everything possible to get a handle on where Cecily might have gone. He drew a complete blank.

He phoned Colby back. "I can't find out anything, but I've put together a network. I'll find her."

"The thing is, she doesn't want to be found. That isn't going to make things any easier."

He didn't want to ask, but he had to know. "Why doesn't she want to be found?"

"Because you're marrying Audrey at Christmas," Colby said simply.

"I'm not marrying Audrey," came the short reply. "I never meant to marry Audrey. She outflanked me while I was getting used to the idea of being a media snack.''

"Well, Cecily doesn't know that," Colby replied.

"Great," he muttered. "That's just great. I leave the country and come home to find myself engaged to a woman I wouldn't have, at any price!"

"That's not the only reason Cecily left," Colby said tersely. "She knew you wouldn't forgive her for not telling you about Matt Holden."

Tate ran a hand through his hair, missing the former length of it. "I've had a rough few weeks."

"So has she," the other man said curtly.

"She could have told me about my mother and Holden!"

"Cecily gives her word and keeps it. There aren't a lot of people on the planet who could make that claim. She promised the senator she wouldn't tell you anything."

The senator. His father. Tate paced with the phone to his ear, his mind busy with possible places she might have gone to. "She might have told my mother where she was going."

"I'd bet good money that she didn't," Colby returned immediately. "She doesn't want you to find her."

Tate stopped pacing. He scowled. "She doesn't want *me* to find her?"

"Actually, she doesn't want any of us to find her. Especially you."

Tate's eyes narrowed thoughtfully. "Any particular reason for that? Other than what I already know?"

"Oh, boy." Colby made a rough sound in his throat. "I still don't think I should tell you. But if something should happen to her…"

"Damn you, tell me!"

Colby took a breath and went for broke. "All right. Cecily's pregnant. That's why she ran."

"You son of a bitch!"

The phone slammed down so hard that Colby shuddered at the noise. He put the receiver down with a grimace. He shouldn't have blown Cecily's cover. But what else could he do? She was pregnant and alone and an attempt had been made on her life. If Tate wasn't told, and Cecily was hurt or lost the baby, he might never get over it. That went double for Tate.

Tate was throwing things. He couldn't remember ever feeling so betrayed. First by his mother, and then by Cecily, and now by Colby. Cecily was pregnant and she'd run away. Why hadn't Colby gone with her, for God's sake, to make sure she was all right?

He stopped heaving furniture around and stood getting his breath, scowling as he thought back to his passionate encounter with Cecily back in South Dakota. He hadn't used anything. And what about that incredibly brash interlude on the rug in her office? Again, he hadn't tried to protect her.

The baby could be his. He caught his breath. Of course it could be his. It *was* his! Cecily had loved him. She wouldn't have gone from him to another man, regardless of the provocation.

But Cecily believed he was marrying Audrey, so she was bowing out gracefully. She was going away to have his child, in order not to be an embarrassment to him. Just as his mother had kept the knowledge of her pregnancy from Matt Holden, Cecily was doing the same thing to him, supposedly for the sake of his own happiness. For the first time, he realized how his father must feel. It hit him so hard he felt as if his stomach had been slammed with a brick.

Cecily was carrying his child, and someone had tried to kill her. He felt sick. He sat down, horrified at the things he'd said to her, at the way he'd treated her. She'd covered her tracks and disappeared. What if he couldn't find her? Missing person cases were left unsolved every day. People vanished without a trace for one reason or another, and were never found. What if Cecily became a statistic? She'd have his child and he'd never see it, or her.

The phone rang again and he picked it up at once.

There was a pause. "Is this Tate Winthrop?" an unfamiliar voice replied.

Tate scowled. "Yes."

"I work for an acquaintance of yours. It's about Miss Peterson."

"Cecily?" Tate asked, surprised.

"Yes," the man said matter-of-factly. "I know who tried to run over your ex-ward, Winthrop. I tried to stop it, but my car was sitting out of the way at the museum parking lot. There wasn't time to act."

"I see." Tate was getting an excess of factual information, and it was making him sick. "Who tried to kill Cecily?"

"A Mr. Gabrini," came the taut reply. "He works for a faction of gamblers based in a nearby state. He's out on bond and facing a stiff prison sentence for fraud, racketeering and money laundering. He wants revenge for Senator Holden's part in his arrest. Miss Peterson is an easy target, and a friend of Senator Holden's. I should also tell you that Mr. Gabrini hired a private detective to bug Miss Peterson's apartment. I didn't know that until today, when I finally ran the detective to the ground."

He let out a breath. "Where's Gabrini?"

"I don't know," the curt voice replied. "But if I were you, I'd make damned sure Miss Peterson was watched around-the-clock. Gabrini's got nothing to lose."

"Who are you?"

There was a chuckle. "You don't remember me, do you? I'm Micah Steele. We had a mutual employer about ten years ago."

Tate searched his memories and found a face to go with them. A battle-scarred blond man the size of a house who spoke four languages and was a gourmet cook. "Yes. I remember you."

"Thought you might. I was working on a related case when Gabrini's name came up, and I started tailing him. Good thing I did. He's bad news."

"He'll be lucky if he lives to go to trial, if I find him first," Tate said, blazing with wrath.

"I'd feel the same way. You might mention it to Miss Peterson, just in case, so that she can keep her eyes open."

"I'd love to," Tate said heavily, adding silently, *if I can find her.*

"I'm at the Justice Department, if you need to talk to me."

"Thanks, Steele."

"You did me a favor once, although I imagine you've long forgotten it. I owed you one. Good-night."

"Good-night."

Tate put the phone down and stood up, feeling like a tiger in a trap. So it hadn't been someone after Colby or Tate. It had been the gambling syndicate out for revenge. His fists clenched at his side. Gabrini was going to pay for that, one way or another. But for the moment, his only concern was Cecily. She was in danger as long as Gabrini was on the loose. Where was she? And how in the world was he going to find her? Even with his contacts, it was going to take time. He thought of the vengeful gambler, who surely had his own contacts. He had to find her first. He wouldn't let himself think about her condition. He'd go mad if he did.

The museum was delightful. Cecily celebrated Christmas with a tiny tree in her rented house and invited her immediate neighbors, an elderly couple, in for pie and coffee on Christmas Eve. It was lonely, but the Martins were kind people and they had a soft spot for an expectant mother whose husband had died on an oil rig.

Cecily felt guilty for the lie, but she had to think of the future. It was a small, rural community, very tight, and she wasn't going to start her child's life with scandal.

Her duties at the museum were mostly custodial, but she had some ideas that would fit within the budget for increasing its holdings and attracting tourists. She'd discussed them with the head curator and he was thrilled with her. He was a widower, several years her senior, with a kind manner and a nice smile. She was optimistic about her chances of making a life for herself here in Cullenville. God knew, she'd had some bad breaks lately. At least, the prospective stalker wouldn't know where she was or how to find her, she hoped. It was a risk to come here, but so far Tate and Colby hadn't managed to track her down. Perhaps the stalker, whoever he was, would give up now. She put a hand on the slight swell of her belly and dreamed of next Christmas, when she'd have a little boy or girl to buy presents for. It would be nice to have someone to love.

It was into the new year before a seething, impatient Tate was finally able to track down a bus driver on extended sick leave who remembered seeing a young woman with a bandaged wrist and a luggage carrier who matched Cecily's description.

The middle-aged man grinned. "Hard to miss that bandage," he recalled. "She was too proud to ask for help, but nobody minded lifting the suitcases for her. She said one of them had a lot of books in it, and that was why it was so heavy. She studied Native Americans, she said.''

Tate's heart jumped with delight. ''Where did she go?''

''Went to Nashville,'' the man recalled. ''I had to show her where to go in the terminal, because she had to change buses. Let me see, where was it she wanted to go? Clarksville? No. Sounded a little like that, though.'' He thought for a minute while Tate waited with barely contained patience. ''Cullenville. That's it. Cullenville. Was going to work in a museum there. Smart girl. Knew all about the first Native Americans who lived in these mountains, too.''

Tate thanked the man, gave him a twenty-dollar bill for his time, and went back to his apartment to make an airplane reservation. Tate had gone to see Audrey to make his situation crystal clear. Surprisingly she'd gone to pieces and admitted to a drug problem that had crippled her ability to reason. She apologized for planting the stories in the tabloids about Tate seducing a teenage Cecily and Audrey's engagement to him and offered to speak to Cecily on his behalf. He put her in touch with a psychologist he knew and helped get her into a treatment center, where, Tate hoped, she was going to stay for some time. He blamed her for contributing to Cecily's flight, but he knew he had to shoulder a large part of the blame. He'd spent a lot of time with Audrey. Now, he had to face the fact that it had only been to keep Cecily from seeing how he really felt.

He'd also been able to put together a profile of Gambini, and it wasn't reassuring. The man had been in trouble with the law since his teens, and he'd managed to slip out of two murder indictments. He had a violent temper and a reputation for revenge, and it was said that he never gave up until he finished what he started. Tate feared for Cecily's safety.

Impatiently Tate started to phone the airport to get a ticket on the next flight to Nashville. It was then he realized that, when he found Cecily, he didn't know what he was going to say to her. It stopped him, but only for a minute. She was still at risk from Gabrini and she didn't know it. He'd have to work out his apology on the way. He made his reservation for the next morning and then sat down in his lonely apartment and recounted his recent sins.

He thought about the baby and his heart jumped. He wondered if it would have his features or hers, if it would be a boy or a girl. His eyes softened, thinking of how Cecily loved children, of how tender and loving she'd be with his child. She'd loved him for so long…

His groan was audible. She probably didn't love him now; he'd seen to that. He got up and paced and wished he knew what to say to her. Then it occurred to him that the man at the very center of this whole damned mess might have some ideas on that theme. After all, he'd coaxed a woman into his arms after a thirty-six-year absence and a lot of resentment. He shouldered into his coat and went out the door.

Chapter Fourteen

Tate rang Senator Holden's home on the way there, to be told that they'd arrived home the night before. Tate didn't ask to speak to his mother or Matt. But he needed advice, and his father seemed like the logical person to give it to him, despite the bad blood between them. He drove himself to Maryland, thinking about Cecily in Tennessee with his baby, and worried sick about how he was ever going to get her back and salvage any of his pride. He was even more worried about Gabrini and his attempt at revenge, chillingly certain that the man would eventually track her.

Matt's housekeeper let him in with a grimace.

"I'm harmless today," Tate assured the woman as she led the way to where Matt Holden was standing just outside the study door.

"Right. You and two odd species of cobra," Matt murmured sarcastically, glaring at his son from a tanned face. "What do you want, a bruise to match the other one?"

Tate held up both hands. "Don't start," he said.

Matt moved out of the way with reluctance and closed the study door behind them. "Your mother's gone shopping," he said.

"Good. I don't want to talk to her just yet."

Matt's eyebrows levered up. "Oh?"

Tate dropped into the wing chair across from the senator's bulky armchair. "I need some advice."

Matt felt his forehead. "I didn't think a single malt whiskey was enough to make me hallucinate," he said to himself.

Tate glowered at him. "You're not one of my favorite people, but you know Cecily a little better than I seem to lately."

"Cecily loves you," Matt said shortly, dropping into his chair.

"That's not the problem," Tate said. He leaned forward, his hands clasped loosely between his splayed knees. "Although I seem to have done everything in my power to make her stop."

The older man didn't speak for a minute or two. "Love doesn't die that easily," he said. "Your mother and I are a case in point. We hadn't seen each other for thirty-six years, but the instant we met again, the years fell away. We were young again, in love again."

"I can't wait thirty-six years," Tate stated. He

stared at his hands, then he drew in a long breath. "Cecily's pregnant."

The other man was quiet for so long that Tate lifted his eyes, only to be met with barely contained rage in the older man's face.

"Is it yours?" Matt asked curtly.

Tate glowered at him. "What kind of woman do you think Cecily is? Of course it's mine!"

Matt chuckled. He leaned back in the easy chair and indulged the need to look at his son, to find all the differences and all the similarities in that younger version of his face. It pleased him to find so many familiar things.

"We look alike," Tate said, reading the intent scrutiny he was getting. "Funny that I never noticed that before."

Matt smiled. "We didn't get along very well."

"Both too stubborn and inflexible," Tate pointed out.

"And arrogant."

Tate chuckled dryly. "Maybe."

"I've told Leta. Maybe I should tell you, too," Matt began. "I'm sorry for what you went through when you were a kid...."

Tate held up a hand. "Neither of us can change what was," he said quietly. "It was almost a relief to know Jack Winthrop wasn't my father. It helped me to understand why he hated me so much. I don't blame you. My mother keeps secrets very well."

"Too well," Matt said gruffly. "I wish she hadn't

kept this one. I've missed so much.'' He added, averting his eyes. It was difficult to say these things, but
they needed to be said. ''If I'd had any idea that you
were my son, I would have swept the floor with your
damned stepfather years ago!''

Tate touched his cheekbone and grinned. ''I take
the point, about not underestimating you because of
your age. God, you hit hard!''

''I had provocation,'' Matt reminded him.

Tate sighed. ''Yes, you did. I was way out of line.
I'm sorry I said those things to my mother. When
she's ready to listen, I'll apologize for every one of
them.''

''She's not angry,'' came the quiet reply. ''She understood what you were going through. So did I.''

He smoothed a place on his slacks. ''I gave Cecily
hell, too.''

''She deserved it least of all,'' Matt pointed out.
''She was involved strictly because she didn't want
to see you hurt. She would have done anything to
spare you.''

''Life hurts,'' Tate said simply. ''There's no way
around the pain of it.''

''So they say.''

''Cecily was in the hospital, did you know?'' he
asked after a minute.

Matt sat forward scowling. *''What?''*

''A car tried to run her over in the parking lot
where she works.''

''Oh, good God!'' Matt exploded. ''Who?''

"A man named Gabrini, apparently, one of the men in the gambling syndicate," he said with barely contained fury.

"Well, is Cecily all right?" Matt persisted.

"She had concussion and a fractured wrist, but she's fine." He looked up briefly. "She told the hospital that she had no family," he added, lowering eyes that would have revealed the pain of that memory. "She and the baby could have died and none of us would even have known."

Matt understood why that was so painful. Cecily had disowned Tate; all of them, maybe.

"Did you go to see her?" the older man asked.

"Inevitably," Tate replied heavily. "For all the good it did me. I didn't know about the baby then." He stared at the carpet. "She gave up her job, vacated her apartment and moved to Tennessee without telling anybody except Colby. It's taken time to track her down. Now that I know where she is, I don't know what to say to her, how to get her back. I don't want to frighten her about Gabrini, but she's in danger. I can't protect her if I'm not there. But given my track record," he added with faint humor, "I don't even know if she'll let me in the door. I thought you might have a suggestion."

Matt was deeply touched that his estranged son would come to him for advice. He wasn't going to let it show, of course. A man had his pride. "I see."

Tate got up and jammed his hands into his pockets, pacing to the window that looked out over the countryside. He pulled the heavy curtain aside and looked out through the elegant white Priscillas that framed the picture window. "I don't know what to do. She left here convinced that I had plans to marry Audrey."

Matt turned in his chair, staring at the long, lean back. "I guess you know by now that Audrey gave the press quite a mouthful of information about Cecily and the so-called Christmas wedding. And she was wearing a ring like the one you have."

Tate glanced at it and turned with a frown. "You noticed this ring in your office that day. Why?"

"Your mother gave it to me the night before I told her I was married," he said heavily. "I gave it back to her. She wears one like it, you know."

So that was the mystery of the ring, Tate thought, staring at it. No wonder it had caught Matt's eye when he'd first seen it on Tate's finger.

"Cecily knows about Audrey's ring," Matt added. "And it's hard to miss that you've been photographed with her in all the best tabloids lately."

Tate's jaw worked. "She engineered most of them. Not all. I was pretty hot at everyone for a while, and she was my ego salve. Now I'm sorry I ever started anything with her. She was tenacious as all hell. Especially now I'm so newsworthy."

"You and the rest of us," Matt agreed with a long sigh. "It's been a hell of a media blitz, hasn't it? But the criminals are all facing tough jail sentences, and Tom Black Knife is back in power, where he belongs.

The Rico statute was used to confiscate the funds they'd drained from the tribal treasury, and it's going to be replaced. But Tom's situation took some sleight of hand, let me tell you! I still don't know where Colby dug up that eyewitness to the old murder who was able to clear him of the charges."

"Don't ask, either," Tate mused. "Colby's resourceful, I'll give him that."

"You used to be good friends."

"We were, until he started hanging around Cecily," came the short reply. "I'm not as angry at him as I was. But it seems that he has to have a woman to prop him up."

"Not necessarily," Matt replied. "Sometimes a good woman can save a bad man. It's an old saying, but fairly true from time to time. Colby was headed straight to hell until Cecily put him on the right track It's gratitude, but I don't think he can see that just yet. He's in between mourning his ex-wife and finding someone to replace her." He leaned back again. "I feel sorry for him. He's basically a one-woman man, but he lost the woman."

Tate paced back to the wing chair and sat down on the edge. "He's not getting Cecily. She's mine, even if she doesn't want to admit it."

Matt stared at him. "Don't you know anything about women in love?"

"Not a lot," the younger man confessed. "I've spent the better part of my life avoiding them."

"Especially Cecily," Matt agreed. "She's been

like a shadow. You didn't miss her until you couldn't see her behind you anymore.''

"She's grown away from me," Tate said. "I don't know how to close the gap. I know she still feels something for me, but she wouldn't stay and fight for me.'' He lifted his gaze to Matt's hard face. "She's carrying my child. I want both of them, regardless of the adjustments I have to make. Cecily's the only woman I've ever truly wanted.''

Matt spread his hands helplessly. "This is one mess I can't help you sort out," he said at last. "If Cecily loves you, she'll give in sooner or later. If it were me, I'd go find her and tell her how I really felt. I imagine she'll listen.''

Tate stared at his shoes. He couldn't find the right words to express what he felt.

"Tate," his father said gently, "you've had a lot to get used to lately. Give it time. Don't rush things. I've found that life sorts itself out, given the opportunity.''

Tate's dark eyes lifted. "Maybe it does.'' He searched the other man's quiet gaze. "It's not as bad as I thought it was, having a foot in two worlds. I'm getting used to it.''

"You still have a unique heritage," Matt pointed out. "Not many men can claim Berber revolutionaries and Lakota warriors as relatives.''

"My middle name," Tate said suddenly. "Who was I named for?''

"My father," Matt said with pride. "He was related to the royal family of Morocco. His wife, my mother," he clarified, "was the granddaughter of a member of the French aristocracy."

"Do you have any photographs of them?" Tate asked.

"Two albums full," the older man said with a grin. "When your mother comes home, we'll drag them out after supper and have a look." He pursed his lips. "You might go and bring Cecily home. Maybe she'd like to see them, too."

Tate hesitated. "I'll have to go to Tennessee."

"I guess you will. Want some coffee?"

"Sure." He liked the fact that his father didn't persist. He liked the quick temper that was over almost as soon as it was provoked. He even liked the way the older man handled himself. He was beginning to feel pride in his father. He didn't realize that the other man was feeling the same thing.

They were drinking coffee and still talking when Leta came home with a shopping bag. She stopped in the doorway of the living room and hesitated there, gnawing her lower lip.

The change in her was phenomenal, Tate thought, rising to greet her. She looked happy, radiant, years younger. Until then he hadn't realized what a difference Matt Holden had made in her life. It became clear at once.

"I came for supper," Tate lied, smiling at her.

Leta put the shopping bag down and glanced at

Matt, who grinned at her. She made an effort at smiling. "It's nice to have you here," she said finally.

Tate took her small hands in his, noting how cold they were. He greeted her in Lakota and bent to kiss her soft cheek. "I am happy when I see you," he said.

She burst into tears and threw her arms around him. "I thought we weren't ever going to speak again!"

He had to fight back the wetness in his own eyes. He hugged her close and kissed her hair tenderly. She'd endured so much for him, when he was small. There was no way he could ever repay that sacrifice. He was deeply sorry that he'd been harsh with her. "I just had to get used to the idea," he said. "But I have. It's all right. Everything's going to be all right now," he assured her. "Everything's fine."

"Except that Cecily's pregnant," Matt Holden offered, grinning at Tate's exasperated glare and Leta's shocked gasp.

"What do you mean, Cecily's pregnant?" Leta burst out. She hit her son's arm with her open hand. She hit him again. "You hooligan, how could you! How *could* you?"

Tate defended himself with both arms. "How do you know it was me?" he teased.

"Who else could it be?" Leta raged. "Do you think my baby would let another man touch her? Would she jump into bed with any other man in the world except you? Are you crazy?"

Tate actually looked sheepish, and there was a new

light in his eyes. Matt, after contemplating the two of them for a minute, sauntered off into the general direction of the kitchen, leaving mother and son alone together for the first time since the tempest had started.

Tate stuck his hands into his pockets and stared down at his pretty little mother. "If you haven't finished hitting me, I think there's a spot or two you missed," he pointed out, touching his arm and grimacing. He smiled. "At least we're speaking again."

"That was your decision," she said gently. "You needed time to adjust to the truth."

He spoke after a minute. "It wasn't easy at first, but it explains a lot about the past. I could never love Jack Winthrop and he couldn't love me. Now I understand why."

She sighed. "You were always a good son. I wanted so many times to tell you about Matt, but I knew what you were going to think of me when you learned the truth," she said, dropping her gaze. "Matt would have loved you."

Tate was lost for words. That seemed to happen to him a lot lately. He took his mother by the shoulders and bent to kiss her forehead. "Don't tell him I said this, because he's arrogant enough as it is. But I would have loved him, too."

Leta hugged him hard. "What's that saying about tangled webs?"

He closed his arms around her with a smile of pure relief. "People get caught in them." He smiled against her hair. "How do you like being a senator's wife?"

"I married Matt Holden. The senator part is taking some getting used to. But now when I talk at rallies or before congressional committees, by golly, they'll listen to me!" she added on a chuckle. "Even if I live here, now, I can do a lot of good for our people back home."

He burst out laughing. "Does my father know you're going to trade on your married name like that?"

"Your father." She repeated the words softly. "You don't mind knowing about him, now?"

He shook his head. "I've always admired him, even when I thought I disliked him." He searched her face quietly. "He barely knew me when all this came up, but he did everything in his power to protect me, just the same. It makes me proud, to have a man like that for my father. So, no, I don't mind. I don't mind at all."

Matt, standing in the doorway, hearing those words from his son, had to turn around and go away until the wetness left his eyes. His son didn't hate him. It was more than he deserved, probably, but there was a new warm place in his heart that was worth all the anguish of the past few weeks.

"I'm glad you're not still angry with me," Leta told her tall son. She reached up and touched his short hair with a grimace. "You and Cecily," she muttered. "Such beautiful hair, all whacked off."

"I was grieving," he said simply.

"So was she," Leta told him. "You haven't treated her in any honorable way. I know I'm one to talk, but I know better than either of you how it is to marry one man and love another and be pregnant with his child." She searched his troubled eyes. "Colby wants to marry her, you know."

Tate's eyes began to glitter. "In his dreams," he said coldly. "The only man she's marrying is me."

"Really?" She was delighted, but puzzled. "Audrey told her about the ring and the wedding dress..."

"I told Audrey and the press that I don't plan to marry her, regardless of rings and wedding dresses. Audrey has problems and it took me a while to figure out why she behaved the way she did." He added quietly, "She's going to spend some time in a drug treatment center drying out. Maybe they can do something for her. I'm sorry for her, but she really complicated things for me."

Leta felt almost weak with relief. "Cecily thought that since you know about your real heritage, marriage to a white woman might not be so distasteful to you," she added. "And Audrey is cultured and quite beautiful."

He actually winced. "Cecily said something like that to me, when I told her that I hadn't seen Audrey lately." He looked, and was very troubled. "She's got it into her head that I wouldn't have wanted her, regardless of my heritage, because she wasn't beautiful enough. That's not true. I've made a real hash of things,"

"Yes," his mother said flatly. "And now Cecily's pregnant and all alone."

"It gets worse. She was almost knocked down by a car while you were out of town on your honeymoon," he said, his voice harsh with emotion.

"*When?* Is she all right?" Leta was frantic.

"She had a mild concussion and a sprained wrist. They kept her overnight for observation. She told them that she had no family living," he added huskily. He drew in a long breath and smiled coolly. "You can't imagine how that hurt."

"Yes, I can," Leta replied. She moved to the sofa and sat down, watching her son drop into the wing chair he'd vacated earlier. "Are the two of you still speaking?"

"She ran away," he said through his teeth. "She thought I was marrying Audrey, so she gave up everything and moved out of town so that she and the baby wouldn't interfere with my life." He glanced at his mother. "Doesn't that sound familiar?"

Leta grimaced and put her face in her hands. "Oh, my poor Cecily!"

"The really tragic part of it is that Audrey was never anything more than window dressing, someone I could use to…"

"To?" his mother prompted, wiping her eyes.

He looked at his clasped hands, at the big silver-and-turquoise ring that had once been Matt's. "Cecily was getting to me,'' he said. ''I had to have a way to keep her at arm's length. She kept her distance when I started going around with Audrey.''

Leta looked worried. ''Poor Cecily,'' she said again.

''I've been free to do what I pleased,'' he said. ''Travel, take dangerous jobs, take risks…I've never had to consider anyone except myself since I left home. I've been independent most of my adult life. I took responsibility for Cecily, but I did it from a distance, mostly. I didn't want to share my life with anyone.''

''You do seem to have gotten your wish,'' Leta told him with disapproval in every line of her face.

''It isn't what I want now,'' he said quietly. ''I don't mind giving up the more dangerous jobs, or my independence. I want my child,'' he said simply. ''I want Cecily. I only wish I could think of a way to make her realize it. I have to have some idea of what I'm going to say to her before I go barreling off to Tennessee after her. There's too much at stake.''

He got up, restless, worried, and went back to the window.

Matt came back into the room, followed by the butler with a huge silver tray that held a silver coffeepot and the accompanying necessities.

''Time out,'' he called, motioning Tate back to his seat. ''Coffee solves most problems, I've found. I've brought a full new pot.'' He sat down on the sofa beside Leta and bent to kiss her with visible affection.

Tate sat down, but reluctantly. He felt lost.

His father looked at him with pleasure, noting their resemblances. He was sorry for Tate's unhappiness, but that was a personal thing that the younger man would have to work through all on his own. He could advise, but he couldn't really help.

"Decided what you're going to do?" he asked Tate softly.

The younger man accepted a cup of black coffee from his mother and slowly shook his head.

"You need a battle plan," Matt advised. "I never left the base without detailed reconnaissance and a battle plan. It's why I came home alive."

Tate chuckled in spite of himself. "She's a woman, not an enemy stronghold."

"That's what you think," Matt said, pointing a spoon in the other man's direction before he lowered it into his cup. "Most women *are* enemy strongholds," he added, with a wicked glance at his smiling wife. "You have to storm the gates properly."

"He knows all about storming gates, apparently," Leta said with faint sarcasm. "Otherwise, we wouldn't be expecting a grandchild..." She gasped and looked at Matt. "A grandchild. Our grandchild," she emphasized with pure joy.

Matt glanced at Tate. "That puts a whole new face on things, son," he said, the word slipping out so naturally that it didn't even seem to surprise Tate, who smiled through his misery.

"You go to Tennessee and tell Cecily she's marrying you," Leta instructed her son.

"Sure," Tate said heavily. "After all the trouble I've given her in the past weeks, I'm sure she can't wait to rush down the aisle with me."

"Honey catches more flies than vinegar," Matt said helpfully.

"If I go down there with any honey, I'll come home wearing bees."

Leta chuckled.

"You aren't going to give up?" Matt asked.

Tate shook his head. "I can't. I have to get to her before Gabrini does, although I'm fairly sure he has no more idea where she really is than I did until today. I just have to find a new approach to get her back home. God knows what." He sipped more coffee and glanced from one of his parents to the other. He felt as if he belonged, for the first time in his life. It made him warm inside to consider how dear these two people suddenly were to him. His father, he thought, was quite a guy. Not that he was going to say so. The man was far too arrogant already.

Chapter Fifteen

But if deciding to go to Tennessee and bring Cecily home was easy, doing it was not. Tate asked for a week off from Pierce Hutton, because he expected to have to work at getting her to come back, and he wasn't leaving her in harm's way alone.

Pierce Hutton gave him a highly amused smile as they went over updated security information from the oil rig in the Caspian Sea.

"So you've finally decided to do something about Cecily," Pierce murmured. "It's about time. I was beginning to get used to that permanent scowl."

Tate glanced at him wryly. "I thought I was doing a great job of keeping her at arm's length. She's pregnant, now, of course," he volunteered.

The older man chuckled helplessly. "So much for keeping her at arm's length. When's the wedding?"

Tate's smile faded. "That's premature. She ran. I

finally tracked her down, but now I have to convince her that I want to get married without having her think it's only because of the baby.''

"I don't envy you the job," Pierce replied, his black eyes twinkling. "I had my own rocky road to marriage, if you recall.''

"How's the baby these days?" he asked.

Pierce laughed with wholehearted delight. "We watch him instead of television. I never expected fatherhood to make such changes in me, in my life.'' He shook his head, with a faraway look claiming his eyes. "Sometimes I'm afraid it's all a dream and I'll wake up alone.'' He shifted, embarrassed. "You can have the time off. But who's going to handle your job while you're gone?"

"I thought I'd get you to put Colby Lane on the payroll.'' He held up his hand when Pierce looked thunderous. "He's stopped drinking," he told him. "Cecily got him into therapy. He's not the man he was.''

"You're sure of that?" Pierce wanted to know.

Tate smiled. "I'm sure.''

"Okay. But if he ever throws a punch at me again, he'll be smiling on the inside of his mouth!''

Tate chuckled. "Fair enough. I'll give him a call before I leave town.''

Colby was quietly shocked to find Tate not only at his door the next morning, but smiling. He was expecting an armed assault following their recent telephone conversation. "I'm here with a job offer."

Colby's dark eyes narrowed. "Does it come with a cyanide capsule?" he asked warily.

Tate clapped the other man on the shoulder. "I'm sorry about the way I've treated you. I haven't been thinking straight. I'm obliged to you for telling me the truth about Cecily."

"You know the baby's yours, I gather?"

Tate nodded. "I'm on my way to Tennessee to bring her home," he replied.

Colby's eyes twinkled. "Does she know this?"

"Not yet. I'm saving it for a surprise."

"I imagine you're the one who's going to get the surprise," Colby informed him. "She's changed a lot in the past few weeks."

"I noticed." Tate leaned against the wall near the door. "I've got a job for you."

"You want me to go to Tennessee?" Colby murmured dryly.

"In your dreams, Lane," Tate returned. "No, not that. I want you to head up my security force for Pierce Hutton while I'm away."

Colby looked around the room. "Maybe I'm hallucinating."

"You and my father," Tate muttered, shaking his head. "Listen, I've changed."

"Into what?"

"Pay attention. It's a good job. You'll have regular hours. You can learn to sleep without a gun under your pillow. You won't lose any more arms." He added thoughtfully, "I've been a bad friend. I was jealous of you."

"But why?" Colby wanted to know. "Cecily is special. I look out for her, period. There's never been a day since I met her when she wasn't in love with you, or a time when I didn't know it."

Tate felt warmth spread through his body at the remark. "I've given her hell. She may not feel that way, now."

"You can't kill love," Colby said heavily. "I know. I've tried."

Tate felt sorry for the man. He didn't know how to put it into words.

Colby shrugged. "Anyway, I've learned to live with my ghosts, thanks to that psychologist Cecily pushed me into seeing." He scowled. "She keeps snakes, can you imagine? I used to see mine crawling out of whiskey bottles, but hers are real."

"Maybe she's allergic to fur," Tate pointed out.

Colby chuckled. "Who knows. When do I start?" he added.

"Today." He produced a mobile phone and dialed a number. "I'm sending Colby Lane over. He's my relief while I'm away. If you have any problems, report them to him."

He nodded as the person on the other end of the line replied in the affirmative. He closed up the phone. "Okay, here's what you need to do…"

* * *

Two hours later, he was on a plane for Nashville. The flight had been delayed due to snow and sleet, and he was impatient. He was irritated beyond belief by the time the flight disembarked at the Nashville airport. He went straight to the rental car desk and got a four-wheel-drive vehicle. Then he set out, in the snow, for Cullenville.

The museum was easy to find—it was right downtown, past one of the town's two stoplights. There he asked for directions to Cecily's house and was told that she had a rental house two doors down. The museum secretary looked at him with pure awe.

"Are you a relative of her late husband?" the woman asked.

His eyes widened. "I beg your pardon?"

"It must be so hard for her, pregnant and just widowed," the middle-aged woman continued. "We've all done what we could to make her happy here. Mr. Johnson, the curator, is a widower himself. He's already sweet on her. But you're probably anxious to see Mrs. Peterson. Shall I ring her and let her know you're coming?"

Tate's eyes were blazing. "No," he said with forced politeness. "I want to surprise her!"

He stalked out, leaving the rented vehicle where it was as he trudged through the small layer of snow and glared contemptuously at the cars sliding around in the street as they passed. This little bit of snow was nothing compared to the six-foot snowdrifts on the reservation. Southerners, he considered, must not get much winter precipitation if this little bit of white dust paralyzed traffic!

As for Cecily's mythical dead husband, he considered, going up the walkway to the small brick structure where she lived, he was about to make a startling, resurrected appearance!

He knocked on the door and waited.

There was an irritated murmur beyond the closed door and the sound of a lock being unfastened. The door opened and a wan Cecily looked straight into his eyes.

He managed to get inside the screen door and catch her before she passed out.

She came to on the sofa with Tate sitting beside her, smoothing back her disheveled hair. The nausea climbed into her throat and, fortunately, stayed there. She looked at him with helpless delight, wishing she could hide what the sight of him was doing to her after so many empty, lonely weeks.

He didn't speak. He touched her hair, her forehead, her eyes, her nose, her mouth, with fingers that seemed bent on memorizing her. Then his hands went to the robe carelessly fastened over her cotton nightdress and pushed it aside. He touched her belly, his face radiant as he registered the very visible and tangible signs of her condition.

"When did we make him?" he asked without preamble.

She felt her world dissolve. He knew about the baby. Of course. That was why he was here.

He met her eyes, found hostility and bitter disillusionment in them. His hand pressed down over her belly. "I would have come even if I hadn't known about the baby," he said at once.

"The baby is mine."

"And mine."

"Audrey is not getting her avaricious little hands on my child…!"

His hand held her down firmly. "I am not marrying Audrey," he said through his teeth. "As if I would! She's in a treatment center. She was bombed out of her mind on drugs. She confessed that she'd planted all the stories in the tabloids and blamed you."

"Wh…what?" she stammered, horrified.

Tate let out a long breath. "Cecily, she's unbalanced. She was spewing lies and the media gobbled them down whole. I never had plans to marry her, regardless of what I let you think. I rejected her and she was out for revenge. It was never more than that."

His hand felt odd against her swollen belly. She started to speak at the same moment that the baby suddenly moved.

Tate's hand jerked back as if it had been stung. He stared at her stomach with pure horror as it fluttered again.

She couldn't help it. She burst out laughing.

"Is that…normal?" he wanted to know.

"It's a baby," she said softly. "They move around. He kicks a little. Not much, just yet, but as he grows, he'll get stronger."

"I never realized…" He drew in a long breath and put his hand back against her body. "Cecily, does it hurt you when he…" He hesitated. His black, stunned eyes met hers. "He?"

She nodded.

"They can tell, so soon?"

"Yes," she said simply. "They did an ultrasound."

His fingers became caressing. A son. He was going to have a son. He swallowed. It was a shock. He hadn't thought past her pregnancy, but now he realized that there was going to be a miniature version of himself and Cecily, a child who would embody the traits of all his ancestors. All his ancestors. It made him feel humble.

"How did you find me?" she asked.

He glared into her eyes. "Not with any help from you, let me tell you! It took me forever to track down the driver who brought you to Nashville. He was off on extended sick leave, and it wasn't until this week that anybody remembered he'd worked that route before Christmas."

She averted her eyes. "I didn't want to be found."

"So I noticed. But you have been, and you're damned well coming home," he said furiously. "I'm damned if I'm going to leave you here at the mercy of people who go nuts over an inch of snow!"

She sat up, displacing his hand, noticed that she was too close to him for comfort, swung her legs off the sofa and got up. "I'm not going as far as the mailbox with you!" she told him flatly. "I've made a new life for myself here, and I'm staying!"

"That's what you think." He got up, too, and went toward the bedroom. He found her suitcase minutes later, threw it open on the bed and started filling it.

"I'm not going with you," she told him flatly. "You can pack. You can even take the suitcase and all my clothes. But I'm not leaving. This is my life now. You have no place in it!"

He whirled. He was furious. "You're carrying my child!"

The sight of him was killing her. She loved him, wanted him, needed him, but he was here only out of a sense of duty, maybe even out of guilt. She knew he didn't want ties or commitments; he'd said so often enough. He didn't love her, either, and that was the coldest knowledge of all.

"Colby asked me to marry him for the baby's sake," she said bitterly. "Maybe I should have."

"Over my dead body," he assured her.

She winced. "This is why I didn't want you to know," she said in a wobbly tone. "You're doing exactly what I expected you'd do. I'm a responsibility all over again, a duty, a liability!"

She didn't even cry normally, he was thinking as he watched the tears run silently, in waves, down her pale cheeks.

He stopped packing and moved to stand just in front of her, his face drawn and somber as he searched for the words to tell her why he was really here.

She bit her lower lip in a vain effort to stem the tears. "Please go away," she whispered. "Leave me in peace."

He scowled. "Cecily..."

"Please, Tate," she pleaded gently. "Just go home and forget that you know where I am. I've broken all my ties in Washington, I've put it all behind me. It's just me and the baby now..."

"You and the baby and your mythical dead husband," he shot back. "What do I have to do to get through to you?"

"There's nothing you can do." She searched his hard face. "You have no idea what limitations a baby would place on you, how it would change your life. You're used to being a loner. You don't share your feelings, your fears, your dreams with anyone. You live alone and you like it. Babies cry at all hours, they have to constantly be watched and fussed over. You'd resent the noise, and the constraint, and the lack of privacy." She turned away. "In time, you'd hate us both for being in your way."

He felt sick to the soles of his shoes as he watched her walk back into the living room. "You don't think I want you and the baby?"

She laughed mirthlessly. "Everything you've said and done for the past eight years has shown me that you don't want a close relationship with a woman. Especially, me.''

He stuck his hands into the pockets of his slacks and frowned, searching for the right words. ''You know why I pushed you away, Cecily,'' he said quietly. ''Not only were we, as I thought at the time, from different cultural backgrounds, I'd been in the position of a guardian to you. It would have been like taking advantage of an affection you couldn't help.''

She was staring out the window at the snow with her arms folded. Her back looked abnormally rigid. ''I wasn't beautiful enough for you.''

Nothing had ever hurt him as much as that simple, painfully honest remark. He just looked at her, speechless. To him, she was the most beautiful woman on earth, inside and out, especially in her present condition.

She turned with a sad smile on her face. ''If you're worried about whoever tried to run me down, I've had no problems since I've been here. I don't think there will be any more attempts on my life. You can safely leave me where I am. I'm happy here, Tate. I'll let you know when the baby comes,'' she added quietly. ''Certainly, you'll have access to him any time you like.''

Doors were closing. Walls were going up around her. He clenched his teeth together in impotent fury.

''I want you,'' he said forcefully, which was not at all what he wanted to say.

''I don't want you,'' she replied, lying through her

teeth. She wasn't about to become an obligation again. She even smiled. "Thanks for coming to see about me. I'll phone Leta when she and Matt come home from Nassau."

"They're already home," he said flatly. "I've been to make peace with them."

"Have you?" She smiled gently. "I'm glad. I'm so glad. It broke Leta's heart that you wouldn't speak to her."

"What do you think it's going to do to her when she hears that you won't marry the father of your child?"

She gaped at him. "She...knows?"

"They both know, Cecily," he returned. "They were looking forward to making a fuss over you." He turned toward the door, bristling with hurt pride and rejection. "You can call my mother and tell her yourself that you aren't coming back. Then you can live here alone in the middle of 'blizzard country,' and I wish you well." He turned at the door with his black eyes flashing. "As for me, hell will freeze over before I come near you again!"

He went out and slammed the door. Cecily stared after him with her heart in her throat. Why was he so angry that she'd relieved him of any obligations about the baby? He couldn't want her for herself. If he had, if he'd had any real feeling for her, he'd have married her years ago. It was only the baby.

She let the tears rush down her face again with pure misery as she heard the four-wheel drive roar out of the driveway and accelerate down the road. She hoped he didn't run over anybody. Her hand went to her stomach and she remembered with anguish the look on his face when he'd put his big, strong hand over his child. She'd sent him away for the sake of his own happiness, didn't he know that? She supposed it was just hurt pride that had caused his outburst. But she wished he hadn't come. It would be so much harder to live here now that she could see him in this house, in these rooms, and be haunted by the memory of him all over again. He wouldn't come back. She'd burned her bridges. There was no way to rebuild them.

Tate got as far as the rented vehicle and slammed his hand hard against the roof, scattering the light covering of snow where his hand hit. He'd lost his temper. That was the last thing he should have done, especially with a pregnant woman who already felt rejected and unappealing. He sighed angrily, staring back toward the house. Well, he couldn't upset her any more than he already had, not today. He'd get a room at the local motel, stash his equipment and come back here on foot. He'd lived on instinct for a long time. He had finely honed reflexes and he sometimes played hunches that seemed illogical to his colleagues. But he sensed somehow that Cecily was in danger, that Gabrini was around, close, somewhere. Feeling that way, there was no chance in hell that he was going away until Cecily was safe. Cecily, and his baby.

* * *

He wondered if he could have been wrong for once as he huddled in a strategically placed appliance carton near Cecily's back stoop. Snow was falling again. He was cramped with his long legs shoved into barely half the required space, and it was cold.

He looked around him at the light covering of snow and regretted his first impression of the way the south behaved in a little icy precipitation. He'd been listening to his police scanner with an earphone and what he learned was a little humbling. There had been ten wrecks since he'd been in town, one of them fatal. It occurred to him that people in South Dakota learned to cope with snow because it came and stayed all winter. Here, where there were only a handful of days in the winter when ice or snow fell, people didn't know how to drive in it. He was sad for the families of the two people who had died in wrecks. He thought about how he'd feel if he lost Cecily, and his heart almost stopped in his chest. She'd been part of him for so long that it would be unbearable to contemplate the rest of his life without her.

A sound caught his attention. It wasn't much of a sound. Just a faint crunch, the sound a foot might make in a patch of ice. His hand went to the .45 automatic he carried in a shoulder holster. He tugged it out, gently, and waited for the loud noise of a passing truck to reach its peak before he cocked it and thumbed off the safety. Wearing black, even a full face mask, he was well camouflaged here by the garbage can.

It was a good thing that he was, too. A small man in dark clothing wearing a face mask like his was approaching the darkened house with an object in his hand that could only be a weapon.

He was good, Tate thought angrily. He moved like an animal, in short, uneven steps that wouldn't have alerted a deer deep in the forest, not the rhythmic movement of a human walk. He looked around him carefully and kept to the shadows. It was painfully apparent to Tate, who would know, that the man had stalked human game before with deadly intent.

He didn't bother to try the back door. He went to a low window where the kitchen was and, still watching stealthily, unfastened the screen and jimmied the window latch. On a moonless night, which this was, with only patches of ice to reflect the little bit of light coming from the street in front of the house, the man was practically invisible.

Tate's heart pounded violently. An adrenaline rush tautened every muscle in his body. He wanted to fire now, to prevent there being any small chance that Cecily would be harmed. But he had to have proof. So far the man had done nothing except force open a window. He had to be in the house before Tate could act. And then he'd have to act quickly, or perhaps cost Cecily her life. The thought stiffened his resolve. All his training, all his covert skills, had combined to lead him to this one brief span of time, when he alone could save the mother of his child from certain death. He couldn't afford one single lapse now. He watched, waiting for the moment to strike.

Inside the house, Cecily was lying in bed in her pretty pink flannel gown wide-awake, her eyes still red from crying. Tate had come after her, and just when she'd thought there might be a real chance for them, he'd admitted that he was only here out of a sense of responsibility. He didn't love her. He wanted the child, perhaps, and he felt it was his duty to provide for Cecily. It was the old, old story again. Tate, running interference. He would never love her. He would never let himself love her. He had excuse after excuse, but it all boiled down to the fact that he didn't want to share his life with anyone. That wasn't going to change, and the sooner she realized it...

She froze. There had been a sound, like wood being broken. She sat up in bed, her heart racing. Could Tate have come back? She got out of the bed and padded softly on the cold linoleum floor to the hallway. She listened, but she didn't hear anything. There was a faint slither, like someone moving in the darkness. Her heart pounded like crazy as she thought of the shadowy person who'd tried to run her down in Washington. Someone from the gambling syndicate, out for revenge? But how would he have found her? Tate had found her, she realized. Someone up to his neck in organized crime could have found her, too.

She swallowed. Her hand went to the swell of her belly as she thought of her child and what could happen. She shouldn't have let her pride force her to do this stupid thing. She'd never run away before in her life. She should have stayed where she was, where she could be protected. In normal circumstances, she could take care of herself. But she had no illusions about her ability to save herself from a professional criminal. She could shoot a gun, but she didn't own one. She had a few karate lessons, during which Tate, who had a belt in tae kwon do, had shown her that sometimes even a lifetime of lessons wasn't enough against a gun or a knife. Her eyes closed as she listened, shivering, for more noises. As a last resort, she could scream, or run. But she had no really close neighbors, and how would she outrun a bullet if the man was armed?

Tate was probably on his way back to the nation's capitol right now, she thought miserably. He would have protected her, and her child, but she'd sent him off in a fury. Great going, Cecily, she told herself. What a headline they'll have now! Former Teenage Love Slave Killed By Vengeful Gambling Syndicate. That would give people something to read with their morning coffee!

She drew in a slow, shaky breath, listening. Something rocked, as if her intruder—she knew it was an intruder now—had knocked against the little telephone table where the living room connected to the dining room. There was another faint noise, and then a jerking sound. There goes the telephone cord, she thought, and almost panicked. What could she do?

She didn't have anything in the bedroom that would serve as a weapon. Her furniture was mostly of the antique sort, because she'd rented this old house furnished. If only she had a club of some sort, it might give her a chance.

She was at the wall beside one of the long, low windows that had disturbed her a little when she'd rented the house. Her sharp eyes focused on the homemade window lock in the bedroom. The metal thumb-latch had broken in here, and the house's owner had taken a broomstick and cut it to fit vertically against the top section of the window to keep it from being opened from outside. It was just right to knock a gun out of a man's hand, perhaps, if she could get it quickly and silently and not get herself killed in the process. She was on her own. She had to help herself. Oh, please, God, she prayed silently, give me strength. Help me!

Swallowing the nausea in her throat, she slid to the window soft-footed and reached up to tug at the stick. It came away smoothly into her hand and she let out a faint sigh of relief. The feel of the wood in her hand gave her confidence. It was heavy and thick, and if she used it properly, it might save her life.

She eased back to the door and bit her lower lip hard to keep panic at bay. She heard soft footfalls in the hall now, coming closer. The bedroom door was standing wide open. She was just beside it and her heartbeat was so loud that she feared her attacker would hear it. She closed her eyes, swallowed again and ground her teeth together. She could do this. She could…!

A shadow moved in the hall. It hesitated. Her teeth ground together harder as she waited. Her hands were trembling on the stick. She couldn't let her nerve fail now! Her mouth was so dry that she could barely swallow. Her hands were sweating on the stick. She gripped it tighter.

The shadow began to move again. It came closer. She held the stick just at shoulder level, waiting, waiting…

A hand holding a pistol came suddenly into view and Cecily acted without even thinking. She brought the stick down so hard that the gun went flying. There was a cry of pain in a strange voice, a loud curse, and she found her hand in a merciless grip as the stick was wrenched from it and raised.

A dark streak came flying at her assailant, knocking him free of Cecily and carrying him headlong to the floor. There was a quick, fierce struggle on the linoleum. The smaller man was suddenly dragged to his feet and knocked down again, with such ferocity that Cecily knew her number was up. There were two of them, and the one still standing was coming toward her.

She cried out, all her courage gone as she realized the skill of this new intruder. She had no weapon. He would kill her…!

"Cecily!"

That voice! She shivered with mingled relief and

horror as she found herself pulled into a fierce embrace, locked to a hard, muscular body, safe. *Safe.* Her arms went under his and around him and she burst into tears.

"Tate," she whispered brokenly. "Oh, Tate!"

He kissed her hungrily, his lips cold from the time he'd spent outside. "I was afraid I wouldn't be in time," he ground out. "I'm bigger than he is, and I had to force the window up. It stuck. God, what a close call! You disarmed him!"

"I hit his arm with a stick," she said, choking. She shuddered. "He had a gun."

"Yes."

He let her go and fumbled for the light switch, throwing the room into brilliance. On the floor, the smaller man was huddled with his hands against his chest, groaning.

Tate pulled off his face mask and retrieved the man's gun, a small automatic, before he pulled a flip-phone from his pocket and dialed the emergency services number, adding a request for an ambulance to be dispatched before he hung up.

"Oh, do you think I broke his wrist?" Cecily asked, puzzled, as she wrapped her arms around her chest and stared at the writhing form on the floor.

"You might have," Tate returned in a voice like steel. "But I called the ambulance because I broke several of his ribs."

He didn't sound sorry, either. He went down on one knee and jerked the mask off the intruder, revealing a thin, unremarkable face now contorted with pain.

"Did you think I was stupid enough to lead you here and then take off without a backward glance?" Tate asked the man furiously. "I checked with the airport and the car rental service. Not that many people rent automobiles and ask for directions to Cullenville. Today it was just myself…and you."

"Damn…you," the man choked. "She…ruined everything. Everything! We had…it made!" He choked again and glared at Tate. "We'll…get her… and you!"

Tate caught the man by the hair and Cecily felt her hands go cold at the way he looked at his fallen enemy. "Do you know Marcus Carrera?"

The other man seemed to go still for an instant. Sure he knew Carrera. Everybody did. The man was a don, a legend, in mob circles. He made Gabrini look like a pickpocket. He swallowed. "Yeah. I know who Carrera is."

"He knows where you live."

Already pale, the man's face went white. "Hey, you can't…!"

"I can. I have." Tate let go of his hair. His face was rigid. "If one hair on Cecily's head is damaged, in any way, I don't have to tell you what to expect. You might tell your friends that you aren't the only member of your syndicate that I've investigated."

"You're bluffing."

Tate just stared at him. "A lot of people owe me

favors. Some of them are in prison. You'll never see it coming. Neither will any of your cohorts."

"You're just...a...crazy Native American. You work for wages for a construction company! What can you do to us!" the man said contemptuously.

"Wait and see." Tate got to his feet.

"My name is...Gabrini. I got family everywhere!"

Tate went back to Cecily, checking to make sure she was all right. "So have I," he said, watching her.

She was still too shaken to say much. She let Tate pull her close and hold her until the shaking stopped. Reaction was only now setting in. It was uncomfortable to find out how vulnerable, and fragile, she really was.

The ambulance arrived when the police cars did. They were accompanied by a man in a black suit who had the look of a federal agent. It didn't surprise Cecily that he went right up to Tate and drew him to one side.

While Cecily was being checked over by a paramedic, Gabrini, who'd already been loaded onto a gurney, was being watched by two police officers.

Tate came back to Cecily while the federal agent paused by the police officers.

"You can take him to the hospital to have his ribs strapped," the man told the ambulance attendant. "But we'll have transport for him to New Jersey with two federal marshals."

"Marshals!" Gabrini exclaimed, holding his side, because the outburst had hurt.

"Marshals," the federal agent replied. There was something menacing about the smile that accompanied the words. "It seems that you're wanted in Jersey for much more serious crimes than breaking an entering and assault with a deadly weapon, Mr. Gabrini."

"Not in Jersey," Gabrini began. "No, those other charges, they're in D.C."

"You'll get to D.C. eventually," the federal agent murmured, then the dark man smiled. And Gabrini knew at once that he wasn't connected in any way at all to the government.

Gabrini was suddenly yelling his head off, begging for federal protection, but nobody paid him much attention. He was carried off in the ambulance with the sedan following close behind. Cecily and Tate filled out the police reports over cups of coffee in the kitchen while one of the officers closed the window and secured it with a small curtain rod crossways at the top.

Tate stared at her over his second cup of coffee with quiet, proud eyes. "You kept your head," he said. "I'm proud of the way you handled yourself. Were you afraid?"

She smiled at the rare praise. "Terrified. But I didn't know you were still in town. I thought I'd go down fighting."

"I underestimated that few seconds of head start

he had. I could have dropped him with one shot, but I had to consider that he might have had time to put a bullet in you before he fell.''

"You saved me."

"You helped."

She sipped her decaf. "Mr. Gabrini was afraid of you," she said.

"He should be. I have some ties that he doesn't know about," he added. "He won't come to any harm as long as he leaves you alone."

She smiled. "Thanks."

"The danger's over. But I'd still rather have you back in D.C., where I can keep an eye on you."

She hesitated. He'd saved her tonight. He did care about her, too, in his own way. But if she went back, he'd feel obliged to look after her constantly. She knew how he felt about marriage, because he'd made his attitude perfectly clear. He lived alone and he liked it. She'd had a good look tonight at the world he occupied, a world of violence and dangerous people, a world in which he excelled. He wasn't going to be able to give up his work because she might worry about him. And what sort of life would she and the baby have, on the fringe of his life? He'd love his son, certainly, but someday he might find a woman whom he could love. She'd cheat him by clinging. She'd had her perfect night with him, a night she'd dreamed of most of her life, and she had his child growing in her body. She could live on the past all her life.

"I want to stay here," she said quietly.

He drew in a short breath, still full of adrenaline from the violence and still fuming because she was rejecting him.

He looked into her eyes. "My parents want you to come home so that they can be near their first grand-child."

Her eyebrows lifted. "That's a new angle," she said. "Pulling out all the stops, are you?"

He glared at her. "Don't think I can't live without you, even if you are carrying my son."

She shrugged, not letting her sorrow show. "I've never thought that, Tate," she said with forced cheer. "How could a mere woman compete with covert ops?"

"I don't do that anymore," he muttered.

"You do that every day," she countered. "You did it thirty minutes ago. You're very good," she added with a measure of fascination in the eyes that searched over his lean face. "I never knew how good until I saw you in action. You live for those adrenaline rushes. I've never seen you as happy as you were when you came back from rescuing Pierce Hutton and his wife in the Middle East. It's quite a change from the nuts and bolts of daily routine around D.C. And you think you could give that up to marry me..."

"Marry you!"

She could see the shock in his face and misunder-stood it. "Sorry," she said quickly. "I know you wouldn't do that. I don't want marriage, either," she lied glibly. "But even though we'd be living apart, I don't want to raise my child in a combat zone with prospective assassins at the door every night. I feel safe here, now."

He was reeling from the way she'd discounted marriage. She'd always wanted to marry him, and now that she was pregnant, she didn't? He was staggered by the knowledge.

He smoothed his long fingers over his coffee cup. "I thought marriage was the one thing you did want."

"Your mistake," she said without meeting his eyes. "I'm happy with my life the way it is. I'll love the baby," she added softly. "You can see him whenever you like...Tate?"

He was out the door before she could finish the sentence. He closed the front door with a hard jerk and she heard the lock fall into place. By the time she reached it, she saw Tate at the curb talking with a police officer and gesturing toward the house. The other man nodded. She was going to be watched, apparently.

She went back and cleaned up the kitchen. Well, he had what he wanted now, an excuse not to offer her marriage. She felt empty and alone, but she couldn't trap him into a marriage that he didn't want with a child he'd never intended to give her in the first place. It was going to be a lonely life, but she had the baby. Tate had his job, and his freedom, for the first time in eight years. With Cecily out of the way, and safe, he could take up his life where her place in it had begun.

Sure enough, the next morning a police officer came by with a telephone technician to fix her phone. Mr. Winthrop, the officer related, had gone last night and made arrangements for a private security firm to look after Cecily. It was no surprise that he hadn't called to say goodbye. She hadn't expected him to. She thought of all the long, lonely years ahead and hoped her new job and the baby would compensate for what she'd lost.

Chapter Sixteen

Colby Lane and Pierce Hutton had the manager of Tate's apartment building open his door for them. They knew that Tate had come back from Tennessee, and that he'd saved Cecily from Gabrini, but nobody had seen him for almost a week. His answering machine was left on permanently. He didn't answer knocks at the door. It was such odd behavior that his colleague and his boss became actually concerned.

They were more concerned when they saw him passed out on the couch in a forest of beer cans and discarded pizza boxes. He hadn't shaved or, apparently, bathed since his return.

"Good God," Pierce said gruffly.

"That's a familiar sight," Colby murmured. "He's turned into me."

Pierce glared at him. "Don't be insulting." He

moved to the sofa and shook Tate. "Wake up!" he snapped.

Tate didn't open his eyes. He shifted, groaning. "She won't come back," he mumbled. "Won't come. Hates me…"

He drifted off again. Pierce and Colby exchanged knowing glances. Without a word, they rolled up their sleeves and set to work, first on the apartment, and then on Tate.

Tate was sprawled across the bed in his robe early the next morning when the sound of the front door opening penetrated his mind. There was an unholy commotion out there and his head was still throbbing, despite a bath, several cups of coffee and a handful of aspirin that had been forced on him the day before by two men he'd thought were his friends. He didn't want to sober up. He only wanted to forget that Cecily didn't want him anymore.

He dragged himself off the bed and went into the living room, just in time to hear the door close.

Cecily and her suitcase were standing with mutual rigidity just inside the front door. She was wearing a dress and boots and a coat and hat, red-faced and muttering words Tate had never heard her use before.

He scowled. "How did you get here?" he asked.

"Your boss brought me!" she raged. "He and that turncoat Colby Lane and two bodyguards, one of whom was the female counterpart of Ivan the Terrible! They forcibly dressed me and packed me and flew me up here on Mr. Hutton's Learjet! When I refused to get out of the car, the male bodyguard swept me up and carried me here! I am going to kill people as soon as I get my breath and my wits back, and I am starting with you!''

He leaned against the wall, still bleary-eyed and only half awake. She was beautiful with her body gently swollen and her lips pouting and her green eyes in their big-lensed frames glittering at him.

She registered after a minute that he wasn't himself. ''What's the matter with you?'' she asked abruptly.

He didn't answer. He put a hand to his head.

''You're drunk!'' she exclaimed in shock.

''I have been,'' he replied in a subdued tone. ''For about a week, I think. Pierce and Colby got my landlord to let them in yesterday.'' He smiled dimly. ''I'd made some threats about what I'd do if he ever let anybody else into my apartment, after he let Audrey in the last time. I guess he believed them, because Colby had to flash his company ID to get in.'' He chuckled weakly. ''Nothing intimidates the masses like a CIA badge, even if it isn't current.''

''You've been drunk?'' She moved a little closer into the apartment. ''But, Tate, you don't…you don't drink,'' she said.

''I do now. The mother of my child won't marry me,'' he said simply.

''I said you could have access…''

His black eyes slid over her body like caressing

hands. He'd missed her unbearably. Just the sight of her was calming now. "So you did."

Why did she feel guilty, for God's sake, she wondered. She tried to recapture her former outrage. "I've been kidnapped!"

"Apparently. Don't look at me. Until today, I was too stoned to lift my head." He looked around. "I guess they threw out the beer cans and the pizza boxes," he murmured. "Pity. I think there was a slice of pizza left." He sighed. "I'm hungry. I haven't eaten since yesterday."

"Yesterday!"

After all she'd been through, the thought of Tate starving chased all her irritation right out of her mind. She took off her coat and walked past him to the kitchen and started doing a visual inventory of the refrigerator. She made a face. "The milk is long since out of date, the bread all has mold and I think you could start a bacterial plague with what's in the crisper here...."

"Order a pizza," he suggested. "There's a place down on the corner that still owes me ten pizzas, paid for in advance."

"You can't eat pizza for breakfast!"

"Why can't I? I've been doing it for a week."

"You can cook," she said accusingly.

"When I'm sober," he agreed.

She glowered at him and went back to her chore. "Well, the eggs are still edible, barely, and there's an unopened pound of bacon. I'll make an omelet."

He collapsed into the chair at the kitchen table while she made a fresh pot of coffee and set about breaking eggs.

"You look very domesticated like that," he pointed out with a faint smile. "After we have breakfast, why don't you come to bed with me?"

She gave him a shocked glance. "I'm pregnant," she reminded him.

He nodded and laughed softly. "Yes, I know. It's an incredible turn-on."

Her hand stopped, poised in midair with a spoon in it. "Wh...what?"

"The eggs are burning," he said pleasantly.

She stirred them quickly and turned the bacon, which was frying in another pan. He thought her condition was sexy? She couldn't believe he was serious.

But apparently he was, because he watched her so intently over breakfast that she doubted if he knew what he was eating.

"Mr. Hutton told the curator of the museum in Tennessee that I wasn't coming back, and he paid off the rent on my house there," she said. "I don't even have a home to go to..."

"Yes, you do," he said quietly. "I'm your home. I always have been."

She averted her eyes to her plate and hated the quick tears that her condition prompted. Her fists clenched. "And here we are again," she said huskily.

"Where?" he asked.

She drew in a harsh breath. "You're taking responsibility for me, out of duty."

He leaned back in his chair. The robe came away from his broad, bronzed chest as he stared at her. "Not this time," he replied with a voice so tender that it made ripples right through her heart. "This time, it's out of love, Cecily."

Cecily doubted her own ears. She couldn't have heard Tate saying that he wanted to take care of her because he loved her.

He wasn't teasing. His face was almost grim. "I know," he said. "You don't believe it. But it's true, just the same." He searched her soft, shocked green eyes. "I loved you when you were seventeen, Cecily, but I thought I had nothing to offer you except an affair." He sighed heavily. "It was never completely for the reasons I told you, that I didn't want to get married. It was my mother's marriage. It warped me. It's taken this whole scandal to make me realize that a good marriage is nothing like the one I grew up watching. I had to see my mother and Matt together before I understood what marriage could be."

"Your childhood was terrible," she recalled.

"So was yours," he returned curtly. "I never told you that I beat the hell out of your stepfather after I took you home to my mother, did I?" he added.

She bit her lip. "No. I really don't know what would have become of me if it hadn't been for you. After Mama died, my life was a nightmare."

He toyed with his coffee cup, his eyes black with

angry memories. "That night, while you were asleep,
I unbuttoned your pajama jacket and looked at what
he'd done to you. Afterward, I drove back to his
house and very nearly killed him. If he hadn't started
crying and begging me to stop, I..." He let out the
angry breath. "That was when I realized how I felt
about you," he added, his eyes meeting hers. "A man
wants to protect what he considers his own. It started
then, that night."

She was surprised by what he was telling her.
"You...looked at me?"

He nodded. His eyes narrowed. "You had the most
beautiful little breasts," he said roughly. "And they
were covered with bruises. I wanted to kiss the
bruises, take you into my bed and hold you, just hold
you, all night long so that you'd be safe. I didn't dare
give in to the impulse, of course," he added with the
first touch of amusement he'd shown since her arrival.
"My mother would have horsewhipped me."

She felt waves of surprised pleasure lance through
her body. "I never knew."

"I was always known for my poker face," he murmured. "But it was sheer agony to be around you.
The older you got, the worse it was. It was inevitable
that one day I'd go mad and take you." He sighed.
"The most hellish part of the whole thing was knowing that all I had to do was touch you and you'd let
me do anything I liked to you."

She traced the mouth of her coffee cup. "I loved
you," she said quietly.

"I know."

There was a world of pain in the words. She looked up into his black eyes and saw an answering emotion in them. "You never told me."

"I couldn't. Until very recently, I wasn't sure I could ever think in terms of marriage. And it wasn't to maintain a pure bloodline," he told her finally with a laugh that was pure self-contempt. "Leta didn't tell you, because I made her promise not to. But one of my Lakota great-grandfathers married a young blond white woman at the turn of the century. He was a member of Bigfoot's band."

Her lips parted. "The band that was decimated at Wounded Knee in 1890!"

He nodded. "He moved to Chicago afterward. He hated his culture for a while, and became a detective, trying to hide his Lakota blood by living white. But eventually he regained his pride and made his background public. He married the doctor's daughter who'd nursed him after the massacre and she gave him a son and a daughter. She could speak Lakota like a native and ride and shoot like a warrior. My mother has the name that was given to her after her marriage: Warwoman."

She was enthralled. "So the bloodline wasn't pure."

He shook his head. "It was an excuse, like all the other excuses. I liked my life as it was. I didn't want ties, especially the sort I'd have had with you." He looked at her with pure raging desire. "I knew if we were ever intimate, there'd be no going back. I was right. I eat, breathe, sleep and dream you, especially now, with my baby growing in your belly.''

She searched his eyes like a woman coming out of nightmare into pure fantasy.

He stood up and shed the robe without a trace of inhibition, letting her look at him for the second time in their turbulent relationship. She was so intensely preoccupied that she hardly realized what he was doing until she was standing equally nude before him. He lifted her into his arms and brought his mouth down tenderly on the swell of their child before he carried her into the bedroom.

There was only faint trepidation in her eyes, but he smiled as he eased down beside her on the king-size bed. ''I'll be careful,'' he whispered, bending to her soft mouth. ''There's no rush. We have the rest of our lives to love each other.''

It was love, too. Every brief kiss, every light, caressing touch, was a testament to what he felt for her. In between soft kisses and tender endearments he coaxed her into the most exquisite intimacy she'd ever shared with him, so that each long, slow, sensual motion of his hips was like ballet. She felt him shudder with the effort it took to control the raging arousal that threatened to burst second by second.

''Tate,'' she moaned huskily, pulling at his hips.

''No,'' he bit off against her open mouth. ''I want it like this,'' he breathed. ''I want it slow and sweet, deeper than it's ever been, so tender...that you sob...when I end it.''

She wasn't certain she could survive it. The pleasure came slowly, in great hot throbs of sensation like waves crashing onto a beach. She clung to his arms and shivered from the tension that stretched her body under the exquisite stroke of his own.

His hands were clenched beside her head on the bed, and he made a rough sound in his throat as he met her wide, glazed eyes.

''Feel how deep I am,'' he whispered hoarsely, his jaw clenching as he moved roughly over her. ''Feel how deep, how completely I...fill you...'' His eyes closed on a harsh cry. ''Cecily...oh, God, I love you...!''

She was sobbing, too, feeling as he did the great riptide of pleasure that went right over the banks of the sensual dam and broke in convulsive ripples against their straining, damp bodies.

I'll die, she thought as she cried out in a voice as alien as his sounded, as they shuddered rhythmically together.

When she could finally give up the last sweet echoes of the massive ecstasy that had trembled in her most secret places, she wept. He held her, smoothed her short hair, comforted her with words and soft kisses as he, too, shivered in the aftermath.

''That was...scary,'' she whispered into his damp throat as he held her.

''Absolutely scary,'' he echoed, stunned by the violence of the climax. His hand contracted in her hair. "We didn't hurt our baby, did we?" he asked, and sounded appalled at the thought.

"No. It's almost five months," she whispered drowsily. "And it wasn't rough. It was..." She shivered.

"Profound," he whispered for her.

"Yes."

He wrapped her close in a frenzy of sudden fear. If he lost her...

And that was the real fear, ripped from the camouflage of a dozen halfhearted excuses for keeping her at arm's length. It was the fear of feeling like this and losing her that had kept him from her.

"Tate?" she whispered, surprised by the convulsive sweep of his arms. "I'm all right. Really, I am!"

His breathing began to slow, but the fear of it was still there. He was remembering Gabrini and how close he'd come to losing her in Tennessee that night. It had haunted him ever since, drove him to drink—he, who only rarely even had a beer. He was afraid of nothing on earth except losing this woman. His eyes closed and he held her firmly against him. "I can't lose you, Cecily," he bit off, without looking at her.

"But, you're not going to, ever!" she said, surprised. She pulled back and met his wild eyes. Her fingers touched his face gently. "I love you more than my life," she said unsteadily. "I could never leave you!"

"You ran," he said harshly. "You left me."

"I didn't think you'd ever love me," she choked. "I only wanted you to be happy, don't you see? I was getting out of the way—" Her voice broke as the memory of those agonizing weeks without him came back to haunt her.

His eyes closed on a wave of pain, and he brought her bruisingly close. "It didn't make me happy. My life was empty. Part of me was dead without you. And then to learn that you were carrying my baby, and in danger, and I couldn't find you!" His mouth buried itself in her damp throat. "I love you so much," he ground out. "So much, Cecily!"

She felt the ripple go through his lean, fit body, with fascination. "You came after me, though. You saved me," she whispered, still feeling the wonder of those husky words as she began to believe them. "I love you, too! I couldn't stop. I don't know how."

The breath he drew in sounded shaken. His hand smoothed gently over her soft hair. "I'll be right with you when the baby comes. I won't leave you, not for an instant."

"I'm very healthy and so is our child," she said. "I'd tell you if there were any problems. There aren't. Except…"

He looked at her worriedly. "Except?"

She smiled against his chest. "I'm sleepy."

"Oh." He smiled back. That wasn't a problem. He drew the sheet over them and began to relax. She sighed and he kissed her forehead. "Deep thoughts?" he murmured.

"I was just thinking how glad I was that I waited for you," she said. She kissed the shoulder her cheek was pillowed against.

"I'm glad you did, too," he whispered. "The way we made love was almost sacred, that first time. Was that when we made the baby?"

"Yes," she murmured drowsily. She touched his chest with drowsy content, loving the muscular warmth of it. "I always knew you'd be in a class all your own as a lover. I was right."

He kissed her forehead tenderly. "I'm glad. But if you want it again, you're going to have to marry me," he added on a chuckle, moving one leg lazily against hers under the sheet.

That brought her wide-awake. She lifted herself to look down into his dancing black eyes. *"What?"*

"You heard me," he said. "I'm not going to be seduced and abandoned. You've ruined me. Now you have to marry me."

She burst out laughing. "You don't look ruined to me," she murmured dryly, letting her eyes feast on the long, muscular length of his body from his strong neck down to his powerful legs and in between. "You look absolutely perfect."

"Flattery won't work," he assured her. "I tell you, I'm ruined. You have to marry me to save my reputation."

She hesitated, aware that he was devouring her

with his eyes, from her swollen breasts to the slight swell of her abdomen.

"I want to. But I'm not sure."

"I know that," he replied. "Tell me why you keep holding back."

"You're a loner," she said simply. "The baby and I would impose restraints on you, on the way you live."

He shrugged. "He's already imposed them," he said with a grin. "I told Pierce Hutton he'd have to find someone else to undertake the dangerous missions. I'll remain head of security, but I'm through with commando missions. I hired Colby," he added with a smile at her surprised expression. "It's the sort of work he loves, and he'll have fewer risks than he does in the job he has now. It might save his life."

"I like Colby."

"I like him, too, now that I know he was only a friend."

She lifted her eyebrows. "How do you know?" she asked suspiciously.

He grinned. "Among other reasons, because you were starving a few minutes ago."

"So were you," she pointed out.

He chuckled. "I'm always starving for you." He stretched lazily and pulled her down on his chest, ruffling her short blond hair. The smile faded as he searched her soft eyes. "I wanted you when you were seventeen," he said huskily. "But I was responsible for you. I couldn't take advantage of what you felt for me.''

She traced a pattern on his collarbone. ''Did you know how I felt, all that long ago?''

''Yes.'' He smoothed a lean hand over her bare back. ''I ignored it at first. But that day I brought you out to Oklahoma...'' He laughed mirthlessly. ''You didn't realize that I almost had you right there in the front seat of the car, did you?''

''No.''

He heard the fascination in her tone. ''If we'd been in a less public place, I couldn't have stopped. It was dangerous to tease me, but you didn't know it.''

''What a waste,'' she murmured sadly.

''Not at all. We both needed time to adjust to the changes it would mean in our lives, Cecily. All I had was the illusion of heritage and a job that could have cost me my life any day. I thought it was what I wanted.''

''It wasn't?'' she mused, smiling.

His arm tightened around her. ''I wanted you. I found dozens of reasons not to have you, because I didn't want to be,'' he searched for a word, ''owned.''

''People can't own you,'' she replied. ''But you can belong to people.''

''Same thing,'' he murmured drowsily. ''I learned early that if you let your feelings show, you can be tormented for them. My father...my stepfather,'' he corrected, ''knew that I loved my mother. He punished me by hitting her, until I got old enough and big enough to stop him."

"Matt feels bad about that."

"I know he does. But he didn't know about our relationship. My mother did all of us an injustice by trying to protect us from the truth."

"She was only trying to spare you heartache and embarrassment."

"Of course she was. But you don't do people any favors by lying to them, regardless of the reason."

She smoothed her cheek against his warm, muscular chest. "Where are we going to live?" she asked, changing the subject.

There was a pause, and then he laughed. "I suppose we're going to need a house. The baby will want one of those gaudy, godawful outside swing sets when he's old enough to play, not to mention a collection of equally gaudy plastic toys."

"They're safer than metal or wood ones," she pointed out.

"We'll see what sort of real estate we can find in Maryland, near Matt and my mother." He toyed with a strand of her hair. "They're already shopping for things to give their first grandbaby. They'll be overjoyed to see us together again."

She closed her eyes with a drowsy smile. "All our baby needs is us."

His hand contracted gently in her hair. "You weren't going to tell me."

"I would have, eventually." She sighed.

"I knew that you loved me. It didn't take long for me to come to my senses," he murmured.

"You'll be bored with a desk job," she said worriedly.

"No, I won't," he denied, rolling over so that she was lying half under him. "I'm going to be a family man now, with new responsibilities." He searched her soft eyes and smiled. "I love you, Cecily. And you have to marry me very soon. I really can't take the chance that you might come to your senses one morning and realize how much better you could do for a husband."

Her heart stopped and then ran away. She had to swallow the knot in her throat before she could even speak. "I couldn't possibly marry anyone else. You really love me?" she asked softly. "You never said so before."

He traced the line of her oval face intently with a long forefinger. "Oh, but I think you knew it at some level."

"I suppose I must have," she said softly. "You knew that I hadn't experimented around, so you had to care about me a little to take me to bed in the first place—and to ignore taking precautions," she added dryly. She grimaced. "But there was always something standing between us."

"I know. I wish I could change the past, but I can't. You ran because of me," he said tightly. "Right into trouble. Gabrini would have killed you."

She looped her arms around his neck. "You saved

me. You've been saving me for years, even from yourself."

He smiled. "You helped me save you," he pointed out, kissing her tenderly. "You're handy in a tight corner."

"I had a good teacher." She traced his eyebrows with tender fingers. "I hope our baby will have your eyes," she said. "They're so beautiful."

"He'll be a duke's mixture," he said softly. "I have Berbers in my ancestry, and French royalty."

There was a note of pride in his voice. "Matt told you?"

He nodded. "He'll love having a grandson to talk to."

"Leta will love having a grandson, too," she murmured. "She can teach him all about Lakota traditions and culture."

He kissed her eyelids closed. "I went to them for advice before I went after you. We made our peace." He lifted his head. "Which reminds me," he said sternly, "I never did get an apology for having crab bisque dumped in my lap, *and having it reported on national television!* That's no way to treat your future husband and, I might add, the son of a native sovereignty advocate and a United States senator."

"You're absolutely right," she agreed, tracing a sensuous pattern just below his collarbone with a teasing finger. "Tate, I'm really sorry about the crab bisque."

His heartbeat increased even before she started

smoothing one long, bare leg against the inside of one of his. He lifted an eyebrow and pursed his lips. "How sorry?" he asked huskily.

She grinned wickedly and smoothed her body completely against his, feeling his immediate response to the blatant seduction. "This sorry..." she whispered into his mouth.

Chapter Seventeen

The next day, Tate brought Cecily to Matt and Leta's house. There was ice on the driveway from an early-morning weather system, so Tate lifted her out of the passenger seat like fragile treasure and carried her right up to the front door. He'd wrapped her in the black leather coat he'd given her last Christmas and pulled the hood up over her hair so that she wouldn't get chilled. In the soft beige dress she was wearing with beige boots, she looked elegant and very pregnant.

"Push the bell," he instructed, rubbing his nose with hers.

"No." She smiled at him teasingly. She was wearing her regular glasses instead of her contacts, and through them, her green eyes looked even more mischievous.

His chiseled lips tugged up at the standoff. "Okay.

We'll do this the hard way,'' he murmured, and dropped his mouth down over her lips. "Give in and push the bell," he whispered.

She looped her arms closer around his neck and kissed him back with an enthusiasm that made him groan against her soft mouth.

Seconds later, she was crushed against his tan raincoat, holding his head to hers, lost in the delight of being held by him, kissed by him, loved by him.

Neither of them heard the door open.

"Wouldn't you like to sit down and do that?" came a deep, amused voice from in front of them.

They broke apart with self-conscious laughter. Matt gave his son a speaking glance before he turned his attention to Cecily, surveyed her curiously and then looked back at his son.

"Is there something you'd like to tell your mother and me?" he asked Tate.

"We're getting married," Tate obliged with a grin.

"No!" Matt said at once in mock surprise and then chuckled as he opened the door wide to admit them. "See what I told you about a battle plan, son?" he asked Tate with glee. "Works every time!"

"Some battle plan," Tate murmured dryly. "I went to Tennessee to bring her home, but she wouldn't come back with me. So I went home and got royally drunk, and when I finally came to, Pierce Hutton had had her delivered to my apartment like a late Christmas present."

"That's some kind of a boss," Matt said with a

laugh. "Leta, we've got company!" he raised his voice.

Tate carried his soft burden into the living room. He was just putting her on the sofa when Leta came flying in from the kitchen.

"My baby!" she exclaimed, hugging Cecily the minute Tate set her back on her feet. "My poor baby, are you all right?"

The concern made Cecily feel like a watering pot. She dashed away the tears. "Oh, I'm such a mess," she said brokenly. "And so happy!"

Leta looked at her tall son over Cecily's shoulder and smiled with pure joy. Tate only grinned, supremely happy.

Tate related the story of Gabrini's capture, and his pride in Cecily's fierce defense of herself made her flush. After the explanations were over, Matt and Leta left Cecily briefly alone with Tate at the table eating pie and coffee while they dealt with an unexpected visitor, a colleague of Matt's in the Senate. Tate seemed to find Cecily fascinating as they sat at the big cherry wood table together.

"You're making me self-conscious," she murmured, eating while he sipped coffee and watched her.

"Pregnancy is a mystical experience to a man," he said simply. "I'm hypnotized by it."

She grinned. "I noticed."

He chuckled. "All that talk about not mixing cultural backgrounds,'' he mused, ''and the first time I had you, it never entered my mind to do anything that would prevent a child. Didn't that seem a little irresponsible to you?''

''Yes, it did. But you didn't know I wasn't experienced.''

''Oh, I knew,'' he said quietly, studying her. ''I knew it to the soles of my feet, long before your body proved it to me.''

She blushed, remembering the sensations she'd experienced with him. Her whole body tingled with memories.

He shook his head. ''It was a revelation, that first time. I still get aroused every time I remember it. Then on the floor of your office,'' he said abruptly. ''I still can't believe I did that.'' He frowned. ''You were already pregnant then. I could have hurt you and the baby.''

''You didn't. And, if you remember, I did the seducing,'' she added with a grin. ''Even under the circumstances, it was something to remember.''

He sighed. ''It still makes me vaguely ashamed. I treated you shabbily, Cecily, and not only then. You've put up with a lot from me.''

''It was worth every tear,'' she teased. ''I have no regrets.''

''I wish I could say the same.'' He clasped his hands together behind his head and sat watching her again. ''You're very sexy with that swell under your waistline.''

She gave him a mock scowl. "Pregnancy isn't supposed to be sexy."

"But it is," he remarked. "You're radiant. You glow." He smiled at her. "I'm glad you want the baby, Cecily. I want it, too. I'm sorry I've given you such a hard time." He moved his clasped hands to his knees and stared at the floor. "My world turned upside down. I wasn't prepared for it. Nothing was as I'd believed it was. My whole life seemed to be a lie. It was hard to adjust."

She put her fork down. "I know." She searched his grim face. "None of us wanted to hurt you. We just couldn't think of an easy way to tell you." She met the dark, searching eyes that came up, and the breath seemed to catch in her throat. He had such beautiful eyes. She wondered if the baby's would be dark like his or light, like her own. "Lies are dangerous, even kind lies."

He nodded. His gaze ran over her face and he smiled slowly. "I wonder which one of us the baby will favor?"

"I was just wondering the same thing. Dark eyes are dominant," she remembered. "Your hair is black and mine is blond, he'll probably have brown hair. I hope he has your eyes. And your height."

"Are you really sure he's a he?"

"Yes, from the ultrasound. Considering that your father was one of three boys a girl was probably a long shot anyway. Did Matt tell you about his brothers?"

That was interesting. "No, he didn't."

"One of them was much older than he was. Philippe died fighting in World War II. Michel died of a heart attack three years ago. They were the only family Matt had left. Or so he thought," she added with a tender smile. "Anyway, boys run in his family and the father, not the mother, determines the sex of the child."

He smiled at her. "As long as we have a healthy baby, I don't care what sex it is." He let his gaze run down to her waistline. "But I meant what I said about getting married soon," he added quietly. "I don't care for casual modern arrangements when a child is involved, although I'd want to marry you now even if there could never be a child. Our son deserves a family name and two parents to raise him and love him. As we've already agreed, I never considered preventing him." He grinned wickedly. "And I'm not sorry, either."

"Neither am I. Okay," she said, smiling. "We'll get married whenever you want."

He sighed with relief, glad that she wasn't going to fight him about it. "I'll speak to the priest here in D.C. who married my parents, if you'd like that. We could have a civil service...."

"No," she said at once. "I'd like us to be married in church."

He smiled. "Fine. And the sooner the better," he added with an amused smile, glancing once more, with unmistakable pride and delight, toward her waistline.

They were married barely a week later, with Leta and Matt and Colby Lane for witnesses. Pierce Hutton and his wife, Brianne, were there with their son, who was several months old. They seemed radiantly happy.

Cecily looked up at Tate as he lifted the short veil of the oyster-colored hat that matched her neat silk suit, and thought that she'd never seen anything as beautiful as the look in his eyes at that moment. He smiled at his new wife just before he bent to kiss her, with such tenderness that tears rolled down her cheeks.

The reception was held at Matt Holden's home, and it was long and rowdy. A number of strangers had shown up for the occasion, some of them very somber, wearing equally somber suits and looking around as if they expected terrorists to vault through the windows any minute. Two other men, very scruffy-looking even in nice clothing, moved like wolves. A big blond man with a faint arrogance of carriage watched the other men warily.

Brianne Martin, with her sleeping child in her arms, moved close to Cecily with mischief in her green eyes. She was fair, like Cecily, but her hair was a darker blond.

"Those two over there belong to the government," she whispered, indicating the stiff men in suits. "The ones by the punch bowl are ex-mercenaries. The big, lean blond man is Micah Steele. He's the last man in the world you ever want to make an enemy of. And that girl over there—'' she indicated a slender woman with brown hair ''—is his stepsister,'' she added with a grin. ''They don't get along at all. That's why she's careful to keep the room between them.''

''Boy, does that sound familiar,'' Cecily muttered with a glance at her oblivious new husband.

''You, too, huh?'' Brianne asked, shifting the baby in her arms.

''Yes, me, too. Tate's been keeping his distance for years.''

She glanced at Cecily's noticeably unbuttoned skirt. ''My, my, imagine a man being able to do *that* from a distance!''

Cecily burst out laughing. Tate heard the sound, glanced at her and smiled with his whole heart in his dark eyes.

''On second thought,'' Brianne whispered, noting the look, ''maybe it *is* possible.''

Cecily only smiled. She and Brianne moved to the sofa and Cecily took the little boy in her arms, thinking that soon she'd have one of her own to love. Tate came up behind them, momentarily alone, and looked down at the baby in Cecily's arms with a smile.

''His name is Edward Laurence, but we call him Laurence,'' Brianne volunteered, ''and Pierce gets absolutely militant if it's shortened. He looks like his daddy.''

"Yes, he does," Tate murmured, dreaming of his own heir who lay under Cecily's heart.

Senator Matt Holden sauntered over to join them, placing an arm around Tate's shoulders with easy affection. "Good-looking kid," he mused. He shook Tate. "So is mine, don't you think?" he added. "I can't think who he reminds me of…"

Tate elbowed him with a grin. "Cut it out. I'm a better-looking copy of you."

"Better-looking?"

"Better tempered, too," Tate said with a warm smile.

"Only on occasion."

"It's nice to see the two of them getting along so well, isn't it, Cecily?" Leta asked as she took her husband's arm.

"Yes, it is," she agreed. "I'm getting used to peace and quiet."

"Think so?" Tate mused. He looked at his father mischievously. "We're getting the papers finalized with the state to open the casino on Wapiti."

"You can finalize them however much the hell you like, but I'll fight you tooth and nail to the very last fence!" Matt returned.

"There's no outside involvement this time, and we've got a referendum coming up on the res to take a vote," Tate told him. "Do your worst."

"You think I won't? I'll be standing right outside the polling place with a placard and every protestor I can muster. In fact, I'll…!"

"Stop it," Leta said, getting between them. "This is a happy occasion. You two can go out back and have this out later."

The two glowered at each other, neither giving an inch.

"Don't they look just alike when they glower like that?" Leta sighed, smiling.

Cecily's eyes were like saucers. "Oh, Tate…!"

He glanced at her with twinkling eyes. Matt did the same. She'd been had.

"You two!" she muttered, handing the baby back to Brianne. She got up. "I'm going to clean house here," she said.

"I have to talk to Steele!" Tate said at once.

"I don't know him, but I'm sure I have to talk to him, too," Matt agreed.

They retreated, chuckling like the devils they were, leaving a fuming Cecily beside her beaming mother-in-law.

Leta hugged her. "They're just pulling your chain," she said. "Matt's compromised, and so has Tate. We'll see what happens now, but I think we'll get our casino. Actually," she said, "it's more of a big bingo pavilion. No faro wheels, no slot machines. Maybe later, but we're starting small. And this time *we're* doing all the groundwork, in the tribe."

Cecily hugged her back. "What a nice wedding present."

"Only verbal, but we have something better for later. Matt and I are giving you a nursery, when you move into that pretty house down the road from us that Tate found you."

"We can have coffee every morning and discuss new campaigns for sovereignty," Cecily agreed with a grin. "Because now I really am family."

Leta sighed. "Really family," she agreed with love beaming from her face.

She went back to Matt and Brianne glanced up at Cecily. "I hope you're going to forgive Pierce for what he did to you," she said dryly. "He and Colby Lane should be shot. They had no business shocking you like that, especially since you're pregnant."

"I wasn't shocked. I was outraged. Parceled back to D.C. with my suitcase and delivered to the father of my child." She sighed as she stared at her husband across the room. "But what a reunion it turned out to be. Your husband has my vote for matchmaker of the year."

"I like him myself," Brianne chuckled and exchanged a long, sweet look with her own husband. Pierce Hutton had dark eyes like Tate's, and his love for his young wife was very evident, even at a distance.

"Tate's very excited about the baby, isn't he?" Brianne added. "I heard him telling Pierce that he was already looking at potential colleges."

"He'll make a good father," Cecily mused, smiling across the room at him. "And a very good husband."

"Who'd have thought it?" Brianne asked softly.

"He always seemed so self-contained. I guess you never really know people, do you?"

Cecily shook her head. "That's part of the fun, finding out the little quirks and surprises that make up complex people. The more I get to know him, the more I realize how little I actually knew about him. He's a very private person."

"So is Pierce. But, you know," Brianne said with mock solemnity, "men may actually be worth all the trouble they cause, in the end."

Cecily laughed, delighted to find such a kindred spirit. "They might be at that!"

The baby was born in the summer, on the hottest recorded day of the year. Tate barely got Cecily to the hospital in time. Little Joseph Matthew Winthrop was born the minute his mother was taken into the delivery room, with a waiting room bursting at the seams with family and some very wary-looking acquaintances.

Pierce Hutton murmured to his wife that every government office in Washington must be represented in there. Leta and Matt were sharing a bench with Colby Lane, who was sharing some news about Cecily's stalker, Gabrini, who'd just been convicted and sentenced to life on racketeering charges after making an unexpected confession of his part in the Wapiti reservation scandal. A nurse interrupted the conversation by appearing in the doorway to tell a beaming Matt Holden and Leta that they'd just become grandparents. It was a fine, healthy boy, and as soon as they had Mrs. Winthrop in a room, everyone could come and see him in the nursery. She darted a worried glance toward a group of taciturn men in sunglasses and dark suits, facing another group in casual dress but looking at windows as if they might be contemplating a break-out. And one of those men bore a striking resemblance to a mobster...

She beat a hasty retreat back into the safety of the surgical ward. That baby was going to have some *very* odd visitors.

In a private room down the hall, a tired but delighted Cecily was watching her husband with his brand-new son. Cecily had thought that the expression on Tate's face at their wedding would never be duplicated. But when they placed the tiny little boy in his father's gowned arms in the delivery room, and he saw his child for the first time, the look on his face was indescribable. Tears welled in his eyes. He'd taken the tiny little fist in his big, dark hand and smoothed over the perfect little fingers and then the tiny little face, seeking resemblances.

"Generations of our families," he said softly, "all there, in that face." He'd looked down at his wife with unashamedly wet eyes. "In our son's face."

She wiped her own tears away with a corner of the sheet and coaxed Tate's head down so that she could do the same for him where they were, temporarily, by themselves.

Now she was cleaned up, like their baby, and

drowsy as she lay on clean white sheets and watched her husband get acquainted with his firstborn. "Isn't he beautiful?" he murmured, still awed by the child. "Next time, we have to have a little girl," he said with a tender smile, "so that she can look like you."

Her heart felt near to bursting as she stared up at that beloved face, above the equally beloved face of their firstborn.

"My heart is happy when I see you," she whispered in Lakota.

He chuckled, having momentarily forgotten that he'd taught her how to say it. "Mine is equally happy when I see you," he replied in English.

She reached out and clasped his big hand with her small one. On the table beside her was a bouquet of roses, red and crisp with a delightful soft perfume. Her eyes traced them, and she remembered the first rose he'd ever given her, when she was seventeen: a beautiful red paper rose that he'd brought her from Japan. Now the roses were real, not imitation. Just as her love for him, and his for her, had become real enough to touch.

He frowned slightly at her expression. "What is it?" he asked softly.

"I was remembering the paper rose you brought me from Japan, just after I went to live with Leta." She shrugged and smiled self-consciously.

He smiled back. "And now you're covered in real ones," he discerned.

She nodded, delighted to see that he understood

exactly what she was talking about. But, then, they always had seemed to read each others' thoughts— never more than now, with the baby who was a living, breathing manifestation of their love. "Yes," she said contentedly. "The roses are real, now."

Outside the window, rain was coming down in torrents, silver droplets shattering on the bright green leaves of the bushes. In the room, no one noticed. The baby was sleeping and his parents were watching him, their eyes full of warm, soft dreams.

DIANA PALMER

66470	ONCE IN PARIS	___ $5.99 U.S.	___ $6.99 CAN.
66452	AFTER THE MUSIC	___ $5.50 U.S.	___ $6.50 CAN.
66149	DIAMOND GIRL	___ $5.50 U.S.	___ $6.50 CAN.
66031	LADY LOVE	___ $4.99 U.S.	___ $5.50 CAN.
66168	PASSION FLOWER	___ $5.50 U.S.	___ $6.50 CAN.
66418	ROOMFUL OF ROSES	___ $5.50 U.S.	___ $6.50 CAN.
66009	THE RAWHIDE MAN	___ $4.99 U.S.	___ $5.50 CAN.
66056	CATTLEMAN'S CHOICE	___ $4.99 U.S.	___ $5.50 CAN.

(limited quantities available)

TOTAL AMOUNT $_____
POSTAGE & HANDLING $_____
($1.00 for one book; 50¢ for each additional)
APPLICABLE TAXES* $_____
TOTAL PAYABLE $_____
(check or money order—please do not send cash)

To order, complete this form and send it, along with a check or money order for the total above, payable to MIRA Books®, to: **In the U.S.:** 3010 Walden Avenue, P.O. Box 9077, Buffalo, NY 14269-9077; **In Canada:** P.O. Box 636, Fort Erie, Ontario, L2A 5X3.

Name:_____
Address:_____ City:_____
State/Prov.:_____ Zip/Postal Code:_____
Account Number (if applicable):_____
075 CSAS

*New York residents remit applicable sales taxes.
 Canadian residents remit applicable GST and provincial taxes.

MIRA

Visit us at www.mirabooks.com   MDP1299BL